The Halsey Brothers Series

Marshal in Petticoats
Outlaw in Petticoats
Miner in Petticoats
Doctor in Petticoats
Logger in Petticoats

LOGGER IN PETTICOATS

The Halsey Brothers Series

by
Paty Jager

Windtree Press
Beaverton, Oregon

This is a work of fiction. Names, characters, places, and incidents either are the product of the author's imagination or are used fictitiously, and any resemblance to actual persons living or dead, business establishments, events, or locales, is entirely coincidental.

LOGGER IN PETTICOATS

Contact Information: info@windtreepress.com
Cover Art by Karen Ronan
Windtree Press
Visit us at http://windtreepress.com

Publishing History
First Edition
Logger in Petticoats 2012 (Ebook only)

Second Edition
Logger in Petticoats 2022 (Print and ebook)

Published in the United States of America

ISBN 978-1-957638-30-0

Acknowledgements

Thank you to all my critique partners, beta readers, and fans. You are the ones who brought about this book and series. You asked for a story for each Halsey brother.

Chapter 1

Sumpter, Oregon
1891

Hank Halsey's stomach churned with apprehension even as his heart raced with anticipation. He studied each person seated around the huge table in Clay and Rachel's dining room. For the first time since their youth, all five Halsey brothers were seated at a Christmas Eve dinner.

Gil, Darcy, and their two, Sadie and Harry, along with Darcy's brother, Jeremy, had ridden in from Galena. Maeve and Zeke now lived in Sumpter awaiting the arrival of their baby. Maeve didn't trust anyone other than her sister-in-law, Dr. Rachel Halsey to deliver her child. Rachel sat at the end of the table feeding her baby daughter, Frankie, mashed potatoes as Clay rested a hand on his daughter's leg. At the end of the table sat Ethan and Aileen and their two, Colin and Shayla.

Hank cleared his throat and stood.

Conversations stopped.

Everyone, including the children, turned their attention to him. A knot formed in his throat, squeezing off his air. He'd kept the stamp mill running when Ethan and Aileen returned to Ireland to reclaim Colin's inheritance, and he took up the slack when Clay tended Rachel and their new baby. He was always the dependable one. The brother they could count on to handle things at the stamp mill at a minute's notice. Now it was his turn to go out on his own and leave the mining and stamp mill in his brothers' hands.

"Well, what's been on your mind?" Ethan asked in his big brother tone that reminded Hank of their father.

"It's been that obvious?" Hank countered still finding the fortitude to have his say. He loved his brothers and their families and while he had to get out on his own, taking on this new venture felt like betrayal.

"You've been cranky as a bear, Uncle Hank," Shayla said, her huge green eyes staring at him.

He glanced once more around the table. Picked up his glass of water and took a long drink. Hank nodded and firmly set the cup down. Now was the time.

"I'm starting a logging operation. The railroad will soon be hauling lumber to areas with no trees. If we stockpile until the line is finished, we'll make as much or more money from the trees on our land as the minerals we're digging." Hank studied the faces of everyone around the table. No one had a scowl, so he continued. "I've been corresponding with a family run operation, and they've agreed to come at the first of the year and start setting up a log camp. As soon as the camp's ready, we'll hire woodsmen and start logging." There, he said it.

"It's about time!" Clay slapped his hands on the table, rattling the dishes and causing Frankie to pucker her face and squall.

"Can I work with you?" Colin asked above the din of Frankie's cries and Rachel shushing her.

"We'll see. I'm not sure the logging company I've contacted will want a greenhorn young man working with them." Hank didn't want anything to happen to Aileen's son or any family member. Until he learned all about logging and could proficiently carry out all the jobs, he didn't want any family members involved.

The women all smiled and his brothers all nodded. This wasn't what he'd expected. Since the stamp mill began as a dream in Ethan's head, Hank had been the brother who could be relied upon to do what was asked.

"You've been eyeballing those pine trees since you spent time helping old man Crawford at the sawmill in Baker City." Ethan put an arm around the back of Aileen's chair. "I can't believe it's taken you this long to finally do something."

"Finally? I've been taking up the slack all of you make when you marry and have children." He'd never carried a grudge toward his brothers or anyone else, but over the last year he'd started harboring a need to be on his own. Living and working in a log camp was the first step in that direction.

"Where're you going to set up the camp?" Gil asked.

"I'm not sure. I have a couple spots picked out, but Mr. Nielson, the boss of the outfit, will make the final decision. I picked him for his logging knowledge and his family. The boys each oversee different stages of the logging and the wife and daughter run the cookhouse." He still wasn't sure having women in a logging camp was a good idea.

"Why are you frowning?" Zeke was always too observant.

"I like everything about the logging operation except the two women." Hank could have turned to dust at that moment from the scathing looks his sisters-in-law shot him.

"Why shouldn't there be women? You said they're part of the family operation." Darcy, the feistiest of the women, pointed her small nose at him like a dog about to attack.

"I-Women can be disruptive." He held up both hands as all four raised out of their chairs.

"We'll show you disruptive." Maeve snatched back the pies she and Aileen had just deposited on the table.

"Aye, no pie for men—" Aileen started.

"Whoa!" Ethan clapped his hands getting their attention. "The rest of us are more than happy to have women around."

"Yeah!" chorused his whipped brothers.

Hank folded his arms across his chest. "I want you all eating crow when one of the Nielsen women disrupts the operation."

"Fine, but they'll be nae pie for a man who distrusts women before he even meets them." Aileen set the pie back on the table and sunk a knife into the golden crust.

Hank's mouth watered, but he knew better than to go against everyone in the room.

"So you've met the family?" Gil asked.

"Only the father. He's Norwegian and believes in hard work and family time." Hank had never met a more jovial man in his thirty-one years. If the rest of the family had his attitude working with them wouldn't feel like work.

"So, the daughter...How old is she?" Darcy asked, passing the pie plates around the table as Aileen filled them.

He knew that tone. His sister-in-law had it in her mind to try and make a match. She'd thrust several women, and in some cases girls, into his life since her marriage to Gil.

"I have no idea other than she's the youngest, and Arvid cares a great deal for his daughter." The man had expounded on her strength, her wit, and her willingness to help her mother to the point Hank had almost felt like the man had matchmaking in his mind as well.

Not that Hank wasn't interested in marriage. He'd witnessed firsthand how his brothers were content and enjoying all the pleasures of being married. But he wanted to prove his worth, bring a new venture to his family, and have his own stake in the outcome.

Hank stood at the base of the mountain the Halsey brother's owned. The thick pine and fir trees colored the mountainside dark green as the cold January sun bathed the snow-covered eastern slope.

"Ja, this is the best place for the camp," Arvid said, stepping off areas and pounding metal stakes through the snow into the frozen earth. "This will be the cookhouse and my quarters." He planted a fourth stake. "My boys will sleep with us until the other buildings are finished." Arvid stood several inches taller than Hank's six-foot-three, and his shoulders spanned a hand's width wider than Hank's.

Hank had yet to introduce Arvid to his brothers, but he didn't have any doubts they would be as impressed with the logger as he was.

"How many buildings are needed? Won't that use a lot of the timber?" Hank knew this mountain and the one next to it, all land owned by the Halsey's and Aileen, held more lumber than they could remove in a year, but he felt a need to keep an eye on the amount used for accommodations.

The man's green eyes glittered with amusement, and a smile stretched across his wide face. "Son, without even hiking up your mountains, I can guarantee you will not run out of lumber for several years. The buildings are necessary to keep your help happy. Happy workers make good workers, ja?"

"Yes." He couldn't argue with the man's line of thinking. "I've never been to a logging operation. You'll have to teach me everything I need to know, starting with the buildings and their uses." Hank watched as the man stepped off another square area, tapping stakes at the corners.

"My oldest, Karl and his brother Dag will have a cabin. Tobias, he's the youngest boy and the one who is good with numbers. He will have a room in the back of the office." The man winked. "This is the building where you count your logs and your money, the beasts of the wood get their mail, and buy necessities."

"What are necessities?" Hank spun the notion of what a logger might need.

"Socks, mittens, clothing, tobacco, whiskey, and paper."

"Whiskey? I'm not sure I want a bunch of drunk men wielding axes and saws." If most of the men were Arvid's size, Hank didn't like the idea of playing bouncer every night if a handful of men got liquored up.

"There's usually only one or two that has a sickness for the bottle. And that's the job of the bull cook to keep them under control." Arvid moved over and stepped off another square. "Paddy will need a cabin."

"Paddy?" Hank pushed up the woolen cap covering his ears enough to scratch his hairline.

"The bull cook."

"I thought your wife and daughter did the cooking?" Hank had never felt so lost in a conversation as he did with this man.

"Ja, Ingrid and Kelda cook."

"Then what does the bull cook, Paddy, do?"

"He lights the stoves and lamps, gets the men up and ready to work, calls them to meals, and takes care of the equipment and supplies. He then banks the stoves and turns out the lights at night. And that's when he tends to the men that have had a bit too much of the whiskey."

"He's basically the man in charge of the loggers?" He must be as big as Arvid and strong as a bull to have the name "Bull Cook".

"Only when they're in the camp. Outside the camp it's me and my boys, and some instances Kelda, who are in charge."

Hank ripped his attention from the man's large booted feet stepping out yet another square and peered at Arvid's face. "Your wife is in charge of the loggers outside camp? I thought she cooked?"

"Nei! Kelda, my daughter. She's been learning the trade since she was big enough to follow me and her brothers about the forest." He winked. "And the men respect her. She can shank a chain and swing an axe as good as they. Of course there's always the newcomer who has to give her a challenge, but she's gives them a good turn."

"Your daughter works in the woods? Isn't that dangerous?" Hank shook his head. It wasn't right for a woman to be in that kind of danger. "While you're working for me I don't want her in the woods."

Arvid narrowed his eyes. "She is one of the best. She can handle any logging job."

Hank stood his ground on this. "She'll not work in the woods while you're here. Keep her in the kitchen." His brother's wives had held occupations usually held by men. But a logger? What did the woman look like? Hank shivered at the thought.

"She will not be happy to hear you forbid her to work in the woods."

"If she values her family having work here, she'll abide." Hank wasn't going to back down.

Arvid watched him intently. "When we met I

told you my family worked together, and I had a daughter."

"Yes, I like that about your outfit, that it's family. But I can't have a woman out in the woods distracting the men or possibly getting hurt."

Arvid shook his head, before his eyes lit with merriment again. "She can cook a berry pie better than any you've ever tasted. The men beg her for pies when the berries are ripe."

Hank found it hard to fathom a woman who swung an axe like a man, baking pies. It just didn't settle in his mind.

A week later fifteen wagons rolled into the meadow where Arvid had staked out the buildings. Big burly men and average sized men jumped out of the first two. The rest of the wagons were loaded down with gear and a few household goods along with one cookstove the likes Hank had never seen. It could take up a quarter of the cabin he and his brothers had lived in for years and now only he resided in.

Arvid strode toward him, his hand extended. "I have brought my family and the best woodsmen I know."

Before Hank could say a word, yelling and the crash of trees resounded through the usually still air.

"Karl has the plans for the camp. He will direct where the buildings are to go. Dag is in charge of the tent where Ingrid and Kelda will cook until the cookhouse is finished." Arvid strode to the back of a wagon, grabbed the head of a huge double-bladed axe like it was a walking cane and strode toward the group of men falling trees.

Hank peered at the chaos around him and soon realized everyone had a job, and they were all setting about doing it. All but him. He hadn't a clue where he should help. His hands itched to do some labor, but from his vantage point it appeared he'd only get in the way.

A man approached him with gnarled hands, a limp, and hair so white it reflected the sun as glaringly as the snow under their feet. The top of his woolen cap, resting on the highest point of his head, came to Hank's shoulder when he stopped and extended a hand.

Hank shook. "Hank Halsey."

"I figured. Yer the only one not doin' a thing. That's generally how it is. The man with the money stands around looking special."

"Now see here, Mr—"

"O'Brien. Paddy O'Brien. The bull cook."

Hank stared at the man. This old coot was to keep drunken men the size of barns in line? "The way Arvid described you, I was expecting—"

"Someone young and as huge as a Ponderosa Pine?" The old man shook his head. "All you young'uns think it takes brawn to make people do what you want." Paddy poked a curved finger at his temple. "It takes livin' life and knowin' the right words to get people to do what ye want. Besides, I've been loggin' longer than you've been out o'knickers, and I know every catastrophe that can happen and every move a logger needs to make to be successful." Paddy turned to leave but spun back. "Remember that when you find yourself in a pickle."

"Wait. I don't like to stand back and watch. I want to learn everything about this camp and logging. What can I do to help?" Hank wasn't sure he liked the man, but he respected his knowledge. Myrle, the widow who helped his family after their parents' were killed, had instilled the fact in all the brothers that older people were a wealth of information.

"You know how to build a cabin?" Paddy asked, his runny-eyed gaze running up and down Hank.

"I've helped build a couple."

"Then go see Karl. He's the tall dark-haired lad with the papers in his hand." Paddy limped away moving with good speed toward the group erecting a large canvas tent.

Before Hank swung his gaze from the tent area, a blonde braid falling down the back of a man's black wool coat and stopping at the spread of a woman's hips in men's dungarees caught his attention. Arvid's wife or his daughter? Hank had to admit he was curious about a woman who worked alongside loggers.

The woman turned.

All his imaginings had given the woman manly attributes. The female face gracing his gaze held a wide, full mouth curved at the edges in merriment. Even across the distance he saw crinkles of mirth around her eyes and joy plumping her triangular face with high cheek bones and a wide brow. She talked to a man with the same color hair and features much like Arvid's. He had to be one of her brothers.

Her gaze wandered from the man's face and held Hank's. He'd never gone weak kneed over a woman, but the second her lips curved a little more and one blonde eyebrow rose as if asking him who he was, his knees melted like the mercury they used at the stamp mill.

"You there!" A deep voice from behind him rocked Hank, and he jerked from her hypnotic hold.

Chapter 2

Kelda watched the man she'd never seen before shake hands with Karl and walk toward the area labeled on Far's map as the cookhouse. Was he the man who hired them to log his mountains? Far hadn't said much about him, only he and his family wanted to reap the benefits of having good stands of pine and fir on their land, and he ordered her not to work in the woods.

Her eyes narrowed as anger changed her curiosity to studying her enemy. He was only a couple inches shorter than Karl. That meant he would be as tall, or perhaps even taller, than she. Few men were taller than her six foot. She towered over other women and found being around them not to her liking.

The outdoors called to her, and if her mother hadn't slowed down from years of long hours cooking, Kelda would be out falling the trees for the camp rather than helping Mor set up the cook tent. She glared at the man, and this man who forbid her to follow the calling of her heart.

"Kelda, we could use your help." Dag pulled on a rope and several men worked the poles into place on the corners of the tent.

"Coming." She grabbed the corner pole nearest her and heaved it up, pushing the tent into position along with the men. The clang of metal on metal rang through the structure as Dag moved around the canvas driving stakes into the frozen ground.

Mor hustled into the tent followed by six men carrying her prized cookstove. "Over here, just like the last time."

Kelda smiled. Mor stood a head and a half shorter than Kelda, but the woman had every man in the camp jumping to bid her wishes, especially Far. That was the kind of marriage Kelda yearned for. One of respect where the man allowed the woman to do what she wanted, whether it was approved by society or not. All the loggers who joined their camp over the years were surprised to find a woman cook and a woman who worked beside them. They wouldn't have a woman working beside them this time. Her fists clamped around the post.

"You can quit hugging that post and help Mor." Dag swatted her on the backside like when she was small. He flashed a devilish grin and ran out the tent flap before she could retaliate. Her brothers still patted her backside when they wanted to goad her.

"Uff da!" Kelda released the pole and ducked out the flap to haul in the boxes of cooking supplies. She walked to the wagon as her gaze slid to the cookhouse area. It didn't take long for her to find the stranger. He wasn't dressed like the rest. His coat was duck cloth and his pants dungarees like she wore. Leather gloves covered his hands as he helped raise a log. *What gives him the right to tell me what I can and can't do?*

"You plan to daydream or get to work?" Mor's question made her jump.

"Work." *Uff da.* She couldn't stare at the stranger every time she saw him and try to rationalize why he disapproved of her without even meeting her. Besides the more she watched him, the more she liked the look in his eyes and the cut of his face. She shook her head. He was her enemy until he understood she wasn't a threat to him or anyone else.

Kelda picked up a crate and packed it into the tent.

Mor followed with a smaller, lighter box. "Don't strain yourself. Let the men lift the heavy boxes." She placed a hand on Kelda's cheek. "You don't have to work like a man. You are a woman."

"Mor, you know I have to keep strong to help Far when he needs it." *I can't allow a man to think he can get the better of me or I'm of no use to Far.*

"Far doesn't need you. He can find someone else when he needs a man. You jump too quickly." Mor opened a box and set things on the long table as soon as Dag and another man had it standing.

"Far only asks you out of courtesy. He hopes one day you will say no," Dag said, shaking the table and leveling it on the frozen ground.

Kelda stared at her brother. "He asks me because he can count on me like he counts on you boys."

"True. He knows family helps family. But Kelda, you can't keep acting like a man. You will never catch a husband." Dag put his hands on her shoulders. "No man wants a woman stronger than he is."

"Maybe I don't want a husband?" She folded her arms across her chest and stared into Dag's concerned eyes.

"We all want a spouse to grow old with. Karl is aching for a wife. He just never has time to look for one." Dag stepped back as men brought in more crates. "Help Mor unpack. Leave the lifting to the men. They need something to do."

Kelda stared at her brother's back as he exited the tent. Did her brothers want wives? If so why didn't they take time off to look for one? She could do their work and give them time to wife hunt. Nodding her head, Kelda decided to bring the idea up with Far. She knew how much he wished for his family to grow with grandchildren. She grimaced. How could they make it work if the boss wouldn't allow her in the woods?

Hank spent the day straining his muscles helping erect the cookhouse. Karl invited him to share the evening meal with them in the cook tent before he returned to his cabin over the ridge. The idea of a meal he didn't have to prepare and filling his belly with warm food before the long ride home appealed to him. Also getting a close glimpse of the two women in the camp intrigued him. What kind of women lived in a logging camp year around?

Hank washed alongside the other men at the

hollowed-out log placed along the outside wall of the tent. He'd learned a few more names as they worked together. The teamster, Smithy, was a surly little man who rode the horses incessantly shouting profanities as the animals dragged the bundles of logs to the construction area. Hank wasn't pleased with the way the man treated the animals, but no one else seemed to see a problem with it so he didn't say anything. For all he knew the draft horses were deaf to the man's shouts.

Delicious aromas wafted from the tent flap as the men entered the canvas cook tent an hour after the sun had set and the tools had been cleaned and put away.

Arvid sat at the head of a long table running nearly the length of the twenty-foot tent. Karl, Dag, and Tobias flanked their father. An empty place remained by Tobias. The workers filed in filling the table near the Nielsen men.

Arvid stood. "Men, I'd like to introduce you to the man we are all working for." Mr.Nielsen waved a hand toward Hank. "Hank Halsey and his family own the mountains we will be clearing. I want you to treat him with respect, but also teach him what it is to be a beast of the woods."

Deep boisterous voices boomed throughout the tent in laughter and welcome. Hank made a point of looking each man in the face and acknowledging him. They were a burly lot, and he didn't want to get on the wrong side of any of them. Paddy sat at the opposite end of the table from Arvid, next to Smithy. His old eyes twinkled in the lantern light.

"Thank you for your warm welcome. I may be

the man paying you, but I want to work alongside each of you and learn how to log. If you see me doing something wrong I want to know." He caught movement behind Arvid and spotted two women advancing toward the tables with large bowls in their hands. His instincts wanted to rush forward and help them carry their burdens, but the men all let out a loud cheer as the bowls were placed one in front of Arvid and one in front of Paddy.

Hank watched the young woman as she smiled at Paddy. The sparkle and joy in her eyes tickled his lips into a smile. She said something to the old man that made him laugh.

"Hank, take the seat by Tobias and enjoy the wonderful stew Ingrid and Kelda have prepared."

Arvid's statement jerked Hank's gaze back to the roomful of men. He strode to the empty seat and sat.

All the men at the table clasped their hands in front of their chests and Arvid began reciting, "I Jesu navn, går vi til bords, å spise, drikke på ditt ord. Deg, Gud til ære, oss til gavn, Så får vi mat i Jesu navn. Amen."

"Amen!" The men chorused. Paddy and Arvid dished up tins of the aromatic stew as the women brought out plates of homemade bread and bowls of butter and jam.

The stew melted in his mouth and the sweet nutty flavor of the bread had him grabbing for a third and fourth slice. It wasn't until his hunger was sated and the others had slowed down that he realized the women didn't sit at the table with them. As if reading his thoughts, Kelda brought out a tray laden with squares of cake.

The spicy aroma reminded him of his mother's cooking and Aileen's kitchen. Ethan's wife loved to bake.

Kelda served the first piece to Arvid, moved to Tobias, and then to Hank. He leaned back as she bent forward between her brother and Hank to place the cake on his plate.

"It smells as good as my mother used to make," Hank said in a tone he hoped didn't sound like he was shining her up.

His comment didn't get him an answer, so he'd yet to hear her voice. He did, however, get a stiff smile. She moved on, the scent of spice, wood smoke, and vanilla remained in her wake.

Tobias elbowed him and wiggled his eyebrows, shoving a forkful of the cake in his mouth.

Hank frowned and dug into his cake, watching from the corner of his eye to see how the other men treated her. Some she joked with, others just smiled and leaned back allowing her access to place their dessert on the plate. The face of a good-sized young man turned red as Kelda leaned in to serve his cake. The man was smitten with her. Hank studied the woman's reaction. She didn't seem the least bit flustered or even take notice of the man. Was she uninterested in men?

"Hank, when will we meet your family?" Arvid had finished his cake and held a cup of steaming coffee in his hands.

Before Hank could say a word, the smaller, older woman appeared at Hank's side with a tin cup and poured coffee for him and on around the table. How did the two women remain looking so fresh when they had to have been at the stove from the minute the tent was set up?

"Do you have a large family? Any sisters?" Karl asked and the table erupted into laughter.

"I have four sisters."

Karl perked up.

"By marriage. They're all married to my brothers."

Karl hung his head a bit and the table roared. Friendly cajoling filled the air.

"So you have four brothers." Dag's raised voice silenced the group. He settled his gaze on Hank then his brothers. "Are they as similar to you as my brothers are to me?"

"More so. We range only a few inches difference in height and all have the same coloring, eyes, and build." He'd noted the blonde hair of Dag and Kelda while Karl and Tobias had dark brown almost reddish hair.

"So when one rides up we will know he is your brother," Karl said, waving a hand. The farthest logger picked up his cleaned plate and passed it down until all the plates on that side of the table were stacked in front of Karl. Tobias did the same thing and soon a large stack of plates arrived in front of Hank.

Kelda walked behind the men, starting at Karl, and they all dropped their eating utensils into her bucket. Hank had to admire the efficient way they cleared the dishes from the table.

"Now the men will retire to the tent we raised, and my family will remain here. You may stay and visit if you choose." Arvid stretched his arms above his head, and the loggers stepped over the half log benches they'd sat on and disappeared out the tent flap.

Curiosity about the family he'd hired battled with the knowledge he still had an hour's ride to make to arrive home. The snow and dark made the usual thirty minute ride twice as long. He started to stand when he caught Kelda watching him. The animosity he saw intrigued him.

"One more cup of coffee, but then I have to leave. My cabin is a good ride from here, and I want to get back early tomorrow morning."

"You could toss a bed roll in here with us," Tobias said, motioning to four cots stacked at the side of the tent.

"You're so sure I'd stay you have a cot ready for me?" he asked, warming to the family's hospitality.

"No those are our cots," Tobias pointed to his brothers, "And Kelda's. But we can find another one."

Hank stared at the men who all nodded at him. The fact they treated their sister like one of them made him shake his head. She was a woman who deserved privacy like all women. He started to say something, but thought better of it. He'd not invade her privacy, too. "I'll head home after my cup of coffee."

Dishes clattered in the background as Arvid and his boys explained the timeline to raising the structures, building the grapple to load the wagons, the chute to get the logs to the landing, and finally falling the first tree.

"Two months? You can have all that done and ready to cut trees in two months?" Hank stared at each man.

"Ja. We are strong fast workers. We only employ men who are the same." Arvid leaned back lighting a pipe that his wife handed to him as she pulled a chair up beside him.

She held her hand out over the table. "I am Ingrid. I am very pleased to meet you."

"Ma'am, I'm equally pleased to meet you. Your husband didn't do justice to your cooking."

Kelda sat down next to Dag. She nodded and stared with earnest into Mr. Halsey's vanilla-brown eyes. "I am Kelda." She withheld any emotion from her voice.

"Miss, pleased to meet you as well." His eyes twinkled when he spoke to her as if they shared a joke.

She worked to keep from smiling back. His good nature made it hard to remember he was her enemy. His face had different planes and angles than her brothers. Their faces were flatter, wider, handsome. Mr. Halsey's face more long, chiseled, and pleasant to study.

An elbow dug into her ribs. She glared at Dag who winked at her.

"Did you make the cake we had with dinner?" Mr. Halsey watched her attentively.

Had he asked this question already? Was that why Dag jabbed her? Heat rushed up her neck and infused her cheeks.

"Yes, with Mor's help." She wouldn't take all the credit. Mor kept her from putting too much salt in when she plotted how to change the man's mind about her working in the woods.

"It was as good as my mother made and equal to my sister-in-law, Aileen's, baking." Mr. Halsey smiled again then focused his attention on her father.

She didn't mind. The longer he talked with her, the warmer her face became until her skin burned like fresh sugar buns from the oven.

Chapter 3

Kelda helped Mor move the cooking supplies into the new cookhouse. Three days they cooked and slept in the tent, now it would be used for supplies and her brothers until their respective cabins were built. She looked forward to tonight when she could sleep in quiet. The older her brothers grew the louder the noises they made at night. Their snoring, talking, and mumblings kept her awake.

She yawned walking across the compound to get another box. Once the cookstove had been placed in the building the men took off to help with the other structures and tree falling, leaving her to carry the needed boxes. She didn't mind. Keeping her body strong for when Far needed her in the woods made her feel more useful than cooking. And he would need her. And the boss wouldn't be able to say anything. She believed Far would stand up to the man when the need did arise.

Kelda's boots scuffed across the hard packed snow as she stared at the men on springboards topping the tall pines. It was her favorite task. Nothing surged the blood like the freedom of standing forty foot above the ground on a springboard and working a saw in rhythm with another person. That exhilaration kept her in shape and ready to help at a moment's notice.

"Oomph!" Air rushed out of Kelda as an elbow slammed into her belly.

"Sorry."

Strong hands held her arms, holding her upright when she wanted to double over. She forced her body to straighten and peered into Hank Halsey's sorrowful brown eyes.

"I was, rolling a rope...I'm sorry, do you need to sit down?" His firm, yet gentle grip on her arms heated her skin clear through his gloves and her coat.

"I-I'll be fine. I've had worse happen to me." Her breathing returned to normal as the initial shock wore off.

"Not by another's hands I hope." The censure in his voice and irritation darkening his eyes gave her pause.

She didn't dare tell him of the indignities she'd suffered at the hands of loggers wishing to discredit her with Far and get her out of the woods.

"Working with logs can leave a body bruised. Once you start actually working the woods you'll see what I mean." This close she found him a few inches taller than her and nearly as broad across the shoulders as her brothers.

"Why?" His hands lightened their hold but didn't leave her arms. His brow furrowed, scrunching his dark eyebrows down at the bridge of his straight nose.

"Why what?" She swallowed as heat curled where his elbow had previously caught her unaware. Why did her body react to him this way? She'd have to ask Mor if there was a sickness that flushed your face and tumbled your insides.

"Why would you willingly work in the woods?"

"Kelda!" The warning in Mor's voice told her she wasted time.

"I have to go." Kelda stepped back. Hank's hands dropped to his side, but his gaze remained on her face.

"We'll finish this after dinner tonight." Hank tipped his hat and walked away.

Kelda, hurried into the tent, picked up the first box she came to, and returned to the cookhouse. Her mind spun with questions. Why did he want to talk about her working in the woods? The expression on his face was so serious. Maybe Far wouldn't be able to talk him into letting her work in the woods. They worked for Mr. Halsey, and Far wouldn't want to stop on this project now. Outrage shook her from head to toe, replacing the tingling heat of his hands with a blast of scorching indignation.

Hank peered one more time around the cookhouse and wondered why with the huge cookstove and all the men seated around the table a sharp cold breeze blew across his skin every time Kelda glanced his direction.

The dishes piled in front of him. Before he

could pass them on to Tobias, the scent of vanilla and woods spun his senses. Kelda's shoulder bumped his as she snatched the plates from in front of him. He shivered. Frosty. The woman was downright frosty, and he hadn't a clue what he'd done. Other than jab an elbow in her gut earlier.

At the time she'd acted like she didn't harbor bad feelings. After some reflection, she must have decided he'd intentionally slammed the air out of her. Which he hadn't. He'd been backing up, dragging the long heavy rope to straighten the coils before rerolling it, the way Dag taught him.

He obviously needed to apologize, again. If he didn't freeze to death before he had the chance. The loggers climbed over the benches and headed out the door. Hank turned his attention to the women. Their backs were to the open area, their heads bent together as the dishes clanged and clattered in the tub and into stacks on the shelf to the side of the drain board.

"Hank, you have been quiet tonight," Arvid said, lighting his pipe and leaning back in his chair.

"When the women get done with the dishes I need to speak with Kelda."

A crash from the washing area captured all the men's attention.

"Kelda, have you been playin' in the butter again? Your fingers seem to be slippery," Tobias joked, and his brothers laughed.

Hank wondered if he'd hurt her worse than she'd made out. She'd been more distracted and fumbling tonight as she served the dinner.

"Why do you wish to speak to Kelda?" Dag asked, his blue gaze holding steady on Hank.

"I owe her an apology for running into her today." A groan rose above the clanging of dishes. "And I think I may have hurt her worse than she said."

Kelda spun from the pile of dishes in front of her and jammed fisted hands on her hips. "You did not hurt me. I told you at the time, I've been through worse than a man's elbow jabbing me in the belly."

Her anger infused rosy color to her cheeks and added sparks to her eyes.

"Then why are you dropping dishes if I didn't hurt you?"

She shot a furtive glance at Arvid and grimaced. Did she want to say something that she didn't want her father to know? Hank made a quick decision. Obviously, the only way to get to the bottom of her anger would be to confront her privately.

"Sir, would you mind if Kelda and I stepped outside?" Hank cringed inside at the sparkle that leapt into the man's eyes.

"Kelda, grab your coat and see what the man wants to say in private."

"Far, that's not a good idea." Karl jumped to his feet. "Someone should chaperone them."

Hank shook his head. He didn't plan to court the woman. He just wanted to find out what was eating at her. He'd learned from his brothers' wives that women liked to talk, and he had a feeling this one needed her cork loosened. "I promise I'm not asking her outside to make advances. We just need to talk in private. It's obvious she's not going to tell me what's eating at her with all of you present."

Kelda already stood by the door, a man's black wool coat buttoned to her neck and a wool scarf wrapped around her head. Her flushed cheeks shone in the lantern light. Her gaze met his solid and unflappable.

"If Kelda isn't back in here in fifteen minutes you can come looking for us." Hank said to appease Karl as he pulled on his coat,

"I don't know what you're worrying about. No man is going to think of Kelda in the way you're talking." The door hadn't fully closed when Dag's voice cleared the threshold.

Kelda's shoulders drooped proving she'd heard her brother's comment. She walked around the corner of the cookhouse to a fallen log at the backside of the building. Hank wanted to catch up to her and wrap an arm around her shoulders. She was a fine woman. Any man would be dang lucky to have her for a wife. He stood in front of her as she sat on the log, her face pointed toward the men's logging boots on her feet.

Hank crouched in front of Kelda, tipping her face up to read her emotions. "Your brother sees you only as his sister. You're a woman any man would be lucky to marry."

Tears glistened in her eyes. "I'm the size and body of a man. Men want a small delicate woman." She wiped at the tears, and her hands clutched his. "Don't make Far keep me out of the woods. It's all I have to make me happy."

Pleading in her eyes and voice sucker punched Hank. "Why would you want to work alongside men in the woods? Women belong in the home."

"I don't care to work inside. I love the outdoors and the labor of logging. Don't keep me out of the woods. It's the one thing I can do well."

The strong grip of her fingers on his proved her strength. He had no doubt she was a skilled woodsman…woman. He pried her fingers from his hands and held them between his palms. "I'm sorry, but I can't allow you in the woods. It isn't proper for a woman to work like that. And what if you prove too weak to handle a job and someone else gets hurt?"

"Ooooo!" Her hands ripped from his grasp and rammed him in the chest. He started tipping backwards and grabbed the first thing in reach—Kelda's arms.

He fell back into the snow dragging Kelda on top of him.

The surprise in her eyes quickly turned to interest as she gazed down into his face. Her body sprawled across Hank, pressing him into the snow. Even with the heavy clothing, her curves were evident as her relaxed body molded over his.

Hank pushed the scarf back from her face and stared into amazing eyes that glistened from the moonlight bouncing off the snow. Her gaze searched his. The rise and fall of her chest quickened. She licked her lips…

He held her head in his hands. Inch by inch, Hank drew her lips closer, wondering if the heat and passion he'd witnessed in her eyes would be in her kiss.

"Kelda!"

The male voice broke through the insanity of his actions. Hank rolled, rose to his feet, and pulled Kelda up with him.

She spun to walk away, but he grabbed her arm.

"Wait," Hank whispered, brushing the glittering snow from her back. When the moonlight no longer sparkled off snow crystals on her coat, he released her arm. "Go. And tell everyone good night from me. I'll head home now."

Kelda hesitated. How could she have gone from rage one moment to wanting him to kiss her?

"Kelda!" Karl's angry tone moved her feet toward the cookhouse door.

"Ja?" She stepped around the corner and confronted her brother. She hoped her encounter with Hank didn't show on her face. She almost giggled thinking of the way he'd flopped backwards from her shove of aggravation.

"Where were you and the boss?" Karl blocked her from entering the cookhouse.

"On the log back there." She swung an arm toward the back of the building.

"What did he need to say to you that couldn't be said in front of your family?" The accusation in Karl's voice plucked at her defiance.

Anger seeped back into her body. Why was Mr. Halsey so thick-headed? Far had worked with many men, and he would not allow her in the woods if she was a threat to anyone. The talk had accomplished nothing. "He didn't need to say anything." She shoved Karl out of her way and plunged into the cookhouse.

Far and Mor sat at the end of the table. Unasked questions hung in the air as Kelda hung her coat and scarf and marched to the stove to pour a hot cup of coffee. She added milk, turning the dark brown a velvety tan.

"I'm going to bed." She took the cup and headed to the small lean-to at the back of the building that held cooking supplies and her cot.

"Kelda." Far's tone held exasperation.

"Leave her be. She's been upset all afternoon. Perhaps talking to an outsider will calm her."

Her mother's words nestled security in Kelda's chest. Her mother understood what it was like to be around men all the time. Men who treated you like one of them. Never a moment to one's self to think woman thoughts, dreams. After landing on top of Hank all she could think of was how strong he felt and her weight on him hadn't even made it hard for him to breathe. But her thoughts couldn't go there. He might show her attention, but he wasn't interested in what made her happy. If he cared about her happiness he wouldn't have ordered her out of the woods.

She dropped the curtain, hooked over a peg, and stopped in the darkness waiting for her eyes to adjust. The stars had sparkled in his eyes as she stared into them. And she was sure the way he held her head and lowered her...so slow... Uff da.

Kissing the boss would only get her harassed by the men, and it was pretty obvious from Karl's reactions he wasn't about to have his little sister find a man before he found a woman. Which brought her to her idea of taking the boys' place one day a week so they could venture into town and hunt up a woman. She'd speak to Far in the morning. There had to be a way to get around the boss's order.

Chapter 4

Kelda grabbed Far's coat sleeve when everyone headed out after breakfast the next morning.

"What does my lovely daughter wish to say to
me?" he asked, smiling down at her.

She loved the way Far made her feel like
a small, pretty girl when he looked at her. She
slipped her arm though his and led him to the
bench at the table. "I know Karl is cranky because
he works long hours and has no time to find a
wife." She held up her hand when Far started to
speak. "Ja, he is cranky. And I have a plan that I
think will make the boys happy. I would like to
offer to help out one day a week for Karl and Dag
allowing them to go to town and hunt for a wife."

Far's eyes twinkled, his lips quivered as if they
wanted to tip into a smile. "What brings on this
kind gesture for your brothers?"

"I like working in the woods and unless someone is sick I rarely get to help. If I work at least one
day a week, I will be more prepared when some-

one is down." Last night waiting for sleep to come she'd reasoned out the best method of getting Far to agree.

His graying eyebrows arched. "Have you forgotten Hank will send us away if I let you work in the woods?"

Kelda worried the inside of her lip between her teeth and studied Far.

"You have called him a reasonable fellow. Can't you make him see how it would benefit the whole camp to have Dag and Karl happy?" She clutched Far's hands. "You know how much I love standing on the springboard and shuttling logs along the chute. I don't want that taken away from me. By anyone."

Far placed his large, wide hand on her head. "Skatten min, my treasure, you know if I agreed with Mr. Halsey I would have never taught you the ways of the woods. You are as good as the men, and I want to be there when you show this to our boss." He tweaked her nose. "But you must not push it on the man. He will become more stubborn the more you force the matter."

"You will allow me to take over one day a week for Karl and Dag?" Her heart hammered in her chest. She missed the woods. Up in the air, topping trees or gaffing logs down the chute, straining her muscles, exhausting her body, and satisfying her mind with a job well done.

"When we start logging, I will figure out a way to get you into the woods one day a week, but this is our secret." He cupped her cheek in his palm and his eyes dulled. "Your mother needs your help. You must help her for me." The last words were spoken so softly she leaned in to hear them.

Mor might be a small woman but her giant husband was scared of her.

Kelda giggled. "I will keep our secret and help Mor."

Far pat her cheek and stood. "Ingrid, keep our daughter busy. She has too much time to think of ways to make us grow old faster."

Mor scurried across the floor, pushing a paper-wrapped package in her husband's pocket. "She is not the one I worry about."

Far leaned down, and Mor kissed his cheek. The love shining in their eyes filled Kelda with warmth from her head to her toes. She wanted a man to love her as openly and honestly as her father loved her mother.

"I am always careful because I do not want to miss a night with you wrapped in my arms." Far winked and Mor blushed. The door opened and he disappeared.

Kelda squirmed watching the blush on Mor's cheeks turn rosy and her eyes glisten. She turned away to attack the mound of dishes left from the morning meal.

"Someday Kelda, you will find a man as caring and loving as your father. When it comes you will know it." Mor picked up a cotton cloth and dried the dishes Kelda washed.

"How?"

Mor placed a fisted hand on her chest. "You feel it in here. Deep, strong, wonderful, and a little painful."

Kelda shook her head. It sounded more like a symptom of eating too many sausages.

Hank rode into camp after lunch. He knew no one cared if he arrived every day or not, but he didn't want to miss anything that happened. Colin had pounded on his door at daybreak. Ethan needed to talk with him before he went to the logging camp.

If Ethan had sent anyone other than Colin, Hank would have ignored the summons and gone to the stamp mill after he'd checked in at the camp, but he didn't want Colin to think Ethan's orders could be undermined.

Rumors David Eccles, the owner of the Sumpter Valley Railway, had mills accepting lumber bids had worried Ethan. He wanted to make sure Hank had contracts with the mills.

Hank patted the contract he'd written last night when he couldn't sleep for thinking of Kelda. He wasn't looking for a wife. This logging operation would take all his time the next few years, and he didn't plan to make a woman wait around for him. But there was something about the tall, blonde woman with a constant smile and sparkle in her eyes that kept him thinking about her. Her adamant plea to work in the woods last night still niggled at his mind.

He'd had his arms full of female when they'd rolled in the snow. He smiled. She'd been soft in all the right places, and he'd darn near kissed her, he'd been so caught up in her vanilla scent and intriguing eyes.

"Watch out!"

A log "thumped" to the ground not ten feet

from his horse. The animal shied sideways and bolted across the camp. Hank managed to stop the frightened creature just short of plowing into Mrs. Nielsen, carrying a basket toward the cookhouse.

His horse snorted.

"Uff da!" She held the basket up like a shield.

Hank bounded off his mount, stumbling and catching his foot in the stirrup in his haste. He finally extracted his foot and stood, flushed and embarrassed in front of the woman. She tipped her head back to peer into his face.

"Mr. Halsey, have you been with the drink?" Her faded green eyes no doubt at one time had held the same spunk as Kelda's.

"No, ma'am. I was thinking..." He trailed off. He didn't want the woman to know he was thinking about her daughter. He shuffled his feet. "My mind was on the contract I want your husband to look over, and I didn't see the tree they were falling. Scared my horse senseless when it fell. Took me by surprise, too."

"Mr. Halsey, a logging camp is a dangerous place if you don't have your wits about you." She shook a thin finger at him.

"Yes, ma'am."

The door to the cookhouse opened. Kelda stepped out wrapping a scarf around her head.

"Mor, I was worried you took so long to get the eggs for the cake." Kelda barely spared him a glance. "Mr. Halsey, did you sleep in this morning?"

He couldn't believe she didn't show any awkwardness about their tumble in the snow the night before. The frostiness of dinner had returned.

"No. I was conferring with my brother on a contract." He patted his jacket pocket where the contract rested. "Any idea where I can find your father?"

"Kelda, his contract has him distracted. Best you take him to your father. He might end up under a tree." Mrs. Nielson patted her daughter's arm, sent Hank a wisp of a smile, and disappeared into the cookhouse.

Hank peered into Kelda's amused eyes. "I don't think your mother likes me."

Her lips quivered between a half smile and a full curve of her lips. "She likes you, or she would not have asked me to take you to Far. She would have let you get hit by a tree." Kelda giggled and her eyes danced with glee.

Her merriment was infectious. He liked the way her face lit when she genuinely smiled. "I see. Then lead on."

She headed toward the shushing sound of saws in rhythm, slicing through trees and the cadence of axes, taking bites out of the tall pines. Her long strides covered the ground with speed. Stepping over downed logs and around underbrush, he saw why she wore men's dungarees. In a dress she would be hampered.

"Timber!" the call barely finished ringing when the top of a tree whistled and whushed to the ground.

Hank tipped his head back. A man stood on the flat cut of the tree nearly eighty feet in the air. Hank gulped and his stomach tightened at the thought of standing on a tree so tall.

A tug on his sleeve drew his gaze from the

man.

Kelda's eyes shone with excitement. "Rudy is a good topper, but I've climbed higher."

Hank's heart sputtered to a halt, and his throat constricted. He stared at the man so high he looked like he could touch the clouds then back at the glowing face of the woman beside him. He swallowed. "Y-you've been that high?"

"Ja. It's like being an eagle. You're high above and can see for a great distance." She peeked at him then stared at the man on the slightly swaying tree. "From up there you would look no bigger than a cat."

Her excitement didn't squelch the fear crawling around in Hank's chest. He'd stick to the ground jobs, and Kelda wouldn't be topping any trees.

"Your father." He'd distract her with the job they came to do. Find Arvid and get back to the camp.

She reluctantly drew her gaze from the man on the tree and scanned the area. "There." Her finger pointed to two men swinging axes one then the other and taking huge chips out of a pine nearly ten feet in circumference. Kelda hurried forward, seemingly unfettered by the chaos of falling trees and men swinging shiny axe blades.

Hank had, until now, stayed in the camp. He wanted to be a logger. Wanted to be out in the woods swinging an axe and doing physical work, but he'd always found a reason to do jobs that kept him close to camp. Watching the unison of swinging axes and the rhythm of the men working the saws made Hank itch even more to be a part of this tradition. It also brought the realization this group of men knew their place and how to avoid the blades, saws, and falling trees as they worked in small groups.

His dawdling watching the men caused him to lose sight of Kelda. Worry for her, moved his feet faster. He dodged the tail end of a tree being dragged to the camp clearing by a pair of horses in time to see Kelda stopping the rhythmic movements of the two chipping away at the large pine.

As he approached the group, they watched him step over limbs and dodge a swinging axe. Hank realized how he handled himself in the woods would determine how far these men would follow him should the need arise. Heaven forbid there wasn't a Nielsen around to run things until the last tree was harvested. But he also wanted the men's respect not their pity or laughter.

He stopped a few feet from the trio. The young man smitten with Kelda worked with Arvid. Hank had learned Peder arrived a year ago from Norway. He was the son of Arvid's best friend still in the homeland.

"Kelda says you have papers for me?" Arvid handed his axe to his daughter. "You and Peder finish."

"Is that..." Before Hank could finish his sentence, Kelda peeled off the black woolen coat and picked up her father's axe. It was obvious from Peder's gaping mouth and wide eyes he hadn't witnessed the woman's prowess before.

She swung the axe, taking a large chip out of the trunk and nodded to Peder to fall into the rhythm. Peder's first swing was ill set and his blade stuck in the wood, breaking Kelda's stride.

"Peder if you can't keep up with me, I'll ask you to step back and let me do this myself." Kelda smiled brightly, plucked his wedged blade from the trunk, and swept the man to the side. She squared up with the tree and swung her axe in long, biting strokes.

Hank followed the lines of her body as it whipped the axe above her head and brought it down into the tree, flinging woodchips and clearing a notch. He couldn't believe she could lift an axe let alone swing it with such precision.

"The papers?" Arvid's deep voice, laced with mischief, jolted Hank from his admiring assessment of Kelda.

"You shouldn't have handed her your axe." As much as he refused to admit she was good with an axe, he had to admire her skill.

"She loves the woods and is better than most of the men. She can't hurt herself working on this one tree. Let her be. She enjoys it." Arvid held out his hand. "The papers?"

Hank forced his gaze from Kelda and reached into his jacket, extracting the contract. "I'd like you to look this over and see if the numbers can be accomplished. I want to get this initialed at the mill in McEwen and signed by the owners in Baker City before old man Eccles seals up all the lumber mills in the area."

While Arvid read the contract, Hank continued to watch Kelda.

A strong gust of cold winter wind bent the pines in the area causing the tree she notched to creak.

"Watch out!" Hank leapt forward, grabbing her arm and drawing her away from the tree.

Arvid burst out laughing. "That tree won't topple. It's stout as that mountain."

Heat spread up Hank's neck and into his cold cheeks. He peered into Kelda's frowning face and slowly released his arms that were wrapped around her body.

"If this is how you behave in the woods, I suggest you stay at the camp with Paddy." The tone wasn't laughing like her father's. Kelda peered at him with disapproval.

The scowl on Peder's face lightened and he smiled. No doubt at the fact Kelda found disfavor with the boss.

Hank stepped back even as his hands wished to remain clasped around Kelda to make sure she was safe. He'd been taught to be a gentleman, but he knew, by the glint in the old man's eyes and the flush that now bloomed on Kelda's cheeks, his actions were beyond those of being a gentleman. He'd just shown the two he carried an attraction to the woman. It was a good thing he was headed to Baker City with the contract tomorrow. He needed space and time to sort out his actions.

He turned to Arvid and cleared his throat. "The contract. Can you, we, provide this amount of lumber in the time I specified?"

The thunk of axe on wood rang out behind him. He didn't dare look for being mesmerized by Kelda's skill.

"Ja. We will probably do even more, but is good to put a safe number on paper." Arvid clapped a hand on Hank's back and handed him the contract. "Go tend to the business of logging. We'll tend to the falling."

"I'll head to Baker City tomorrow. I'll be back here in a couple of days. Are there any supplies you need?"

"Ask Ingrid. She always has a list." Arvid placed a hand on his daughter's shoulder, stopping her rhythmic axe. "Take Mr. Halsey back to the camp and Mor."

Kelda nodded and picked up her coat, shoving her arms in the sleeves before Hank could reach out and help. She walked back through the trees and chaos faster than their trip out, as if she wanted him to get stuck behind or perhaps hindered. He didn't mind following. It gave him a chance to fully study and admire her graceful, muscled body. Her baggy clothing hid the muscles he knew powered the robust swings of the axe and the agility of her movements avoiding trees and near collisions with the other loggers.

Once out of the trees and crossing the camp yard, Hank doubled his stride to walk shoulder to shoulder with her. "I'm sorry I pulled you away from the tree, but my actions are exactly why it's foolish for you to be in the woods. I'm sure I'm not the only man who's tried to save you from harm." The apology wouldn't soften her obvious anger but it was warranted. Not only did it allow him to voice his concern but to also show her he wasn't callous.

She stopped, fisted her hands on her hips, and stared at him. The deep green of her eyes flashed with anger and something he thought for a moment was embarrassment.

"Why can't you be like other owners and stay in the office counting the trees and your money? No one else has cared if I work in the woods."

"There are no trees to count. Every one of them is being used on the buildings for this camp." His lips quivered to smile, but he remained determined not to let on her ire amused him.

She huffed. "Well, then stay here and make sure the buildings are fit for their uses."

"I have longed to learn the logging trade. I'm not going to sit tight in the camp or the office while I have a firsthand ability to learn." He hadn't told Arvid of his long dream of being a logger. He wasn't even sure where it came from, but he'd wanted to be a "beast of the woods."

She cocked her head to one side and stared at him. Slowly a smile twitched and grew on her lips. Lips he'd dreamed about the last few nights. Lips that he knew would be sweet, soft and irresistible once he'd tasted them.

"You want to be a beast of the woods do you?"

"Yes."

"Then you better find a bunk when the workers' cabins are done so you aren't riding in here after a half a day's work is done." Her gaze raked him up and down. "Once the falling starts we work twelve to fourteen hours a day. As long as the sun's shining."

"Those hours don't scare me. I've worked that and more at our mine." He squared around to continue the verbal jousting.

"Mine. Then you know how to work a pick and not an axe." Her toes pointed toward his and her flirty green eyes snapped with challenge.

"True, but I'm a quick learner."

"You will need to be to stay out of trouble in the woods."

"I won't be getting into trouble as long as you stay in the kitchen." There was no way her father or brothers could do their jobs if they were keeping an eye on Kelda in the woods. His decision to not allow her out there was a solid one.

Daggers flashed in her eyes. "You'll have to start at the lowest jobs before you'll be allowed to work with Karl or Dag. It's how they determine if you're cut out to be a beast." Her gaze drifted over him as though assessing his skills.

Hank's palms itched to reach out and push the golden strand of hair fluttering in the wind back under her scarf.

"Kelda, if you are done showing Mr. Halsey around I need your help." Mrs. Nielsen stuck her head out of the cookhouse door.

Hank flinched at the realization they stood staring into one another's eyes. He cleared his throat and turned to the woman as Kelda scurried past her mother and into the building. "Mrs. Nielsen. I'm taking the contract to Baker City tomorrow, are there any supplies you need?"

A smile much like her daughter's lit the woman's face. "Ja. It is Arvid's birthday on Saturday, I would like to make his favorite lefse, but I need more potatoes."

"Anything else?" Hank couldn't help but get caught up in Mrs. Nielsen's excitement over her husband's birthday.

She looked around then leaned closer. "Would you be here on Saturday for dinner and to help with the boys if they drink too much?"

He raised a brow. "Drink too much? Do they get mean?"

"Nei. But they poke fun at their sister when they have too much drink, and I know Arvid will pull out the akevitt, a Norwegian liquor he has for special occasions."

Hank didn't like the idea of playing keeper to the Nielsen family, but if he could spare Kelda some torment from her brothers, he could hang around after dinner.

"I'll be here."

"Mange takk, thank you. I love my men, but there are times I would like to use my cast iron pan on their thick heads." She pulled her gray head in and the conversation ended.

Hank smiled. He'd no doubt the woman, if angered enough, would smack her men around with a pan. She'd inflict little injury, but if her daughter, who wielded an axe like the beasts of the woods, decided to try out her mother's punishment it could cause a great deal of discomfort to the one on the other end of the pan.

Chapter 5

Kelda woke Friday morning feeling like she'd yanked a dull saw through a tree all night. Wanting to be in the woods and instead bending over the large tub filled with the pans from the bread cooling on the table didn't help her disgruntled mood.

The door banged open.

Kelda jerked and spun around.

Hank stood in the doorway, a bulging burlap sack slung over each shoulder. "Where does your mother want these bags of potatoes?"

Kelda hustled forward to take one.

"No." He shook his head. "Just tell me where to put them."

"The storeroom." Kelda hurried between the table and the wall to the backroom where the supplies were kept. She pulled the blanket back and Hank hesitated.

"Just place them against the wall right here." She glanced up and caught Hank scanning her cot, the two dresses hanging on pegs, and her brush on an upturned crate. Luckily, her unmentionables were tucked in the trunk at the end of her bed.

"You sleep in the storage room?" His tone verged on anger as he dropped the bags on the floor.

"Ever since I felt uncomfortable sleeping in the same room as the boys." She shrugged. It was the only life she knew, and it was a good life.

Hank shook his head. "Haven't you ever wanted a room of your own with frilly curtains and a fancy bed?"

Did he think she was lacking in feminine interests? The thought horrified her. "It won't happen as long as I'm working for my family and that's what matters."

He took a step toward her. His hand lifted then settled back at his side. "Family is good, but sometimes don't you just want to do something for yourself?"

"There are days when I'd like to be anywhere but here, doing, whatever a woman does when they aren't cooking or logging, but those are only wishes that won't feed my family." Her insides twisted. She'd never voiced her thoughts to any-one. Keeping them locked away made them easier to ignore. Now that she'd voiced them, she won-dered if she'd ever do the things other women did. Dinner in a fancy restaurant, kiss a man, have a baby.

"The next time I go to Baker City you can come with me." His dark eyes held something she'd never seen in a man's eyes or anyone's eyes. What could that deep smoldering mean?

"I can't. I'm needed here." She stepped back, and her knees buckled against the edge of her cot. Her body plopped down hard, causing the boards to crack and thud to the floor. Humiliation burned a scorching path up her neck, infusing her cheeks.

Hank bent to offer assistance as Mor scurried into the room.

"What is—" Mor grabbed the broom to the side of the door and whacked Hank across the back.

"Ow!" Hank spun from looming over Kelda and grasped the broom from Mor.

Kelda pushed out of the bed frame and grabbed Hank's free hand to pull herself to her feet. He leaned down, giving her more leverage, and she popped up beside him, clutching his strong hand. Her mother's stern glare at their twined hands sprang Kelda's fingers open. She released Hank and peered at her mother.

"Mor what are you doing beating on Hank with a broom?"

Mor's eyes narrowed and she glared at Hank. "What is he doing in your room? And you sprawled on the bed?"

"Mrs. Nielsen, it's not what you're thinking. I brought the potatoes you asked for." He pointed the broom handle at the two sacks leaning against the wall. "It's crowded in here. Kelda backed to move out of the way and ran into the bed, landing on it."

Kelda's face heated again. Not only did her large body ruin her bed but her mother had thought she and Hank... She'd had dreams of Hank kissing her ever since the night they sprawled in the snow. As much as she wanted to hate the man for not allowing her to work beside her brothers and father, she couldn't wipe away the niggling idea a man, this man, could want her. That Mor believed Hank had those thoughts about her daughter delighted and frightened Kelda.

Mor's knowing gaze took in the splintered bed frame sticking out from under the wool blankets. "I'll get Paddy to fix the bed." She pointed a thin finger at Hank's chest. "Out of here. Next time you bring supplies, leave them inside the front door. If I catch you back here again, I will use the cast iron pan and not a broom."

"Yes, ma'am." Hank nodded to Mor then faced Kelda. "Are you all right? That was a nasty fall—Ouch!"

Mor struck Hank's shins with her pointy-toed women's boots. "I said get out. You can talk with her in the eating area."

Hank hobbled out of the supply room. Mor grabbed Kelda's arm.

"He's a good man, but do not let him lead you down the wrong path. You both are past the age of marrying."

"Mor! I fell. That's all." Kelda couldn't remember any other time in her life when her face had heated so many times in one day. Her chest ached with not an undesirable pain, but one that felt too large for her chest.

"Kelda?" Hank's questioning voice riveted her gaze to the blanket separating the two rooms.

"Go. But do not lose your head." Mor inclined her gray bun toward the doorway.

Kelda slipped out. Hank bent near the front door, rubbing a hand up and down his shin. He straightened when her boots clomped across the packed dirt floor.

"Did you hurt yourself when you fell?"

His concern added to the tightness in her chest. "Only my pride. I'm not usually so clumsy."

A grin spread across his handsome features. "It was kind of comical. Not you falling, but the bed and then your mother flailing me with a broom."

Kelda couldn't hold in the fit of giggles. Hank's deep laugh joined her and all felt right.

Mor stepped out of the room with an apron full of potatoes, and they both laughed harder.

"Go to work, Kelda has potatoes to peel," Mor said, dumping the potatoes in the wash tub.

"I'll see you at dinner." Hank opened the door and disappeared.

Kelda stared at the door a moment before joining Mor and peeling the potatoes.

Hank didn't know what came over him other than the fact every time he got close to Kelda his body overruled his good intentions. He stomped to the newly finished office and jerked open the door.

Tobias glanced up from stocking shelves behind a counter at the side of the room.

"Are those the items the loggers purchase?" Hank needed a distraction. After learning of Kelda's living conditions and never having been treated like a woman, he'd offered to take her to Baker City. At the time he'd said it, he just wanted to show her how a woman should be treated; not like a man or like an employee. After the desire she'd flared in him and then the beating he'd received from her mother, he wasn't sure that was such a good idea. But after having made the offer, how the heck would he get out of taking her without looking ill-mannered?

"Ja. The beasts are charged a penny more than what you pay for the goods to offset the labor of selling the items." Tobias peered into Hank's eyes. "There have been some bosses who charge five cents over their cost to pad their wallets."

"The penny is fine. Add it to your pay since you'll be the one running the sales and making the payroll." Hank walked past the younger man and into the small area that was to be his office. The room could easily fit a desk and a bed. He'd bought a desk in Baker City while purchasing potatoes and formally signing the contract with the Oregon Lumber Company. Until the railroad made it to McEwen to haul the lumber to Baker City and the mill, he'd have to pay the loggers and stockpile the logs. He'd talked it over with his brothers. It was risky to start logging now before the railroad was close, but if he waited, others would jump in and then they'd have to sell and transport the lumber even farther which would cut into the profit.

"Mr. Halsey?" Tobias stood at the office door.

"Yes?" Hank shook off the worries that made him wonder if he should have waited a year.

"I've counted every log that's been used for building, and Karl gave me the measurement for the chute we'll build next. I've calculated the logs we'd need for that. Would you like to take a look at my numbers?" The younger of the Nielsen brothers had a strong mind but was a bit timid. The work in the office suited him better than the hard labor and hollering orders to the other men even if he was the same size as Hank.

"Yes, I'm still not certain what a chute is. Could you tell me about it?" Hank, took the wooden stool behind the counter while Tobias pulled out a large piece of paper with a drawing on it. He spread the paper across the counter and began explaining.

"This being an operation on a mountainside with no large streams to float the logs down, we will build a channel of logs shaped like a trough that the logs we fall will slide down and land in the stack yard. Smithy and the other teamsters will drag the logs to the chute with the horses and then greasers and gaffers will see that the logs keep moving down the mountain."

The idea seemed ingenious but... "How fast do the logs come down the chute? What stops them at the bottom?" Hank didn't like the idea of the logs slamming into visitors or the women.

"The chute is built to keep them moving but not at such a steep pitch the logs can't be controlled especially when the weather warms and the logs could get warm from friction. At the bottom, the chute curls up to stop the logs." Tobias smiled broadly. "We've only lost one man to a chute operation and that was his own doing. He didn't give the force of the logs the respect they deserve."

This wasn't the first time he'd heard one of the crew talk about the logs in such a reverent fashion.

"Have you worked out in the woods or always in the office?" Hank couldn't wait to get out in the woods and be a part of the group that came in sweaty, dirty, and exuberant every evening for dinner.

"All Nielsen's have to work at every job for a while. It is how we find out what we are good at and can be called upon when there is someone sick or injured to fill in." Tobias studied him intently. "Are you planning to learn all the jobs?"

"Yes. I want to learn everything, so in the future I can step in and help when needed." Hank planned on making logging his future whether just on his family's mountain or by traveling. He was tired of mining. His future was in the trees he'd marveled at from a young age.

"You'll start out greasing the chute, move to gaffer and then up the line. The last thing you'll learn is climbing a tree with a rope." Tobias shuddered. "I hate that and will leave it to Kelda. She loves climbing the trees high in the air."

"I noticed that when she took me out to talk to your father the other day." Remembering the exhilaration in her voice talking about the sights from high in the air chilled his bones more thoroughly than standing in a winter blizzard.

"She'd be out there every day falling trees if Far would let her." Tobias shook his head.

"It's not your father keeping her in the cookhouse, it's me. I won't have a woman working out in the woods." Hank wasn't surprised when the young Nielsen raised his brows.

"You told this to Kelda?"

"Yes, she knows where I stand on this." Hank wondered if she was coming around to his thinking. They had shared a laugh a few moments ago.

"That explains her anger the other night after you two talked." Tobias shuffled some papers. "You might want to watch yourself around her. Kelda doesn't like having anyone tell her she can't be in the woods." He scratched his head. "I'm surprised Far hasn't said anything to the rest of us.

"If Mor could still work the long hours or had other help than Kelda, Far would have Kelda out there working. She is the best." Tobias nodded and rolled up the diagram of the chute.

"You would work beside her. A woman?" Hank stared at the young man.

"Ja. Far only hires the best. His children are the best, and he likes everyone to know."

Kelda might be one of the best, but he'd make damn sure she never worked alongside the men. She had to be a distraction. He couldn't keep his eyes off her the other day when she was swinging an axe. He frowned. Neither had Peder. Allowing Kelda in the woods on a permanent basis would only cause problems.

<h1 style="text-align:center">Chapter 6</h1>

Kelda stepped out the back of the cookhouse to toss the dish water and caught sight of Hank and Tobias unloading a bed into the office. Tobias already had his cot set up in the small room beside Hank's office. Did Hank bring him a bed?

Curious, she leaned the dish pan against the back of the cookhouse and wandered toward the office, drying her hands on her apron. Hank stepped from the office and hefted a trunk up on his shoulder.

"Are you moving into the office?" she asked, walking up behind him.

Hank spun. She ducked to avoid the trunk corner colliding with her head.

"Yes. I want to be here from the start of the day to the finish and the ride back and forth to my cabin is taking up too much of my day." He motioned with his free arm for her to enter the office. "It's cold out here. Tobias has a fire stoked in the office."

Kelda stepped around Hank and the trunk and entered the office. Tobias looked up from behind the counter and smiled.

"Hank and I will live in the office." Tobias held out a tin cup and motioned to the coffee pot on the small pot-bellied stove in the corner.

Hank brushed past her, disappearing with the trunk into the room that was to be his office. When he returned, she swept her gaze the length of him and would have sighed audibly if not for her brother watching them keenly and her vow to not be friendly with the man.

"Your office won't be very private if you sleep in there." She sipped her coffee and watched him over the rim of the cup.

A smile curved his full lips. "From what I've seen around here so far there isn't a whole lot that is private in this camp."

She had to agree there. Everyone's business seemed to be everyone else's. "True." She took another sip. "You could have slept in a bunkhouse with the other beasts."

"I like my privacy. I've been living alone for so long now that I'd make bad company for a room full of men. Besides I grew up with five brothers and our parents in a one room cabin. I prefer having walls around me and not snoring, noisy bodies." Hank held up a hand, "No offense, Tobias."

"I understand."

"Me, too." Kelda stared point blank into Hank's eyes. "That's why I don't mind sleeping in the storage room."

A spark lit and quickly disappeared from his dark eyes. What had her comment triggered in his mind?

"I better get back. I stepped out to toss the dishwater when I saw you unloading. My curiosity pulled me away from my chores. Mor is probably yelling out the door wondering where I wandered to."

"Come by any time," Hank said, taking a step toward her.

Their gazes latched, and she wished she had more experience with men other than working beside them. There was something in his eyes she couldn't cipher, but it made her heart quicken.

The door to the stove slammed shut. Her eyes flinched closed from the noise and cut off the connection from Hank. Without another word or glance she strode to the door and out into a flurry of snowflakes. A late winter blizzard veiled the camp in white as freezing wind blew down off the mountain. She needed the jolt of cold to knock her back to her senses and to help her remain neutral to the man.

Her teeth chattered by the time Kelda arrived at the back door of the cookhouse. She picked up the dishpan and entered the building to find her mother flushed.

"Where have you been we have to get the lefse made for Far's birthday dinner." Her mother worked the masher up and down in the large pot of boiled potatoes.

Kelda moved her mother aside and took the utensil. Her height helped when it came to mashing the large pot of potatoes. "Get the other ingredients ready, I'll mash these."

"Where were you?" Mor placed salt, butter,

sugar, canned milk, and flour on the table.

"I spotted Tobias and Mr. Halsey carrying a bed into the office. Mr. Halsey will now be sleeping in his office." Kelda smashed the potatoes making them as fine as she could. The idea Hank would now be sleeping at the camp meant she would see him more. Her heart banged against her ribs. When had seeing him become so important to her? His being around all the time would make it harder for her to work in the woods. How would Far find a way for her to work for her brothers if the boss was always under foot?

"I invited him to Far's birthday not to move in." The unease in Mor's voice drew Kelda's gaze.

"What is wrong with him sleeping here? He will be ready to work earlier and not be exhausted to ride back to his cabin." How could she dread his staying one moment and stick up for him the next? She frowned and mashed harder on the potatoes.

Mor placed her small thin hands over Kelda's. The size difference was that of a woman and child, with Kelda's being the woman and her mother's the child.

"Daughter, I have eyes. I see the way the two of you look at one another."

"Mor—"

"Don't deny it. Even your brothers have come to me worrying you will be hurt." Mor shook her head. "Your father sees only good from this. But I… Kelda promise me you'll be a good girl and not get compromised."

Kelda sucked in air and stared at Mor open-mouthed. "H-how…I…" She was at a loss for what to say. Her mother thought Hank would…She would...

Her heart slammed into her ribs like a ten pound axe, vibrating her body and knocking the air out of her.

"It is hard to remain good when a man shows you how special you are." Mor's eyes glassed over all dreamy.

Was she thinking of her youth with Far? Had Mor and Far kissed and touched before marrying? She wanted to ask and learn more about the feelings between a woman and a man. Mor shook from her reveries and carried the pot of potatoes to the table.

Kelda's hands trembled and her knees wanted to give way. If this was how mooning over a man made her feel, she had to stop these thoughts. She couldn't be weak and do the work Far expected of her.

Hank took the time to clean up and put on a new shirt before tramping through the snow flurries to the cookhouse. From the way Mrs. Nielsen talked about the birthday meal it was a special occasion.

The others were already seated around the table when he stomped through the door. He nodded at each one and clasped Arvid's hand wishing him a happy birthday. Before he sat, he scanned the back of the room and found Kelda in a dress that accentuated her wide shoulders, firm breasts, and smaller waist than he'd imagined. The dark skirt flowed over her hips to the floor. He grinned at the man-sized boots peeking out from under the skirt as she walked toward the table carrying a plate piled with rolled up pancakes.

"Hank, this is lefse a Norwegian favorite," Arvid said, taking several of the pancakes.

Ingrid placed sliced venison roasts at both ends of the table as Kelda followed with pitchers of gravy and bowls of potatoes.

The feast continued longer than usual meals with each man being served a glass of beer and ending the meal with a cookie Tobias called fattigmann. They were fried, lightly coated with powdery sugar, and had a spicy bite Hank liked.

After the loggers left, the family remained around the table. Ingrid and Kelda joined them and Arvid poured a yellowish liquid into small cups. He passed them out until each person at the table had one.

Hank raised the glass and sniffed. It had a spicy fruity aroma.

"Hurra for deg som fyller ditt år!" The family chorused and tossed back the liquor in one swallow. Ingrid and Kelda included.

"Happy birthday!" Hank added and swallowed the drink. The taste wasn't unpleasant but burned in a way different from whiskey. He coughed and Tobias pound on his back with a wide flat hand. It was like being swat with a wooden plank.

Kelda giggled and pointed at him,

Tears seeped from his eyes and his nose ran.

The men all laughed and held out their glasses to be refilled. He didn't want to be labeled as someone who couldn't hold his liquor and held out his glass. A clucking sound caught his attention. Ingrid shook her head slightly and pointedly looked from her boys to Kelda.

She'd invited him here to keep her daughter from embarrassment. But what better way to keep them from talking about their sister than him making a fool of himself with his drinking?

He shrugged, kept the glass extended, and downed one more swallow. This time it burned clear to his toes and tingled. A sure sign he'd hit his limit. Two whiskeys were all he could handle, and this liquor would appear to have the same effect on him.

Arvid raised the bottle to refill, Hank pulled his glass back.

"You do not have to ride to your cabin tonight. Tobias tells us you have put a bed in your office." Arvid shook the bottle at Hank.

"But I do need to be up and ready to finish the work that accumulated while I was in Baker City. I don't mind celebrating with a couple of drinks but that's my limit." Hank pushed his glass over to reside by the women's.

Karl slapped a wide hand on the table, bouncing the glasses and gathering everyone's attention. He quirked an eyebrow and stared at Hank. "The boss wants us at a disadvantage I think."

Hank shook his head. "No, I just like to be clear headed."

Dag winked. "Do you think we won't notice you looking at our sister if we drink and you don't?"

He couldn't stop his head from spinning Kelda's direction. The tip of her ears fairly glowed they were so red. Her embarrassment had to be apparent even to her giggling brothers wiggling their glasses for refills.

Arvid refilled the cups, and they all downed another round.

Hank's mind spun with how to keep Kelda from anymore of the trio's mischief. The only way would be to get her out of the room, but that would mean giving them even more fodder to goad her with if he suggested they leave together.

"Kelda, I used more lard than I planned on the fattigmann, would you go to the cold storage and bring more for in the morning?" Ingrid looked at Hank as she spoke to her daughter.

He took that as a prompt to go with her. Mrs. Nielsen's actions puzzled him considering the way she had behaved the day he and Kelda were alone in the storage room behind the kitchen.

Kelda immediately rose and headed to the door. Hank followed. He started to reach out and help her with her coat and realized the group at the table watched. Instead, he put his own coat on and picked up the lantern.

"I can get the lard myself," Kelda said, reaching for the lantern.

"I need the fresh air."

She scowled and marched out the door ahead of him. He didn't look back. Didn't want to see her family's reactions.

He ducked his head and plunged into the flurry of snow. The usual packed snow in the camp was covered with six inches of fluffy snow. Kelda scooted her feet along, kicking up white plumes. Hank hurried beside her, bumping his shoulder into hers. "Let's go sit in the office for a while. At least until your brothers wander off to bed."

"But Mor—"

"Sent you out here so your brothers wouldn't tease and embarrass you and sent me to keep you company." He led the way to the office. The heat from the small stove stung his cold cheeks when he opened the door. He waved her in, followed, and set the lantern on the counter.

Her forehead was wrinkled in thought. Hank grasped her coat, drawing it off her shoulders. Kelda's wide green eyes peered at him with so many questions he wanted to pull her into his arms and kiss her. Not a good direction for his thoughts to go. He stepped away, placing her coat across the back of the only chair, and motioned for her to sit. He made a mental note to make a couple more chairs. This would make a nice place for men to gather and visit.

"When did Mor tell you to keep me company?" Her question came out so soft he barely caught it.

"When she invited, or rather, demanded I come to your father's party. She said when the boys get to drinking they tend to pick on you." He pulled the stool from behind the counter over and sat. It made him taller than her, but still not as tall as standing.

Her brow slowly smoothed, and her eyes regained the sparkle and good humor he usually witnessed bestowed on others. "Was that before or after she whacked you with the broom?"

Laughter came easy when he was with Kelda. He caught his breath and thought. "Before."

Her eyes glittered with newfound merriment. "I am surprised she let the two of us out together. But then she did..." Kelda's voice trailed off, and her eyes widened as she stared at him.

"She did what?" He reached out gathering her cold hand between his. The strong fingers and calloused hand were smaller than his, but not tiny like Darcy's or fine-boned like his other sisters'. It fit his nicely. He looked down at their clasped hands then into Kelda's face.

The uncertainty in the shadows of her eyes slowly softened into a dreamy stare as a wistful smile played at the edges of her lips. The sight reminded him of school girls.

"How old are you?" He'd believed her close to his age, but now, seeing her like this, he wondered if he'd been wrong.

"Twenty-six this May. Why?" She leaned forward, her gaze intent on his face.

"Just wondered." He ran his thumb back and forth over the back of her hand. For all the work she did her skin was remarkably soft.

Her breath caught and she swallowed. "A-and you? How old are you?"

"Thirty-one."

"Oh. That's how old Karl is. He's cranky as an old bear he wants a wife so bad." She tipped her head to the side and watched him. "Is not having a wife what makes you so cranky about me working in the woods?"

Hank snorted and dropped her hand. Leave it to her to think everything was about her being in the woods. "No I'm not cranky about you working in the woods because I want a wife. I happen to like not having a wife. It gives me the freedom to do what I want." He stared into her eyes. "I'm too busy for a family."

She shook her head. "Karl is busy too, and that's all he thinks about. Do you think some men just need a woman?"

If not for the innocence shining in her eyes, he would have thought she was hunting for a way to get intimate with him. And darned if he didn't want to push her just a little.

"Do you mean they need a woman in their bed?"

Her intake of breath told him what he wanted to know. While she may live and work with men, her family had kept her from anything sordid.

"No! I meant to cook, clean, be company, and raise their family." Her cheeks tinged a deeper pink, and she tucked her hands deeper into her lap.

Hank felt a tiny bit of regret for his words, but this woman had a way of making him want to best her. "Where do you think that family the woman cares for comes from?" He knew pressing into this line of talk would have him standing in the cold before he could sleep, but he wanted to know her views.

Her face deepened in color, and her gaze dipped to her hands. "I know about making babies. I just…" Her gaze sought his. "I think sometimes people are just so lonely they settle."

Hank peered into her solemn eyes. "Would you?"

She shook her head. "I know there are few men who would be comfortable having a wife the size of me who works in the woods. But I'd rather be lonely than live with someone who didn't look at me the way Far looks at Mor."

He knew that look. It was the way light sparkled in his brothers' eyes when they spotted their wives. He nodded. There were times it was painful to watch the happiness his brothers found. But he had plans, and a wife didn't fit in them. Hank focused on Kelda's face. The innocent, wistful smile curving her lips sliced heat through his body and corralled it in his crotch area.

He stood and walked to the wood box to put distance between them.

"Why do you want to work in the woods?" she asked.

Her change of subject was welcome. The stove door creaked, and Hank shoved a log into the potbellied stove. The clank of metal on metal rang through the small area as he gathered what he wanted to say together in his head.

Hank sat on the stool and stared at the dull black stove. "I've always been fascinated with anything made from wood. Furniture, houses, tools, utensils, toys. The list goes on. Then to stand in the forest and peer up a tree...I just like the idea of being a part of something that affects so many lives."

"You could make the furniture or toys." Kelda leaned forward, placing her elbows on her knees, her chin in her hands, and watched Hank.

"I want to be a part of the process of harvesting the wood. To pick the right tree and leave behind smaller trees to grow and be harvested later. I want to treat logging like farming. I've seen mountainsides where all the trees are cut. The ground washes away if there's a strong rain and there is nothing left for the owner to continue making money."

"Far doesn't allow the men to cut down every

tree. We only take ones of certain circumference." She'd witnessed the mountain sides Hank talked about.

"I know. I asked around and learned your family does the kind of logging I've thought about." His gaze left the stove and peered into her eyes. "I want our property to keep on supplying Halsey's with a living for many more years."

"Are your brothers farmers?" She'd learned very little about his family from Far or her brothers. He didn't talk much about them or her family didn't feel she needed to know.

"No. Ethan and Clay run the stamp mill and mine."

She scrunched her forehead. "What's a stamp mill?"

"The rock we take from the mine is crushed at the stamp mill helping us extract more gold and silver from the rock and mine."

"That sounds like hard work." No wonder his body was as well-defined as her brothers.

"It can be. We also take in other miner's rock and crush it for them for a percentage."

"You said you had four brothers. What do the other two do?"

"Gil is the marshal of Galena. Zeke and his wife are Pinkerton detectives."

Kelda inhaled. She'd read about the Pinkerton's in the newspaper. "How did they become Pinkertons?"

Boisterous singing erupted outside and grew in volume as it drew closer.

"It's a long story. I'll tell you some other time. It sounds like your brothers are coming this direction." Hank slipped two coffee cups from pegs behind the stove and filled them, handing one to Kelda.

She took the offered drink and sipped.

The door burst open. Tobias had his arms slung around Dag and Karl's shoulders. The three were grinning like small boys with toads in their pockets.

Hank set his cup down and opened the door to the room with Tobias's cot. Her brothers disappeared into the room. Whispering and giggles floated back to them.

"I think Tobias will not be feeling well tomorrow," Kelda said, holding back a snicker.

"It doesn't appear that he will." Hank sat back down at the stool and took a sip of his coffee.

Two loud thunks, a groan, and a creak came from the room before Dag and Karl lumbered back into the office.

"He's not feeling well," Karl said, using the counter to lean against. Dag leaned next to him, grinning like an idiot.

Kelda tried to keep from laughing at the sight of her inebriated brothers, but their goofy smiles and rolling eyes tickled her insides. A laugh burst out. She held her hand in front of her mouth to try and stop the onslaught of mirth but she couldn't.

"What'r you laughing at?" Karl asked, taking a step toward her and swaying.

"You two. I've never seen two sillier looking creatures in my life." Kelda knew her brothers drank more than they should on several occasions throughout the year, but she usually disappeared to her area in the storeroom and didn't see the outcome.

"Silly? We'll show you silly, little sister." Dag moved fast for someone who moments before used the counter to hold him up. His arm snaked around Kelda. He planted a foot on the chair and flopped Kelda over his leg. "We'll see how funny you think a spanking is."

"Get your hands off her!" The menace in Hank's voice stilled Kelda's heart.

She tilted her head. Hank's usual affable face darkened with rage. The glint of anger in his eyes and his clenched fists startled Kelda. Before Dag's inebriated senses took in Hank's words, Hank stood her on her feet and moved her toward the door.

"If I see either of you lay a hand on your sister again, I'll see to it you're docked wages." Hank plucked her coat from the back of the chair and draped it over her shoulders. "I'm taking you back to your mother." He slipped his coat on and opened the door.

Kelda leaned into Hank as he escorted her across the camp with an arm protectively around her shoulders. The scene swirled around in her mind like a tide pool. No one had ever stood up to her brothers when they teased or tormented her. When they picked on her out in the woods, Far just chuckled and told them to take it easy. She studied Hank's stern face as he stalked across the snowy ground. Why had her brother spanking her upset him so? They were drunk and being stupid. They never hurt her. Well, physically, but her pride usually took a battering from their antics.

He stopped at the door of the cookhouse and

drew in a deep breath. "I—"

"Come inside, it will be warmer." Kelda put her hand out to open the door. She wanted to see his face when he talked to her. The darkness made it hard to see the intent in his eyes.

"I don't want to say what I have to say in front of your parents." Emotion deepened his voice and fluttered her stomach.

"I'm sure by the state of the boys, Mor has tucked Far into bed and she'll be by his side." Kelda patted his arm and swung the door open. A lantern sat on the table, its flame turned down low. "See. No one."

She slipped the coat from her shoulders and hung it on the peg by the door. Hank shut the cold and snow out and grasped her shoulders.

"I meant what I said to your brothers. If they lay a hand on you again, tell me, and I'll dock their wages. If anyone else puts their hands on you, I'll send them packing." He stared into her eyes.

The anger and concern swimming in his eyes squeezed her chest. "They're always swatting me or—"

"You're not a child nor are you their toy. You're a woman, and you deserve to be treated like one. As long as I'm paying the men in this camp they will keep their hands off you and treat you like a lady."

His announcement made her giddy with the thought he saw her as a woman. No one had ever treated her with such high regard. Elation washed through her having someone voice the words she'd been secretly wishing to hear.

"Mange Takk. Thank you for calling me a lady.

I've never..." Tears burned her eyes. She didn't want to cry. Didn't want him to see how badly she needed to hear those words.

"Shh..." Hank's arms wrapped around her. One hand pressed her against his chest while the other rubbed circles on her back.

The heat of his body pressed to hers and his hand soothing her back warmed her better than a red hot stove and filled her with contentment. She snuggled into his embrace, taking in his musky scent, and enjoying this moment of being cherished by someone other than her father.

"Feeling better?" His husky whisper next to her ear slithered tingles of anticipation down her neck.

She raised her chin to peer into his eyes. His dark eyes sparked before his lashes lowered, hiding his emotions. Hank's face grew near and their lips touched. A quick brush of soft skin to soft skin. The connection rippled pleasure through her body.

A thud in the back room jolted their lips apart.

Chapter 7

Hank stared into Kelda's dreamy gaze. The kiss had been everything he'd dreamed of—sweet, innocent, and intoxicating. Damn. He kissed her. First he stood up for her with her brothers and now this. His gaze darted to the back of the room to see what caused the sound that sprang them apart. Ingrid stepped out of the room she shared with Arvid and picked up a skillet. He didn't have time to make an excuse or find words to get out of the predicament he'd made.

"I'll talk to you tomorrow." He ducked out the door without a glance at Kelda.

He balled his fists and stomped across the camp. He'd known having an unmarried woman in the camp would cause trouble, he just hadn't thought it would be him that got caught in the trouble. Hank started for the office, but when the bright light in the one window tossed a shadow on the wall inside of one of Kelda's brothers, he turned his toes toward the only other building with a light on. Paddy O'Brien's cabin. He didn't want to have a chat with Kelda's brothers when they were liquored up. And he could really use some of Paddy's wisdom about how far over the line he'd stepped as the boss of this outfit.

Kelda stared at the door. Flutters tickled her insides and heat warmed her lips. Hank called her a lady, and then he kissed her. Two things, she'd dreamed of ever since she'd realized she would never fit into women's shoes, happened tonight.

"Kelda, what are you doing allowing that man's hands on you?" Not even Mor's harsh tone could invade Kelda's happiness. She touched her lips and sighed.

"He called me a lady and told the boys if they laid hands on me again he'd dock their wages." She glanced at Mor. Her small body was clad in her nightdress, and she clutched a frying pan. Was that why Hank hightailed it out the door?

"Ja, he called you a lady. That's what you are." Mor put a hand on Kelda's arm. "Come on over and have a cup of tea with me."

She followed Mor to the table and sat while her mother put the tea kettle on the stove and placed cups, saucers, and honey on the table.

Mor sat across from Kelda and reached over, taking one of her hands. "I know Far and the boys have always treated you like one of them, but I wanted you to be tough since you took a liking to the outdoors and begged to work with the men." Tears glistened in Mor's eyes. "I know how much you want to be working in the woods with Far. I see it in the yearning in your eyes every morning when the men walk out that door."

The tea kettle whistled. Mor pat her hand and stood, shuffling to the stove and picking up the kettle. The whistling subsided as Mor poured water into a tea pot and spooned in the tea leaves.

Why did Mor have tears in her eyes as she talked to me? What made her sad?

Kelda studied her mother's slow movements. She remembered a time when Mor flitted around the cookhouse like her skirt was on fire. These days her movements were slow and methodical. Some days Kelda believed Mor second guessed her ingredients and looked a little muddled when she started to get something and would come back with a different item. Was that why Far wanted Kelda to remain in the cookhouse and not outside helping?

Mor poured the light brown tea into the cups and sat. She raised the cup to her lips and sipped. Kelda stirred a spoonful of honey into her tea before she sniffed the aromatic steam rising from the cup and sipped.

"It's good of you to sit with me while I have a cup of tea," Mor said, the worry lines gone from her brow and her eyes shimmered a soft green.

Had she forgotten their earlier discussion? Not wanting to talk about it anyway, Kelda nodded. "I needed a warm drink to help me sleep."

Mor patted her arm. "Yes, it always helps me to sleep."

Kelda vowed to watch Mor closer during the day and to tell Far she knew why he wanted her to stay in the kitchen.

Paddy stared at Hank. The old codger had laughed when Hank told him about docking the Nielson boys' wages. Now he stared into Hank's face with the cunning and intensity of a wolf.

"You stood up for Kelda with her brothers?"

Hank curled and uncurled the brim of his hat in a tense fist. "It's not right the way they always touch her and make fun of her. She's a woman and being around men all the time has to wear on her. There's no need for them giving her aggravations."

"She made the decision to stay here. Arvid offered to send her to a teaching school." Paddy held out a bottle of whiskey he'd been sipping on when Hank invaded his privacy.

Hank shook his head. "Why didn't she go? She seemed wistful about living somewhere other than a storeroom the other day."

"The Nielsen's are a strong family. They support one another and she loves the woods." Paddy chuckled. "Could you see her standing in front of a bunch of children?"

Hank started to nod his head then a flash of her swinging an axe stopped him. Her face glowed with good health and happiness when she swung that axe and made wood chips fly. He shook it off. "I think she'd make a fine teacher."

Paddy outright guffawed. When he reined in his humor, he took a sip of whiskey and squinted one eye at Hank. "Yer tryin' to put her somewhere she's not wantin' to be. If she had a notion to leave she could have left a long time ago, but she didn't."

"She told me she's had to battle with other

loggers. That's not right." Hank couldn't forget she was a woman, and as one, he'd been brought up to protect her.

"If she wants to be a logger she has to, from time to time, put some of them in their place. They don't brawl, but they can get into some axe swingin' or climbin' matches. That little lady has lost to few."

"What happens when she loses?" Hank had a feeling that was Kelda's problem. She lost to the men and therefore felt she had to work harder to prove her strength.

"She's only lost two times, but then she hasn't gone against her pa." Paddy winked.

"Who did she lose to?"

"Dag and Karl."

"She went against her brothers?" The men were both larger and brawnier than her. She was more foolish than he'd thought.

"It's the way of the woods. You have to best the best in order to take over their jobs if you've a mind to be a wood boss." Paddy took another sip and stared pointedly at his bed.

"Will I have to go up against Dag and Karl?"

"Only if you have somethin' to prove. Bein' the boss you don't have to."

Hank stood, cramming his hat on his head. Now he had more than just the kiss he shouldn't have taken to keep him up tonight.

He opened the door and Paddy called to him, "If you don't want the others givin' you what for, you need to stop moonin' over Kelda."

Hank pulled the door firmly shut behind him and stalked to the office. Not only did he kiss

Kelda, but the whole damn camp speculated over his interest in her.

The light in the office barely glowed in the window. The brothers must have finally gone to their cabin. He opened the door and hung his hat and coat on the pegs by the door. Hank pivoted to add wood to the stove and stopped short.

Karl sat on the stool, his head resting on his crossed arms on the counter. Damn. He'd have to wake the man and get him to his bed. The bright side, it was better than lying in bed and pondering the evening.

"Karl." He shook the shoulder the size of a regular person's head.

"Mmmfff. What?" Karl's head came up, and he shoved the stool backward as he rose to his feet. The sound of the furniture hitting the floor was muffled by the hard packed dirt.

"Karl, you need to go to your cabin and get to bed so you can work tomorrow." Hank tugged the man toward the door. The brothers had arrived at the office earlier without any overcoats. No doubt, in their drunken state they left them hanging at the cookhouse.

Karl dug his heels in and jerked his arm out of Hank's grasp. "What are your intentions toward my sister?"

Hank let out a whoosh of air. He knew this question would be coming soon after kissing Kelda, but he wasn't ready to say anything until he thought his actions through. "I don't have any intentions. She's a woman and should be treated like one."

Karl stared at him his mouth open enough he

could have caught flies had it been any other time of year. "I know she's a girl. But if she wants to work alongside the rest of us she has to be able to take teasing."

Frustrated Hank stood nose to nose with Karl. "She is not a girl. She's a woman. Kelda deserves the same respect you give your mother. And teasing is one thing, but the things I've heard you say to her...they shouldn't be said to anyone you care about. Are you so blind you don't see how your words hurt her?"

"There you go, sticking up for her. What do you care? You're the boss, you aren't her family." Karl pushed his face closer and blew disgusting breath into Hank's face.

He wanted to back up and draw in fresh air, but he wasn't about to back down. Not when this jackass wasn't giving him any good reasons for his behavior. "I am the boss, and I want every man or woman who is working here to be comfortable and do their job. Harassment will not be tolerated."

"Harassment? Uff da! We're just having fun with our sister and you come in here and act like we're tanning her hide." Karl backed up when Hank stretched to his full height and leaned in.

"Dag was trying to tan her hide earlier." Hank opened the door. "Out! We'll discuss this in the morning with your father present."

The expression of disbelief that washed over Karl's face would have been comical if Hank wasn't wound tighter than his pocket watch.

"Good night." Hank pulled on Karl's sleeve, dragging him to the door and pushing him out into the snow. He was a big boy and could walk the twenty yards to his cabin in the dark.

Hank placed the bar across the door and drew in the rope pull. If someone wanted him or Tobias they'd have to pound on the door, and if he was lucky Tobias would see to it. His head ached. How had this evening turned from a celebration of life to his feeling like he'd put a chain around his neck?

He placed a log in the stove, picked up the lantern, and wandered into his office. He left the door open to allow the heat in. One look at his bed and he knew he wouldn't sleep. Something wasn't settling in his mind and from past experience that meant until he figured it out he wouldn't sleep. Hank took a seat at his desk and pulled out a paper and pencil.

What disturbed him the most about tonight? He sat back and reran the night's events over in his head. Everything was going well until Karl and Dag came to the office drunk and Dag pulled Kelda over his knee.

The way her eyes widened and a glint of fear dulled their sparkle there wasn't a chance in hell he'd have let her brothers harm her. His chest had squeezed with the need to do something. He rubbed the heel of his hand over his breastbone re-experiencing the panic that had gripped him. There was no call for women or children to be hurt by a man's hands.

Then the wonder in her voice when he called her a lady and the tears...he'd never been able to handle a woman's tears, so he'd pulled her into an embrace. Her body fit his so well, he forgot himself and when her face peered up at him, he couldn't resist a brief kiss. His body heated remembering how supple and soft her lips had felt.

Then Mrs. Nielsen arrived with a frying pan. That had brought him back to his senses. How was he to face the two women tomorrow? And he'd told Karl they'd discuss the way they treated Kelda with their father.

Hank moaned and dropped his head into his hands. How had he managed to undermine his authority in one night?

Chapter 8

Kelda tossed and turned most of the night. She'd barely slept when Mor started banging around at the stove. The ache in her head had nothing to do with the akevitt and everything to do with how her brothers would react around her today and for the duration of their work for Hank. He'd thrown a threat at them they'd never had before, and one that she knew would be darn near impossible for them to adhere to. There wasn't a day went by that they didn't punch her shoulder or smack her backside out of playfulness. She didn't care for it but realized it was their way of showing affection. Even a couple of the long time workers punched her shoulder when they worked together.

She had to talk to Hank and explain the way things worked in a logging camp. If she didn't have the men's respect as a logger she might as well resign herself to the cookhouse or head out to the teaching college Far suggested six years ago.

Mor entered the supply room and gathered the

ingredients for hotcakes.

"I'm coming, Mor." Kelda swung her legs over the edge of her bed and stood.

"Your father had too much celebrating last night. I don't know if he'll eat breakfast," Mor said, turning and exiting the room.

Kelda dressed quickly and stepped out of the supply room. A young man burst into the cookhouse.

"Where's Hank?" he asked breathless and stomping his feet.

"He's at the office. I'll take you." Kelda grabbed her coat, tossing it around her shoulders and led the stranger across the compound to the office. She tried the door but the bar was down and the rope pulled in.

She pounded on the door. "Hank! Hank!" She turned to the young man. "Is there something wrong?"

"Maeve's having her baby, and Pa sent me to get uncle Hank."

Kelda beat her fist on the door once more. Why wasn't he answering? Was he ashamed of kissing her last night? "Hank, wake up!" She turned to the young man. "I'm Kelda."

"Pleased to meet you, I'm Colin."

Surely Tobias would answer. She pound again. "Tobias! Wake up!"

Turning her attention to Colin, she said, "I'm afraid they all had too much to drink last night celebrating my father's birthday."

The bar on the other side scraped the wood and the door swung open. Hank stood inside dressed in rumpled clothes. His surly gaze barely landed on her when Colin stepped between them.

"Uncle Hank, Pa wants you to come. Maeve's having her baby, and she's having a time of it. Uncle Zeke's a handful." Colin began his foot shifting motions again.

Hank grabbed his hat and jacket and pulled the door closed. "Let's go." He turned his gaze on Kelda. "Let your father know where I've gone. I'm not sure when I'll be back."

She nodded. "Send our blessings to your family."

His gaze went cloudy, but he nodded and hurried toward the corrals holding the horses.

Hank's departure would prevent the discussion with her father until he was of good humor. Relief rolled down her neck and loosened the muscles of her shoulders. Perhaps by the time Hank returned everyone will have forgotten his threats, and they could go back to normal. She touched her lips. Everyone but her. After experiencing her first kiss she was pretty sure there would be few kisses that would equal the event.

Hank pulled his horse onto its haunches in front of the house Zeke and Maeve bought in Sumpter. By the line of horses tied out front the whole Halsey family was supporting Zeke. He wasn't sure why he was pulled into this, but he was damn happy it had happened. He'd spent most of the night trying to find a way to best dig himself out of the hole he'd made. Unfortunately, he kept coming back to the fact he wasn't going to let his principles slide. Kelda was a woman, and therefore everyone in the camp should respect her as one.

No touching her.

And that included him.

Gil opened the door and slapped him on the back. "Good to see you. Maybe you can talk some sense into Zeke."

Hank handed his hat and coat to Darcy and received a hug from her, Shayla, and Sadie.

"What's the problem?" While he'd been greeted jovially, tension hung in the usually happy atmosphere that surrounded the Halsey families. If something had happened to Maeve the greeting would have been more somber. What the hell was going on? He'd have to work harder at staying in touch with his brothers and their families.

Gil led him into the kitchen where Zeke, Clay, and Ethan sat at the table.

Darcy handed him a cup, and he sat in the spot at the table that wasn't occupied as Gil took the seat next to Ethan.

"The baby isn't turned the right direction. Rachel wants to cut Maeve open and take it out." Clay put a hand on Zeke's shoulder. "Our brother is holding things up."

Hank peered into Zeke's pale, weary face. The two had always been close and seeing his brother's pain Hank wondered if maybe it wasn't best to remain unmarried. He didn't think he could go through the agony of someone he loved hurting.

"I'm sure Rachel knows what she's doing or she wouldn't have suggested it. If you don't give her permission you could lose both the baby and Maeve." Hank didn't allow his gaze to drift to others at the table. He stayed focused on the need to help his brother make the right decision. "You didn't keep me up nights telling me all about Maeve's attributes and how you couldn't see yourself growing old with anyone but her for nothing. Zeke, you want her by your side. You need her by your side." Zeke latched onto his gaze. The pain dulling his eyes put a knot in Hank's belly. "If it was anyone but Rachel, I'd be scared, too."

Hank's heart rat-a-tatted inside his chest as he waited for Zeke to say something.

Zeke finally nodded. "Tell Rachel to do what she needs to do."

Darcy darted from the room before he finished his sentence, and the men at the table all let out a collective sigh.

Darcy raced into the room. "Ethan and Gil start hauling hot water and the items stacked on the table by the stairs up to Rachel and Aileen." As usual his pint-sized sister-in-law was all bossiness.

"Hank and Clay keep Zeke company." She deposited a pot of coffee in the center of the table and followed the other men out of the room.

Zeke ran a hand through his hair. His agitation and fear hung in the room like a dense fog.

"How's the log camp going?" Clay asked. He'd clearly made the decision that the talk should be of something other than Maeve.

"It's nearly completed. Arvid says the next project is the chute to transfer the logs down the mountainside, and then we'll be falling and stockpiling the logs." Hank wasn't keen on discussing the logging operation but realized it would help Zeke.

"When are you going to allow us a tour?"

Clay peered at him with unseeing eyes. Hank still marveled at how well his brother had adjusted to a sightless life. Of course having the love and companionship of a woman who wouldn't let him use his blindness as a crutch helped.

"As soon as we're an actual working camp."

Ethan returned to the kitchen. He placed a hand on Zeke's shoulder. "Rachel said it won't be long now and you did the right thing." He sat at the table, and Colin pulled a chair up next to him.

Silence overtook the room as each man stared into their coffee cup. Hank peered at each of his brothers. They all had wives they cherished more than their own lives. If he married, he could one day be sitting here worrying about a wife. The thought conjured up Kelda. He shook his head. Was that something he wanted?

"Uncle Hank who was the pretty lady who helped me find you?" Colin asked, a bit of mischief twinkling in his eyes.

How had the scamp known he didn't want Kelda brought into any conversations with his family?

"Kelda? She helps her mother in the cookhouse." Hank couldn't stop the heat rising up his neck as all three of his brothers turned their gazes on him.

"Colin, did you say she's pretty?" Clay asked. "How pretty?"

"She has big green eyes that sparkled and made me want to smile back at her." Colin peered at Hank. "She's a bit bigger than Ma, ain't she?"

A knot formed in Hank's gut. He didn't want to talk about Kelda. He wasn't sure how he felt about the woman and damn sure didn't need his brothers speculating.

"Yes, she's taller than your ma." He stood to get more coffee then remembered the pot was on the table and sat back down. All his attention was on the brown liquid pouring into his cup.

"How pretty?" Clay asked, his tone more teasing than inquiring.

"She's not ugly." Hank steeled his face to remain noncommittal as Kelda's face popped into his head.

"She was real friendly and helpful," Colin added, hopping out of his chair and grabbing cookies off a plate on the counter.

"Set that plate here. We could all use some of your ma's cookies," Ethan said, his gaze never leaving Hank's face. "Hank, you aren't very talkative about this pretty, friendly woman."

"Nothing to say. She helps her mother cook." Hank picked up a cookie and took a bite to fill his mouth so he couldn't say anything else.

Clay's hand brushed back and forth on the table cloth before bumping into the cookie plate and snatching a molasses cookie. "You're not saying much is saying a whole lot." He tipped his head. "Don't you think so, Zeke?"

For the first time since Hank arrived, Zeke appeared to be slowly coming around to his normal demeanor. That didn't bode well for Hank. If these three brothers ganged up on him over his not talking about Kelda, he wasn't sure he'd be able to keep all his frustrations bottled up. They'd always talked things out.

"Yeah, his not saying is speaking real loud."

Zeke grabbed a cookie and offered him a smile before taking a bite.

"Colin, tell us more about this woman. What's her name again, Hank?" Clay had always been the instigator to dig up what no one wanted to talk about.

"Kelda, her name's Kelda. She told me while we were standing waiting for Uncle Hank to open the door." Colin's face turned thoughtful. "Why'd it take you so long to answer the door, Uncle Hank? She pounded more than once and hollered."

Ethan leaned forward placing his forearms on the table. "Didn't you want to talk to her?"

"I figured Tobias, who also lives in the office, would answer the door." Hank snarled and snatched another cookie. Why couldn't they just drop the whole discussion? He should have told Colin he didn't have time to come here, but he wouldn't have been able to live with himself it things hadn't turned out well. The Halsey family was always there for one another. This was a good way to avoid the Nielsen men for a little longer. Damn! When he'd dreamed of starting a logging operation he'd never thought it would disrupt his life so much.

"That doesn't answer why you ignored a woman calling your name." Ethan continued to stare. "You and her have a falling out?"

Hank snorted. "Can't have a falling out when there's nothing to fall out of."

Clay slapped the table. "That's the problem. She doesn't like you and you like her."

Hank shook his head. "Brother you are so wrong it's a wonder you can walk across a room."

Ethan snapped his fingers. "She's after you and you're not interested."

"You're all wrong and all your fishing isn't going to get you anywhere."

Darcy entered the room. "Zeke, your son and wife would like to see you."

Zeke leaped out of his chair knocking it over. He grasped Darcy's hands in his. "They're both fine?" The pleading in his voice jammed a knot of emotion in Hank's throat.

"Yes. Maeve will have to take it easy for some time, but they are both doing well."

Gil walked up behind Darcy and wrapped his arms around her. "You've got two fighters on your hands, Zeke. Go see them."

Zeke dashed out of the room and thundered up the stairs.

Hank wanted to hang around and see how Maeve and the baby were doing, but he wanted to see Kelda and make things right with her family. This incident reminded him how important family is, and he wanted to make sure he hadn't caused her any trouble.

He stood.

"Where are you going?" Darcy asked, moving to the cookstove.

"Back to camp."

"Did you eat breakfast before coming here?"

He shuffled his feet.

"I thought not. No one here has had any breakfast either. You men go tend to the animals, and I'll have your meal on the table in twenty minutes." Ethan, Gil, Clay, Colin, and Hank all stared at her. "Go, shoo. There's chores to do, and I don't want you under my feet while I work."

They bundled into their coats and headed out the door.

"What chores need done?" Clay asked.

"I don't know, but I'm heading to the log camp. Gil, tell your wife thanks but I need to get back." Hank untied his horse from the picket fence.

"There's no sense in riding off without a meal." Ethan caught hold of his horse's bridle.

"You don't need me here, and I really do need to get back. There's some unfinished business needs tending." He swung up on his saddle.

"This have anything to do with Kelda?" Clay asked.

"Who's Kelda?" Gil asked.

"A pretty lady at the logging camp," Colin piped in.

Aggravation finally boiled over. Hank couldn't stop the words from bursting forth. "Yes, it has to do with Kelda, and the fact I threatened her brothers last night."

Ethan grabbed him by the back of his coat and hauled him off the horse. He and Gil took him by an arm and marched him to the barn with Clay and Colin in their wake.

"Hey! I have to go!" He tried to shake them loose but one was slightly larger than him and the other only a couple inches and pounds smaller.

In the barn they let go. He spun ready to fight. That's what he needed, a good brawl to work off the frustration that seemed to smother him lately.

Ethan put up his hands. "We're not going to fight you. There's more than this woman that has you ready to swing at us."

Hank stared as his brothers all stood with their arms crossed waiting. Colin scanned the group and imitated the grown men.

Hank shook out his raised fists and tense shoulders and leaned against a wagon wheel. "I don't know what's going on." He grabbed his hat and slapped it against his leg. "I knew there would be women at the camp. I thought an older woman and girl the way Arvid talked about them." Hank couldn't stop the memory of his first sight of Kelda. "His daughter is a grown woman. And as stubborn as she is pretty." He glared at the men present. "She would rather work out in the woods among the men than help her mother cook."

"She works in the woods? Is that what's eating you?" Ethan uncrossed his arms and took a seat on an upturned bucket the other's followed by finding a comfortable spot to roost.

"Yes. No. I told her father if she worked along-side the men, I'd find another outfit to log our mountains." He stared at his brothers. "It's not safe for her out there. She likes to top the trees. That's... It's not safe."

"And her father agreed to your terms?" Gil shook his head.

"Yes. I think he was looking for a way to keep her out of the woods. This makes me her enemy and not her father."

"If you threatened her brothers for touching her then you're the enemy to them all." Clay stated the obvious with a noncommittal tone.

Hank cleared his throat and stared around the barn. "You could look at it that way, I guess."

"You guess? Hell, Hank, I can't believe you're

ready to rush back over there from what you just told us." Ethan scowled. "This is a mess. We believed you could handle being a boss on your own, but what you're telling us now, I'm wondering if maybe one of us needs to come over and check on things."

Anger shot Hank to his feet. "I can handle this. It's not as bad as it sounds. I'd planned to have a talk with the Nielsen family his morning before Colin showed up." He ran a hand over his unshaven face. "They're more reasonable than you'd think. All but the women."

Clay chuckled. "When have women ever been reasonable?"

Gil and Ethan both agreed.

Darcy's voiced called from the house.

"I'll eat, but then I have to get back to the camp and get things straightened out." Hank stood and strode to the house. He wasn't any happier about the conversation he must have with the Nielsens, but he had to do it or lose the trust of his family.

Chapter 9

Kelda cleared the table as a few of the loggers left the cookhouse and Far walked gingerly into the room he shared with Mor to get the Bible. It was Sunday, and he always read from the Bible for those that wished to hear. Then they would head out and work just like any other day.

Her brothers were quiet all through the meal. She wasn't sure if it was due to their drinking or Hank's order. She could tell from the way the rest of the outfit acted normal they didn't know about Hank's edict. Except for possibly Paddy whose eyes twinkled and a mischievous smile curled his lips when he glanced her direction.

She had to speak to Hank as soon as he returned. There was no reason for him to announce the firing or pay dock. Once the others heard this, it would not only upset the camaraderie she had with the men, it would put her at a disadvantage when she went back into the woods. She refused to allow the man to not only take her out of the woods but to undermine her authority with the loggers. As Arvid's daughter, she had the respect of the beasts, but her putting up with their good-natured ribbing and banter also gained her respect. She'd lose that if Hank continued with his threats.

Once the dishes were cleaned and put away, Kelda snatched her coat and scarf from the peg by the door and slipped outside. She'd wait for Hank's return and confront him before he had a chance to make things worse. Unsure of the best place to wait, she pushed through the fluffy new snow toward the office. There would be a warm stove, quiet, and a window to watch for Hank's arrival.

In the office, she hung up her coat, shoved another log into the stove, and pulled the stool to the window. She'd been busy ever since the young man Colin arrived and took Hank away. Now, she had time to wonder why Hank was needed for a birthing. The boy said something about Zeke, one of Hank's brothers. Was the family so close that everyone was required for a birthing?

Her heart squeezed. Would there ever be a day when she would hold her child in her arms? The thought had always saddened her. That was until last night when Hank kissed her. He found her pleasing. A tickle started in her stomach and spread. It was hard to remember to be mad at him for calling out her brothers when he showed her the attention she'd never thought she'd ever expe-rience.

The men filed out of the cookhouse and soon Far and her brothers followed. She chewed on her lip. Once the men were all in the woods there wasn't a reason for her to remain in the office.

How long would the birth take? He may not even return today. The thought started a small spear of panic bubbling in her throat. What if he came in late in the night? He'd be able to talk with everyone while she was helping Mor with the morning meal tomorrow.

She pulled her coat back on. Her hand reached for the door as she heard the cadence of a horse entering the camp. Would Hank think she was snooping if she walked out of the office? But what could she be snooping in? There was little of importance and nothing she didn't already know about in here. Kelda stepped to the window and peeked out. Hank dismounted and scanned the camp. Weariness added lines to his face. His long legs carried him toward the cookhouse.

She had to talk to him before he spoke with anyone else. Kelda flung the door open.

"Hank!"

He spun at his name. His gaze collided with hers. Her heart raced at the aggressive stride and unflinching stare.

Hank stopped at the threshold. "What are you doing in the office?" He stepped forward moving her into the room.

Now that he was in front of her, she couldn't find the words she needed. Her heart raced as memories of the kiss the night before heated her skin.

He closed the door, took off his coat, and hung it on a peg. Without looking at her, he checked the stove and used a poker to stir the coals. Hank straightened and walked toward her.

"About last night..." his voice trailed off.

"Yes, that's what I wanted to talk to you about." Her gaze drifted to his mouth and the soft lips that had placed the chaste yet burning kiss on her lips.

He cleared his throat and turned. "Last night. The kiss..."

"Yes?" Why was his back to her? She couldn't see his eyes. Couldn't read his thoughts.

"It shouldn't have happened."

The denial in his voice dropped her heart into her stomach.

"I-I..." Her mind raced with the rejection. She'd never let him know how much that kiss had meant to her. She swallowed the pain, using it to fire up her anger. "I wanted to talk to you." Fisting her hands she rammed them on her hips. "You can't threaten my brothers or the men by docking their wages. Or firing a man who touches me."

He spun around and his eyes narrowed. "You like them handling you that way?"

"Nei. But I don't want to be given special treatment either." She crossed her arms and glared back at him.

"Special treatment? It's not special. It's how a woman should be treated. You are a woman." He took a menacing step toward her.

Kelda didn't back away. She'd have it out with him. She didn't care if he never touched her again as long as he left her life alone.

"I am a woman, but also a logger, and won't have you undermining the respect I've earned."

"You're not a logger. Not while my money's making the payroll." He moved so close his nose nearly touched hers. Their boots did bump.

"When we move on to another job, I will and I won't have the men thinking I've lost my talents while you've had me sitting around pretending to be something I'm not." She sucked in air as his arms snaked around her, drawing her flush to his body.

He stared into her eyes. His brow furrowed as his frowning gaze probed. The heat of their melding bodies spread through her.

"What am I pretending you are?" he said so soft, so seductive, her legs weakened.

"A w-weak woman who needs a man to tell her what to do." Staring into his eyes, feeling his hard body against hers, and not giving into the urge to nuzzle against the day's growth of whiskers on his cheek was harder than clinging to a tree forty feet in the air.

"I'm not telling you what to do. I'm looking out for your safety." He tipped his head and staring into her eyes, lowered his lips to hers.

For someone who just said kissing her was a mistake, he was doing a mighty fine job of kissing her, again. The warmth of his breath rushed across her cheek as he angled and opened his mouth.

She'd never kissed anyone until Hank. While she was stunned at this new openmouthed kiss, her body jolted when his tongue touched her lips. She gasped and he slipped in. Kelda moaned as her body sagged against his. Her hands clutched his shirt front, clinging to stay on her feet. The assault on her senses would have puddled her on the ground if not for his arms banded tightly around her.

He continued to probe the inside of her mouth.

The sensation of his tongue against hers vibrated through her, whirling her senses.

Hank drew back from the kiss. Why the hell did he do that? He wanted to push her away so he could concentrate on the business and not her. He'd thought one more kiss and he'd get her out of his thoughts. It didn't work. The farther he took the kiss, the more he wanted and the more she responded.

He placed his forehead on hers and waited for his desire to recede so he could think clearly. He'd just gone over the line. When he spotted her in the office doorway, he'd wanted to chase away any fancies she might have about the kiss the night before. Now... he couldn't deny last night's kiss or this one.

Holding her arms, he set her away from him. He'd gone and done it this time. Her kiss swollen lips curved into the infectious smile he loved. Her eyes sparkled like ice crystals in the sun.

They hadn't even begun to fall trees and he'd started a hurricane of troubles. He had to slow things down. Keep his distance from this woman.

"I'm sorry. That should never—"

Kelda placed her fingers on his lips. "Don't say it. I'm sure you've kissed many other women and enjoyed it more."

He started to protest but realized she was giving him an out. Something he needed. "I think Karl's right. We should have a chaperone around."

Her forehead wrinkled. "Nei. I don't like my brothers knowing what I'm doing."

"I don't want to be flogged by your family for inappropriate behavior." He dropped his hands from her person and took another step back. He'd need to keep distance between them from here on out. If he kept kissing her every time they were alone, he'd find himself escorted to a wedding. His.

Her eyes widened as he distanced himself. Her face scrunched up, and her eyes narrowed with a glint of satisfaction. "If you don't want me telling Far about your kisses, you better not follow through with your threats to my brothers or the others." She crossed her arms. "And allow me to work in the woods."

Anger raced up his spine. Had she planned to seduce him all along to get her way? "I'll forget my threat about them touching you, but I won't change my mind on you working in the woods. It's too dangerous." To calm down he walked to the back side of the counter and leaned over it, keeping space between them. "My family agrees that you or any woman isn't going to work in the woods as long as we're paying the wages."

"You've talked this over with your family?" Her eyes widened and jaw went slack.

Her surprise made him chuckle. "You think I don't talk things over with my family when we're all in this venture together?"

"You've said very little about your family so I figured you weren't close." Her gaze held his. "Who is Maeve, the woman who had the baby?"

Hank had forgotten where he'd spent the better part of the morning. "She's Zeke's wife. She and the baby are fine. Thanks to Rachel, Clay's wife."

"Why wouldn't she be fine? My mother had my brothers and me without any problems." Her curiosity pulled him into the conversation when he would have rather slipped on to another subject.

"The baby was turned the wrong way and not coming. Zeke feared for both of them and was refusing to let Rachel cut Maeve open to get the baby."

"Oh my! How could your brother let someone cut open his wife?"

Hank chuckled. "Rachel is a doctor. She knows what she's doing."

"A doctor?"

He could see her thinking all he'd said through.

"You have a sister-in-law who is a doctor and one who is a Pinkerton and you still refuse to let me work in the woods?" Her eyes narrowed on him.

"Yes. Their jobs aren't dangerous." He'd fibbed a little. Maeve's job was dangerous but she'd be out of danger now that she had a child to tend to.

She shoved her hands on her hips.

The door opened and Tobias shuffled in. His green face and arms anchored around his stomach caught Hank's sympathy. Kelda moved to her brother, helping him into his cot and sitting beside him.

Hank took this as his chance to slip out and apologize to Karl and Dag. If his words didn't get any farther than those two he had a chance to keep out of marriage. If he slipped up and Kelda told her family about the kisses, he had no doubt if the Nielsen's didn't drag him to the altar his family would.

Chapter 10

Kelda served the meals so she was always on the side opposite of the table from Hank. She feared getting too close to him and having her body give away her feelings. Since the day he kissed her and said they should have chaperones, he'd made it clear that he didn't want any advances from her or to be alone with her. But she knew he watched her as she went about her chores. Her cheeks heated thinking he wanted to kiss her again as much as she wished to be kissed.

Then as the days went by without a word or encouraging smile from him, she began to wonder if his suggestion of their distance was because he couldn't control his actions around any woman. His forced distance left an emptiness as if a dear friend had died. She wanted to confront him but couldn't work up the courage for fear of what his reasons may be. Even though she'd only recently been called a lady and treated like one, something she hadn't experienced until he came into her life, she missed it.

Warmer March winds blew down the slopes melting the snow and making the camp a muddy mess. The chute was nearly completed. Everyone was in a jovial mood knowing the real work would soon begin. Kelda longed to be one of the workers along the chute to push the first harvest of logs down.

Everyone filed out of the cookhouse to begin another day. Kelda tugged on Far's sleeve holding him back. "I want to be at the top of the chute and push the first logs down."

He smiled and tweaked her nose. "The boss will be at the bottom watching the first logs be stacked. He'd notice if you weren't there."

"Far, you haven't forgotten my offer to work for the boys once a week?" Dread squeezed her chest. She wasn't going to remain in the cookhouse the whole time they were here logging.

He placed a hand on her shoulder. "I will find the time when you can work in the woods. I don't want my best topper to lose her skill." He winked, gathered her against him for a hug, and disappeared out the door.

"What are you and Far whispering about?" Mor asked. She'd become more agitated and easy to upset over the last few weeks.

Kelda could tell by the empty stare in Mor's eyes this was going to be a day when her memory failed. She put an arm around her dainty parent and smiled. "I believe a certain mother has a birthday coming up."

Mor stared up at her. "Whose mother?"

"Mine. Your birthday is only a week away.

What would you like for your special day?" Kelda squashed the worry building in her. The last week Mor had spoke in Norwegian more and struggled with recipes she kept in her head.

She set her mother to drying dishes as she washed. She didn't want to take over the cooking but that would happen as Mor continued to slowly forget things. Hopelessness swelled in Kelda's chest and made it hard to breathe. She would end up here, cooking, washing dishes, and hating every minute of it when Mor could no longer work.

Her mother began telling a story in Norwegian. Kelda didn't listen. She washed the dishes and felt her life slowly dissolving into nothingness.

Hank paced back and forth in front of the finished chute waiting for his family to arrive and the first log to be ushered down the contraption. There was only one thing that dampened this day—Kelda. The last two weeks she'd been more than reserved. She'd lost her glow and spark. When he asked Arvid if she was feeling ill, he said Mrs. Nielsen wasn't feeling herself and Kelda had more to do.

His gaze slipped over to Paddy and the loggers, who would pile the logs, and took in the Nielsen's; Arvid, Ingrid, Tobias, and Kelda who all stood on the opposite side of the chute. Kelda held his attention. Her eyes were downcast and her body appeared thinner. Had his decision to keep his distance from her caused this decline? He wanted to walk around the chute and pull her into his arms and tell her why he had to keep his distance. It wasn't that he didn't want to hold and kiss her; it was he didn't need or want the distraction of her to interfere with his running of the camp. He'd learned from his first rash threat to her brothers that he couldn't keep a level head when it came to her welfare.

The jingle of harnesses drew his thoughts from the woman. Ethan drove a wagon loaded with people into the camp. Maeve and the new baby sat beside him. The oldest children bailed out of the back as soon as Ethan put the brake on. Sadie, Shayla, and Colin raced over to him.

"Uncle Hank! Uncle Hank!" He picked up the girls, hugging them and squeezed Colin's shoulder. Darcy, Rachel, and Maeve walked up holding their youngest children. Each one put an arm around him and pecked his cheek. Aileen laughed as his brothers slapped him on the back.

"Before we start, I'd like to introduce you to the family, or part of the family we're doing business with. Karl and Dag are up top cutting the trees we'll see come down this chute." Hank led his family around to the Nielsen's. This would be his family's first introduction. His family had trusted his judgment in hiring this logging crew, but he also wanted them to approve of the family. With that thought his gaze landed on Kelda as it did whenever they were close.

He introduced everyone and was once again struck with the loss of excitement on Kelda's face.

"Hi, Miss Kelda. You remember me?" Colin asked, stepping closer to her and doffing his hat.

Kelda smiled briefly and nodded her head.

Hank wanted to lead her away from everyone and find out what was ailing her. He glanced at

Rachel. Maybe what she needed was a doctor.

"Sound the horn, Arvid and let's see the first log," he said, sidling his way to Rachel. When the logger blasted the horn, Hank leaned close to Rachel. "Take a minute before you leave and talk with Kelda. She's not acting right."

Rachel stared into his eyes, then smiled and nodded.

Hank hoped she didn't get the wrong idea by his actions. He watched Ingrid to see if she worried about her daughter. The woman seemed confused by all the commotion. Kelda wrapped an arm around her mother drawing her away from the chute and excitement.

A muffled rolling noise grew in volume. A log came into view sliding down the chute. A man stood fifty yards up the wooden trough. The log slowed alongside him, and he used a gaff hook to shove the log on down the chute. It shushed down, slid up the curved end of the chute, and stopped at a low spot where two men gaffed the log and rolled it off the channel. Another man wrapped a chain around the end of the log and used a draft horse to drag the tree over to the flattened area where the logs would be stacked.

His family cheered and clapped.

Ethan slapped Hank on the back. "It looks like your dream is becoming a reality."

"I couldn't have done any of this without Arvid and his family." Hank's gaze settled on Kelda. She led her mother back to the cookhouse.

"Everyone is welcome to cookies to celebrate!" Arvid said, shaking hands with his brothers and chatting.

Rachel hung back with Hank. "Why do you want me to visit with Kelda?"

"She's losing weight and has lost the sparkle in her eyes that I first noticed." Hank stopped Rachel. "I think there's something up with the mother, too. She's been more dependent on Kelda."

"That could be Kelda's problem. Taking on responsibilities."

"You two coming?" Zeke shouted, holding the door open on the cookhouse.

Hank hustled Rachel along. Inside the building, he took Arvid aside. "Rachel is a doctor, would you mind if I had her visit with Mrs. Nielsen and Kelda?"

Arvid's bushy gray eyebrows rose. "Why?"

"They've both been acting out of sorts." He could tell the man wasn't happy that someone else noticed his women folk were behaving different.

Arvid ran a hand over his face. "My Ingrid has been having trouble remembering things and living in another time. It's hard for Kelda to work beside her and see the changes and take up the extra work."

Hank stared into the man's face and understood he wasn't ready to come to terms with his wife's failing mind.

"Can you at least allow Rachel to talk with Kelda?" His gaze strayed to where she was pouring coffee and trying to smile, for there wasn't a gleam in her eyes. "She's losing weight."

He glanced back at Arvid and found himself being studied.

"You show a lot of concern for my daughter."

"I show concern for anyone I can see isn't

behaving their normal self."

Arvid nodded. "Have your doctor talk to her."

Before Hank could give Rachel the nod all the women moved in unison toward Kelda.

Kelda turned from placing the coffee pot on the cookstove and found herself surrounded by the Halsey brothers' wives. They were all uniquely different yet held the same air of assuredness she felt in Hank's presence. They were all pretty and feminine. She looked down at her logger boots and large hands. With these women around why would anyone even look twice at her?

"You look worn out. Here, let us help." Darcy, the tiniest, and yet the one that exuded the most authority, slid Kelda onto a chair. Aileen, the one closest to her size with red hair and freckles, slipped a cup of coffee into her hands.

Aileen then picked up the plates of cookies and carried them to the table where the men sat talking. Kelda's gaze slid to Hank. She'd caught him watching her several times. The concern wrinkling his brow added a glimmer of lightness to her otherwise dismal thoughts.

"Do you mind if I ask you some questions?" Rachel, the doctor, asked.

Kelda shook her head. "I'm not sure what you'd care to ask me but go ahead."

Rachel picked up her hand and felt her wrist. "Are you eating?"

"When I've got time. Why?" Kelda slowly pulled her hand back.

"Do you have any pains?" Rachel's eyes held empathy.

"No pains." She slid a glance toward Hank and

found him watching intently. "Did Hank ask you to talk to me?"

"Yes. He's concerned about you and your mother." Rachel placed a hand on Kelda's forehead.

"I'd say the two are overworked," Maeve said, returning from depositing her baby in Zeke's arms.

"Ah agree," added Aileen, stepping up behind Rachel. "Ye need to have Hank take ye to Baker City and look for another to help cook. If it's been a two person job and yer doin' both jobs yer goin' to wear yerself out."

Kelda stared from one woman to another. They didn't understand. It was a family operation. Only she and her mother cooked. Where would they put another woman? Another cot wouldn't fit in the supply room. She shook her head. "We're fine. We can do this."

Rachel took Kelda's trembling hands. "Honey, you can't. It's obvious from how worn out you are. You don't look a thing like the woman Colin has been talking about ever since he rode over here to get Hank."

She stared at the doctor. "Colin has been talking about me? Why?"

Aileen smiled. "Ye made an impression on my laddie." She nodded toward Hank. "And from what the men say on Hank, too."

Kelda shot a glance toward the man they talked about. He sent her a slight smile. If he'd made some move to try and console her the last month rather than keep his distance, she might have not gone so far under in self pity. But as it was, she wallowed in it every single minute of the day.

Darcy trotted up to the group. "Why all the

serious faces?"

"Hank needs to find help for Kelda and her mother," Maeve said and turned on her heels taking decisive steps toward the table.

Kelda sprang out of the chair. "Nei. Don't."

Hank rose to his feet. "Don't what? What's wrong with her?" In two strides he was by her side. Raising the eyebrows of every family member both his and hers and eliciting a chuckle from Paddy.

"She's worn out," Rachel stated.

Maeve and Aileen put their hands on their hips.

Darcy stepped forward, putting an arm around Kelda's waist. "You and Kelda need to go to Baker City and hire someone to help with the cooking and dishes.

"I don't think..." Kelda started to protest, not so much the help but the trip alone with Hank.

Far stood up. "Kelda and Ingrid have always been the cooks. There's no need for anyone else."

Rachel stepped forward. "Mr. Nielsen. Look at your wife and daughter. Really look at them." She put her hands on Mor's small shoulders. "They are both tired and losing weight. Their clothes aren't hanging on them proper."

Far sank back down. "I don't know what to do with her." His loving eyes brimming with tears stared at Mor.

Kelda rushed to his side, slipping her arms around him. "I'm trying to care of her, Far."

He patted her arm and kissed her head. "Ja. It is too much for you to handle alone. You go with Hank and find help."

She shook her head.

"Ja. You find a good helper."

"There's no room for another person in the supply room." She thought she whispered to Far but the collective gasp burned a path of mortification up her neck.

"We'll build a cabin for you and the help will stay in the supply room." Hank's voice held a promise she knew he'd not break.

"There's no need to build another cabin. If you bring back another woman, she and Kelda can use my cabin. I'll stay in the supply room," Paddy offered. "If the cooks are goin' to be bunkin' far from the cookhouse makes sense I'll be here to start the stove."

Kelda stared at each adult face. They smiled and nodded. Her gaze landed on Hank. His expression was unreadable, but he also nodded.

She knew the trip to Baker City would take at least two days, maybe more if they didn't find a suitable cook right away. "I can't be gone from the camp that long. Mor can't handle cooking by herself."

Aileen and Darcy stepped forward. "We can cook until you get back."

"That's—"

"Necessary," Darcy said. "Aileen and I know how to cook for large numbers we'll figure out sleeping arrangements since we won't be able to travel and it will give our husbands a chance to poke their noses into what all Hank's been doing around here."

Kelda sent a pleading look Far's direction.

He shook his head but uttered, "Ja, we need to

feed the beasts and you need help." He sent a look to Mor who was studying everyone as if she just noticed them. "We need help."

Ethan stood. "After a full tour of the camp, we'll figure out where the women will stay and decide when you two will head to Baker City."

"Why can't Aileen or Darcy go to Baker City with Hank and hire a cook? I'm sure they have experience with such matters." Kelda wasn't sure why her heart raced at the idea of being with Hank and her mind chanted it was a bad idea.

"You need to find a person you can work with." Darcy refilled coffee cups. "That's why you have to do the hiring."

Kelda knew when she was outnumbered. She peeked at Hank and wasn't reassured by his pensive glower.

Chapter 11

Hank pulled the wagon up to the cookhouse. Aileen and Darcy had arrived at the camp the day before and settled into Paddy's cabin. The bull cook had hauled his belongings over to Smithy and Oscar's cabin.

Aileen stepped out the back door and flung dirty water from the dishpan. Her flushed face turned his direction. "She's 'bout ready."

Hank climbed down as Aileen walked up to the wagon. "She's a bonnie lass but plum wore out. Make sure she eats and rests while she's gone."

His heart swelled for his sister-in-law's concern for Kelda. "I'll do my best to make her relax." Had he ever witnessed the woman doing anything other than work? He had no idea what she liked to do to relax.

The door opened, and Kelda stepped out carrying a valise. She wore the black men's wool coat over a dark heavy dress, one he'd never seen before. He stepped forward and took the valise from her hand. His fingers brushed hers. The widening of her eyes and race of his heart told him this would be an interesting trip.

Kelda scampered up into the wagon while he placed the bag in the back.

Darcy popped her head out the door. "Enjoy yourself, but bring back a strong back and good worker. I don't know how you and your mother handled this."

"Thank you for all you're doing." The sag in Kelda's shoulders eased a bit. "Remember Mor can wander off if you don't keep an eye on her. I told her I'd be gone a couple days but she may forget."

"Dinnae worry 'bout yer mother. We'll treat her like our own." Aileen patted Kelda's knee.

Hank climbed onto the wagon and clicked at the horses. They set out at a steady walk. The muddy track between the snow-lined sides would make the trip a slow one. Kelda's head twisted as she stared back at the camp.

"I'm not kidnapping you," Hank said, trying to break the tension he sensed in Kelda.

"It feels like it. Did you talk to your family before they arrived for the first log and say, let's all take sides against Kelda and her family."

The glint of anger in her eyes relieved him. Finally, some sort of emotion and spark in eyes that had been dull and unemotional for a month.

"No. When Rachel arrived I asked her to look at you and your mother. You've both been losing weight, and I didn't like that the laughter had left your eyes." He reached a gloved hand over, laying it upon her hands resting in her lap. "Kelda, I care very much that you're happy." Too much.

Her features didn't lose any of the anger. "Then why have you treated me like I have a disease? After you kissed me"—she drew in a deep breath as if fortifying herself—"you said we'd need a chaperone. A room full of loggers is a pretty good chaperone. All you had to do was say a word or two to me at a meal or smile." She pulled her hands out from under his and jammed them in her coat pockets. "I wouldn't have thrown myself into your arms if you smiled." She glared at him. "I do have pride."

How did he tell her it was himself he didn't trust? Especially with the two of them alone for three and possibly more days. They'd arrive at Baker City before dark and use tomorrow and possibly the next day to find a cook's assistant, then the next day to return. That was a hell of a long time for him to restrain the desire he had for this woman. At least on the return trip they'd have a third party in the wagon with them.

"I wasn't trying to punish you. I'm the one to take all the blame for the kiss." He grasped the reins in both hands and stared forward. He should have insisted Ethan haul her to Baker City. She'd have been in better company.

"Why?"

Her quiet question jerked his gaze to her downturned face.

"Why what?"

"Why did you kiss me then act like I didn't exist? Was my kiss so bad? Or are you a man who can't leave a woman, any woman alone?"

Hank snorted. "I can count the women I've kissed on one hand. I am not a womanizer."

"Then why are you ignoring me?"

"I'm not. We're talking right now."

She slugged him in the arm.

"Ow!" He rubbed his arm. "That's not fair. A man doesn't hit a woman."

She slugged him again. "Think of me as a man and maybe you can talk to me."

"That does it!" Hank yanked on the reins, hauling the wagon to a stop and grabbed Kelda, flopping her over his lap. Just as he raised his hand and her round bottom came into view, he realized why her brothers found the need to paddle her backside. It wasn't out of humiliation or anger but retaliation for the feisty woman's antics. They didn't spank her out of cruelty but love.

"Hell!" He spun Kelda to a sitting position on his lap and took his frustration out in a deep, soul searching kiss. Her cold fingers threaded through his hair, knocking his hat off. When he was dizzy from lack of air, he drew back, but held her on his lap.

"Woman, you make me forget I'm a gentleman." His hands rested on her hip. He enjoyed the feel of her snuggling against his chest.

"You do it to yourself." Her green eyes held the sparkle he loved.

"How is that?"

"You make us both crazy by not talking or even acknowledging the other and then when we are alone we have to make up for lost time." She tentatively kissed the underside of his jaw. Her soft sweet kiss jolted him more than the heated kiss moments before.

He gently moved her to the wagon seat. "We

need to get going or we won't get to Baker City before dark." He retrieved his hat and centered his thoughts.

Kelda squirmed on the seat, until her hip settled against Hank's. He'd bestowed another heart stopping, body throbbing kiss on her, and she wasn't going to let him shove her away again. If his kisses weren't given freely to any woman as she'd presumed, then his kissing her was as special to him as it was to her. Why had he put up a wall after their previous kisses? What did he fear? Her? Where kisses led to? One thing was certain, she'd find out what put the wall up and stone by stone knock it down.

"If you've kissed so few women how did you learn to do it so well?" She touched her still tingling lips.

A smug smile curved his lips. "I kiss well?"

"Since you're the first man I've ever kissed and it is very pleasing, I'd say you kiss well." Her toes curled in her boots remembering the sensations this last kiss had hummed through her body.

Hank laughed and slid his arm around her back, dropping his hand to her hip and pulling her even tighter against him. "That's one thing I admire about you, you always say what's on your mind. Most women chat about things and you don't know what they're getting at."

She smiled. Far liked her directness too. Mor always told her to hold her tongue. Was this just another male trait she'd picked up?

"How are we going to let people know we're hiring a cook?" She'd wondered about this ever since she decided she wasn't hiring an assistant but a full cook. That way she could sneak out and work in the woods when Far allowed. Her heart hummed with the prospect of being in the woods, swinging an axe. She tamped down the happiness, not wanting Hank to ask questions she would find hard to evade.

Her giddiness took a swift dive realizing sneaking into the woods would hurt their friendship. She had to weigh what made her happy. At the moment she relished the time spent kissing and talking with Hank, but at the same time she yearned to be in the woods doing what she did best—topping trees.

"Ethan sent a telegraph to the Morning Democrat for an advertisement. We should have people showing up at the Commercial Hotel tomorrow."

"Hotel?" Her heart raced. "Are we staying in a hotel?"

"That's usually where people stay when they go to town." He glanced at her.

"I've never spent more time in a town than us passing through and picking up a few supplies." This would be a new adventure.

"Have you ever been to Baker City? It's fairly large compared to most towns."

"No. This will be my first for a lot of things."

Hank's arm loosened his hold and he cleared his throat. Why did her comment have him shifting to put distance between them?

"I'll take you to the Warhauser restaurant. It is the finest between Portland and Salt Lake City."

Trepidation fluttered in her stomach. "I only have this dress. I can't wear it to a fancy restaurant."

His gaze traveled over her face, resting on her eyes. The sincerity and heat in his gaze lodged a knot of joy in her throat. His caring chinked away at her notion no man could ever love her for her.

"I'll buy you a new dress and women's boots."

"You'll be spending way too much just for this extra trip." Giddiness bubbled in her chest thinking she could have a pair of women's shoes. At the same time her conscience slapped her with reality. She could not accept clothing from him. He was her boss. "Nei! I couldn't accept such items from you."

"It will be my early birthday present to you. Didn't you say your birthday was in May? That's not that far away. And we may not have another chance to get back to Baker City again before then." He squeezed her back against him. "You can't refuse a birthday present. That would be rude, and you, Kelda Nielsen, are not rude."

"I may not be rude but I am smart enough to know taking such luxuries from you would look like I allowed you liberties." She stared into his dark brown eyes. The mischief dancing there dissolved.

"I don't expect anything from you other than to accept my gifts. You've worked hard and kept the workers well fed and happy. Giving you an early birthday gift is the least I could do." He placed a brief kiss on her head. "I am not a man who expects favors for gifts. I give them freely."

Kelda believed this even if she knew her brothers and even her father may not. Hank had always been true to his word with her. He did, however, keep things locked up inside. Not good for a person, she'd learned that the hard way. She should have said something to Far about the workload getting too much and her concerns about not being able to work in the woods.

The morning passed with Hank pointing out landmarks and telling stories about his brothers. They ate a snack of cookies and an apple as they drove. By late afternoon traffic on the rutted muddy road increased. Buggies, wagons, horses, and people on foot slogged through the mud. Patches of snow in sunless areas brightened the otherwise dull colors of brown, beige, and faded green.

The closer they traveled to Baker City the less snow she saw between the trees and on the hillsides. On the backsides of some buildings mounds of dirty snow piled in the shadows.

Hank had his full attention on keeping the horses moving forward in the congestion for other vehicles and mud.

Kelda stared at the tall stone buildings dwarfing the smaller wooden structures. People hurried across streets, high stepping through the mud and knocking their shoes on the wooden walkways before entering buildings. She'd never witnessed so many people in one place. Their clothing ran from the everyday dresses under shawls and wool capes to fancy silk and lace dresses topped with fur trimmed capes and fancy full length coats. The men were equally diverse in their working clothes and expensive wool suits with wide-brimmed hats and fancy, tall, narrow-brimmed hats. The variety of people blended into a spinning collage of colors.

The wagon stopped. She turned her gaze to Hank.

"I'll turn the wagon and horses over to the livery boy, and we'll walk to the hotel." He jumped down and hurried to her side as she started to climb down.

"We're not out at the camp. You don't have to prove you can do everything a man can." Hank placed his hands on her waist, lifting her off the wheel spoke she stood on.

She didn't mind his helping. It made her belly tingle, but she grew up fending for herself and it would take some getting used to having a man treat her like she was spun sugar.

His hands lingered on her waist when he placed her feet on the ground. "I plan to show you how a lady is to be treated so don't go barreling off. Wait for me to return and escort you."

The warmth shimmering in his eyes curved her lips into a smile. "I'll wait right here."

"Better yet, wait on the walkway out of the mud." He escorted her to the board walkway across the street and returned to the livery.

Kelda slowly spun taking in the activity, sights, and scents. The horse manure of the livery along with the sweet dry hay mixed with the faint overtones of cooking.

Hank returned with a young man who climbed onto the wagon seat and waited for Hank to retrieve her valise and his satchel from the back. He walked over to her and nodded to his arm. Kelda slipped her hand through the crook of his elbow and they followed the board walkway into the milling people.

Avoiding the elbows, packages, and skirts of the passing throng took as much dexterity as avoiding the axes, saws, and trees in the woods. They traveled the length of the walkway to another street. Here, Hank turned right and she spotted the Commercial Hotel. The building was two-stories tall with a balcony across the front. She was thankful it wasn't a fancy hotel. She already felt out of place in the city.

They entered and Hank marched to a counter. "I'm Hank Halsey. You're holding a suite for me."

"Yes, sir, Mr. Halsey." The dapper dressed man behind the counter smiled and spun a large book toward Hank.

Hank signed the register and slid more money than Kelda had ever seen at one time across the counter. "We'll be taking all but one meal from your restaurant. There will also be people arriving tomorrow morning for interviews. We'll conduct the interviews in the suite. Please contact us when the first person arrives."

"Yes, sir." The man placed part of the money in a box and pocketed the rest.

Kelda tugged on Hank's arm. He glanced her way, and she rose onto her toes to whisper in his ear. "That man is stealing part of the money."

Hank smiled. "I'll explain later."

"You're in the corner suite. Number twenty." The man held out a key.

"Thank you." Hank accepted the key and walked toward the stairs.

Kelda hurried to the base of the stairs. He nodded for her to go first. Holding the front of her skirt up, Kelda ascended the stairs noting the plush carpet that ran the length of the treads and muffled their steps.

Lights unlike anything she'd seen before hung on the walls. She continued down the carpeted hallway having spotted numbers on the doors and stopped in front of the one numbered twenty.

"Go ahead and open the door." Hank stopped beside her.

Kelda turned the brass knob and pushed. The room was large and held a table, two chairs, a commode with metal knobs and a funny pipe, a door on the wall to the right, and one large bed with a quilt and fluffy pillows.

One bed.

Chapter 12

Hank turned from placing the bags at the foot of the bed. Kelda's silence had to be from her taking in the nice room. His gaze landed on her angry face and his heart nearly stopped.

"What's the matter?" He took a step toward her, but she raised her hand, holding him back.

"Why is there only one bed?" Her gaze didn't meet his. It remained riveted on the bed.

"This is my bed. You—"

"I am not climbing in that bed with you. Mor would...she..."

"Kelda." He pushed aside her hands and grasped her shoulders, turning her toward the door on the west wall. "Your room is through there. I purchased a suite. It's two rooms that are attached." Hank slid his hands down her arms, capturing her hands. He led her to the door, twisted the knob, and pushed the door inward, presenting another room much like his. He ushered Kelda inside, and then stepped back in his room and picked up her valise.

The thought of bedding with him had shown him a side to Kelda he'd not witnessed before. He'd best mind his manners and keep his randy thoughts in his head and not allow his body out of control.

The sound of her moving around in the other room lightened his mood. If she was inspecting the room then she must be over her initial shock.

Hank stepped through the adjoining door with her valise. Kelda looked up from her inspection of the quilt and smiled shyly.

"I'm sorry for the way—"

"No apology necessary. I didn't realize you weren't aware a suite is connecting rooms." Hank placed the bag on her bed and moved to stand in front of Kelda. He picked up one of her hands. It seemed he had to touch her every chance he had since they broke through the awkwardness.

"I would never force you to sleep with me."

"I know, it's just...Mor has been telling me to not let you compromise me, and I jumped—"

He tugged her into his arms and held her. "Kelda, I will do my best not to compromise you, but you have a way of making my mind go to mush."

She wound her arms around his neck, pressing her body to his. He wished they had their coats off so he could feel her curves. He mentally shook. Wrong. He needed the barrier between them. His body wanted her and his mind had to be the restraint.

He kissed her tenderly and removed her entwined arms from his neck. Hank stepped back watching her lashes gradually rise and her dreamy eyes focus on him.

"Get out of your coat, put your things away, and freshen up. We'll go down to the restaurant and have dinner. I promised Aileen you'd be well fed and rested when you return." He walked toward the door.

"Hank, if you keep kissing me like that I might allow you to compromise me."

Her breathy statement tumbled his heart and stalled his feet. He glanced over his shoulder and damn if he didn't want to scoop her up in his arms and lay her down on the bed behind her.

He swallowed and cleared his throat. "Keep talking like that and you're going to make it damn hard to get through these next few days."

Her cheeks grew deeper in color, but her eyes shone with a brilliance he'd yet to see. "You have fifteen minutes to get ready for dinner." He stepped through the threshold and shut the door before he did something they'd both regret.

Kelda stared at the people seated about the restaurant. It was her first time eating in such an establishment, but she wasn't about to let anyone besides Hank know that. Most of the women wore what she presumed were evening attire for such a dress was not one to work in. If a person bent over their bosoms would fall out and the thin, shimmery material would be cold. Not to mention all the lace and fancy buttons that would catch on a bucket or laundry tub.

When she and Hank walked in, those present

stared. Her nerves had her clutching Hank's arm tightly, but he never said a word. Now, as they ate and she studied the people and room, her nerves had calmed. The waiter brought over a slice of apple pie for each of them.

"Is there anything else I can get for you?" the man asked, his gaze straying to Kelda. She returned his smile, and his ears reddened.

"No. We're fine."

Kelda studied Hank. His words had come out gruff and clipped.

"Is something wrong?" She picked up her fork and slid it into the pie.

"No. Why?" Hank shoved a hefty bite into his mouth.

"You sounded mad when you replied to the waiter." She watched him chew, enjoying the motion of his jaw and the way his eyes searched her face.

He put down the fork and reached a hand across the table. Unsure what he wanted, she placed her hand in his. The racing of her heart when they touched no longer shocked her. She'd come to expect it. He held her hand while his gaze continued to hold hers.

"It's good to see the sparkle in your eyes again. I've missed it."

She ducked her head. He only knew half of what had caused her to be so sad. She couldn't tell him about feeling trapped in the kitchen when Mor started forgetting things. That she'd feared never setting foot in the woods again. He didn't want to hear of her desire to be topping trees. Once they hired a cook, she could sneak out with the help of

Far and spend a day here and there in the woods. Her stomach knotted. If Hank knew these were her thoughts he'd be angry.

"Hey, you're turning cloudy on me. Is there more that's bothering you?" He released her hand and tipped her chin up.

"I-I don't want to just hire an assistant. I want to hire a cook. I only want to help."

His full smile nearly took her breath away. "I think that's a wonderful idea. You could go to town once in a while and enjoy life outside the logging camp."

She held her smile. That wasn't what she wanted, but she'd let him think so. "With Mor getting more and more forgetful, I'll need time to care for her. I can't do that and be the one running the kitchen."

His expression became serious. "I'm sorry your mother isn't doing well. I'm sure Rachel will do all she can to help you."

Kelda nodded. The waiter hovered near the table.

Hank sent him a scathing glare and captured her hand. "I'm ready to go back to the rooms. Are you?"

"Ja."

Hank rose and held out her chair before placing a hand on her lower back and maneuvering her out of the restaurant and toward the staircase. The heat of his hand sent tendrils of warmth spreading through her body. How could such a simple touch stir so much within her?

At their door, he pulled out the key and clicked the lock. He stood back for her to enter.

Once inside his room she wasn't sure what was appropriate. While she was tired, she didn't believe she could fall asleep right away.

The door closed, and she heard the lock click tight. Light footsteps grew near and arms circled her waist. Hank pressed against her back and kissed her neck.

"Tomorrow, before the interviews, I'm taking you to the bootmaker and a dressmaker."

"Nei. You don't need to spend money on things I don't need."

He kissed her behind the ear and her knees buckled slightly. Hank held her tight against him, keeping her from sagging to the floor.

"I told you. They will be my early birthday gifts. Besides, I'm taking you to dinner tomorrow night at the Warshaur. I don't want you feeling underdressed."

She spun in his arms. "You don't have to lavish me this way. I'm content just to be with you and feel special."

He kissed the tip of her nose. "You are special. I can't believe all these years there hasn't been a logger ask you to marry them. You're beautiful, smart, and have a favorable disposition."

She sighed. Only Far and Mor gave her such compliments. "I have had a couple try to kiss me when they'd had too much to drink. But no one has ever taken notice of me besides you."

"Not true." His brow wrinkled in a frown.

"What do you mean?"

"Paddy thinks the world of you, Peder turns red every time you get near, and my nephew is smitten with you. You don't see it, but nearly every man you smile at becomes enthralled."

She could have sworn his voice dropped to a growl.

"Paddy is like an uncle. We have had many a grand time together playing tricks on the boys. And Peder...He's a boy." She stared at Hank. From the first time she laid eyes on him her body responded to the sight of him. His first words had warmed her skin, and his touches tormented her hours later when she was all alone. It might be bold and perhaps a bit bawdy but she wanted Hank. And the sooner she let him know the more likely he would come around to her way of thinking. "I want a man."

The fire that lit his eyes right before his lips captured hers scared and exhilarated. The meeting of their lips burned to the tips of her toes and swirled back up to settle low in her body, burning, churning, and leaving a yearning ache.

His hands roamed up and down her back, settling on the curve of her backside then drawing her hips closer. The weight of his exploring hands raised the level of desire pulsing through her. He pulled out of the kiss, leaving her breathless and wanting. She clung to his shoulders for fear she would slither to the floor at his feet.

Space eased between them as he gradually left her standing on her own.

"Go to your room."

The order shook her from the dreamy state caused by his kiss. "What?"

He turned her and gave a gentle shove. "Go to your room, or I won't be held accountable for my next actions."

Kelda snapped her gaze to his face. He appeared to be in pain. "Are you not feeling well?" She took a step toward Hank.

"No! Don't come near me. Go to your room and lock the door. I should never have kissed you. Go. I'll see you in the morning." He spun, placing his back to her.

How could kissing her be so wrong or painful? Tonight wasn't the time to discuss this. He'd not continue any conversation. She walked through the adjoining door, closed and locked it. That's when she heard a deep throaty growl on the other side. What had she done to aggravate him so?

Hank put his hands on the back of the chair and stood gripping the wood until his desire for Kelda slackened and he could sit and take his boots off. He'd never had desire so strong for a woman. Or jealousy. Watching the waiter nearly fall all over himself when Kelda smiled at him had taken a great deal of restraint to not say something. He hadn't wanted to embarrass Kelda. It was evident she didn't notice the admiring glances from the patrons in the restaurant.

Tomorrow night in a new dress, women's shoes, and perhaps her hair down, she would turn even more heads. He'd have to prepare for it and remember she only had interest in him. Her statement she wanted a man and her heated gaze had been his undoing. He couldn't stop his need to show her he was the man for her.

He slipped out of his clothes and stood looking at the big bed. What he wouldn't give to have her

in it with him. But he'd promised not to compromise her. He kept his promises and even if he had
to visit the bathing room down the hall and take a
cold dunk in the tub—several times a day—he'd not
go back on his promise.

Chapter 13

Kelda stepped out of the bootmaker's shop feeling as if she walked on clouds. The man had two pairs of women's shoes in her size. He said there were several women in the town who had feet as long as hers. The boots were lighter and fit her feet better than the men's boots she'd worn all her life. Her body swayed and her gait was less labored.

Before the bootmakers, Hank bought her two dresses at the dressmakers. The woman would deliver them to the hotel after making some alterations. One dress would only be used for special occasions. Now she knew why the women the night before wore the shimmery dresses. The material slid light and sinful against her skin. Of course she didn't have the proper undergarments for such a dress. Thinking of all the items Hank had bought, guilt stabbed at her conscience.

When they arrived at the Commercial Hotel she started for the stairs.

"Mr. and Mrs. Halsey, you have several people waiting for an interview," the clerk called out.

Kelda's feet stalled at the man's assumption. She started to open her mouth, but Hank intervened.

"We'll go to our rooms and get settled. Send the first person up in ten minutes." Hank placed his hand on her back, propelling her up the stairs.

She craned her neck to object to not correcting the man, but his expression said keep moving. Outside the room as he unlocked the door, she questioned him.

"Why didn't you tell him we weren't married?"

Hank opened the door and motioned for her to enter. "There's no need for him or anyone else to think any different." He followed, closed the door, and faced her. "It doesn't hurt they think we're married. We have separate rooms and beds which keeps your reputation in tact when we return to the log camp."

Kelda studied him. It didn't make that much difference if the hotel staff thought they were married, but the people they interviewed would know different when they returned to the camp.

"What about the people we interview? They have to know the truth or they could say things to Far or my brothers that would get you hurt."

Hank hung up his hat and coat and plucked her cape from her shoulders. "You're right. We'll introduce ourselves right away and keep a professional appearance during the interview. I'll ask the basics. You can ask the questions about cooking." He handed her the cape. "Best to keep all your belongings in the other room so there are no questions. In fact, you stay in there, and I'll summon you after the first person arrives."

Kelda took her cape and left Hank scanning his room. What was he thinking? She closed the door behind her and sat on the bed staring at her narrow, lightweight boots. No one had ever given her so many things at one time. The delight that had lit his face with each item she accepted had felt like she'd given him a gift.

A brisk knock reminded her why they were here. To find a cook.

Kelda stepped out of the adjoining room as a small, frail looking woman sat in the chair Hank indicated.

"Sit here and I'll retrieve another chair from your room." He passed her shaking his head.

Kelda had the same first reaction. This woman had to be her mother's age and less robust. Hank returned with the third chair and placed it alongside Kelda's. He sat and began the preliminary questions.

It took less than fifteen minutes and the woman was at the door to leave.

"Please ask the clerk to send up the next applicant," Hank said before closing the door on the woman.

"She is a definite, nei." Kelda said. "How could she even think she'd be able to cook for sixty loggers is unbelievable."

"I agree." Hank crossed the room and filled two glasses with water from the faucet.

She had never been in a building with running water. It was one of the novelties she'd tell her family about.

He handed her one glass and set his on the table as a knock sounded on the door.

Noon came and went, and they had yet to find a suitable cook.

Hank ushered the last person out the door and turned to Kelda. "Let's go down to the restaurant and get something to eat."

She stood. "My growling stomach had me preoccupied talking to the last one."

He tweaked her nose. "I heard it."

Her cheeks reddened. "Do you think Mrs. Hamilton heard it?"

"No, she was across the table." He grasped her elbow. "Do you need to freshen up before we go down?"

"Nei." She took a step toward the door.

Hank wanted to pull her into his arms and kiss her, but his head thankfully overruled his body. Instead, he followed her out the door and down the stairs.

"Have you found who you're looking for?" the clerk asked as they crossed the lobby.

"No. Are there any more people waiting?" Hank scanned the people sitting on the cushioned chairs in the lobby.

"No. But if someone comes in I'll ask them to wait until you return." The clerk's helpfulness was no doubt due to the tip he'd slid the man the day before.

"Do you think it's going to take us longer than two days to find a cook?" Kelda asked as Hank seated her at a table in the restaurant.

"I hope not. Neither one of us can afford to be away from the logging camp that long." Hank took a seat across from Kelda.

Halfway through the meal a commotion rose out in the lobby. Hank stared at the man about his size leaning on the counter, clearly intimidating the clerk. The man's clothes were that of a laborer.

"Cook! Here!" The man said in an accent that sounded vaguely familiar but more guttural.

The clerk pointed to the restaurant and the man stalked through the door, his eyes scanning the room. The waiter pushed through the kitchen entrance, and the man marched across to the door and disappeared.

Five minutes later the man slammed through the door. "Ingen forstår meg," he muttered walking passed their table.

Kelda's gaze fell on the man and she smiled. "Jeg gjør."

The man spun and stared at her. They began talking in what Hank believed to be Norwegian. The more animated Kelda became the more he wished he knew the language. The man turned to Hank and held out a hand.

He glanced at the hand then at Kelda.

"Meet Lars Eiker, he is our new cook." Kelda smiled at the man who beamed down at her.

Hank didn't like the needle pricks of jealousy piercing his chest. "Our cook? That was kind of fast."

"He was told about the job by another Norwegian who can speak and read English but then he had trouble getting the clerk to understand why he was here. The clerk sent him to the kitchen and they sent him away." Kelda grasped Hank's hand. "He's perfect. He can speak with Mor in Norwegian, he was the cook on a ship to come to America, and he has been cooking at ranches and mining camps as he crossed to Oregon."

Hank had to admit they were all good qualities for the cook they needed. But the man looked to be only a few years older than Kelda and from the way he smiled and watched her, he would like nothing better than to work side by side with her.

"I don't know. You have only his word for all of this."

"He needs to find a steady income and a place to make a home to bring his wife and her family over." Kelda squeezed his hand. "We can help him reunite with his family."

Knowing the man was already married lifted Hank's doubts. "Okay. Tell him to meet us out front at eight tomorrow morning."

Kelda relayed the information and the man beamed. He shook Hank's hand again with even more enthusiasm and marched out the door.

"What is your father going to say when you bring home that hulking man?" Hank led Kelda out of the restaurant.

"He'll be pleased to know we're helping a fellow countryman."

Hank stopped at the counter. "If anyone else arrives tell them the position has been filled."

The clerk looked bewildered but nodded.

"Wait here. I'll get your cape, and we'll go for a stroll. I don't know about you but I'm in need of fresh air." Hank led Kelda to one of the cushioned chairs.

"That's a wonderful idea." The smile she bestowed on him warmed his heart and had him leaning toward her. She cleared her throat reminding him they were in public.

He pulled back and stared into her glittering eyes. "I'll be back quickly."

"I'll be waiting." She sat primly on the cushion, and he took the stairs two at a time.

Kelda couldn't believe her good fortune. Lars would be perfect. He had the skill to cook by himself, as well as the strength and stamina. He knew the recipes that her father loved, he could speak with Mor since she'd slipped into speaking Norwegian more than English, and she could tell he would keep her secrets of working in the woods from Hank.

Shame flared, causing a slight throb in her head. It was wrong to go behind his back when he'd done so much for her. She squeezed her eyes shut and tried to push the guilt aside. She thought back to the month when she believed she would never set foot in the woods as a logger again. The sadness that had engulfed her was worse than any anger she'd receive from Hank.

"Here you go." Hank arrived in front of her, his coat and hat on, and held out her cape.

"Mange takk." She stood and he slipped the garment around her shoulders, fastening the top button for her.

He handed her the pair of leather gloves he also purchased that morning. The softness enveloping her hands made her sigh.

"You're spoiling me." She looked up. The happiness lighting his eyes stammered her heart.

"You deserve to be spoiled." He placed her hand in the crook of his elbow and strolled out of the hotel.

She enjoyed walking linked arm in arm with Hank. He was taller than her and made her not so conscience of her height. He maneuvered her around obstacles and allowed her to browse store windows when she saw something unique. They spent the rest of the afternoon wandering the streets and returned to the hotel as the street lights started to flicker on. The electric lamps in the hotel settled a yellow haze over everything.

Hank stopped at the clerk's desk. "Is there a bathing room located on the second floor?" he asked.

Kelda stared at Hank. A bathing room? What could that be? Surely not a room just for standing in a wash tub.

"Yes, sir. It's at the end of the hall. One on the left and one on the right. Towels and soap are on a shelf."

"Thank you." Hank placed his hand on her back to once again navigate her up the stairs.

"Mr. Halsey, Mrs. Maroony delivered these while you were out." The clerk held up two wrapped packages.

Kelda held out her arms to take her new dresses. Hank plucked the packages from the clerk and continued moving her along. She was beginning to feel like a cow the way he manipulated her.

At the door of their room, she asked the question swirling in her head. "Why don't they just bring a wash tub up to the room if you want a bath?"

He waved her inside and chuckled. "The bath is for you. Another way for me to pamper you." He motioned to the adjoining door. "Gather all the items you need for a bath." He glanced at the packages and dropped one on the bed.

"What are you doing?" Kelda put her hands on her hips. She didn't mind being pampered but she was getting tired of being bossed around.

"This is the dress and undergarments you'll wear to dinner. Go get the other things you need, and I'll show you to the bathing closet." He sat the package down and took his hat and coat off.

Did she want to bathe in a closet? It would be nice to take a bath without worrying about someone barging in. Sunday night was her bath night at the camp. Everyone knew it and stayed out of the cookhouse. She usually dragged the wash tub into the supply room for added privacy but it was dark, small, and cold. The water grew cold before she finished.

She removed her cape, gloves, and boots before gathering her brush. Kelda looked around. Everything else she would need was in the package from the dressmaker. She stepped into the next room. Hank had a bundle of clothes under one arm and held out the wrapped package to her.

"You're taking a bath as well?" Her heart raced wondering if the bath closet had more than one tub in it.

"Yes. The clerk said there was a bathing closet on each side of the hall. It's been a while since I've had a good soak." He opened the door and nodded for her to exit ahead of him. She stepped out, and he moved around her to walk to the end of the hall. He tried the door on the right and it swung in.

Kelda peeked around him and spotted a long white tub to the side of the room.

"Come on in. I'll start the water and show you how to turn it off." Hank peered at her from over his shoulder.

She scurried into the room and scanned the interior. Hooks protruded from the wall beside the door. A wooden chair sat at the end of the tub and a colorful braided oval rug covered the wood floor beside the tub. She set the package on the chair and ripped the paper open, drawing the clothing out and hanging it on the pegs.

"This is how you turn the water on and off." She pivoted and watched Hank turn knobs above the head of the tub. "Turn them off when you have enough water. When you're finished pull this string and the stopper will come out and allow the water to drain."

"This is all...I've never seen anything so marvelous." She ran her hand over the smooth cool surface on the side of the tub.

"Ethan built a water and bath closet for Aileen in their house." Hank straightened. "Enjoy your bath."

"I will. But does this cost extra? If we need to share water, I can take a quick bath and you can use my water." His generosity this trip was more than she dared to think of repaying.

"Baths come with the price I paid for the suite. Take your time. I'll be across the hall. I didn't lock the door on the room so you can go back whenever you want." He dropped a light kiss on her forehead and walked to the door. "Lock this after I leave."

She nodded and crossed to the door. He smiled and stepped out, drawing the door firmly shut. She slipped the hook into the eye and turned back to the steaming, gushing water. The tub was half full. She turned the knobs, shutting the water off and quickly undressed. It would be wonderful to wash her hair without having someone pour buckets over her head.

Chapter 14

Hank sat in the room waiting for Kelda to return from the bathing closet. He'd bathed, shaved, and now waited impatiently for her to return. He'd told her to take her time, but his stomach growled and he wanted to see her in the dress he'd purchased. The blue gown had been advised by the dressmaker, and Kelda would be stunning in it.

He stood to head down the hall to see if she was having problems when the knob on the door turned. He held his breath and waited.

The door opened quickly and Kelda slipped in shutting it tightly behind her. She had the brown wool dress she'd worn the last two days around her shoulders like a shawl. Her old undergarments were tucked under the arm not holding the dress about her.

"Why are you wearing the other dress like that?" he asked, stepping toward her.

Her face reddened. Her lashes lowered, and she stared at the carpet where her bare toes dug into the colorful yarn.

"I can't fasten the dress."

Hank crossed the room and removed the wool dress from her shoulders. He glanced at her back and realized the dress had a long row of small buttons which held the garment on.

"Not a problem." He stepped behind her and started at the bottom. The silky undergarments he'd purchased to go with the dress skimmed his knuckles as he worked the buttons. She'd adamantly refused a corset and the dressmaker had provided a bust improver which was to support her assets. His fingers worked up her back, pushing her silky hair to the side. Kelda gathered her loose hair, pulling it over a shoulder. The long golden locks sparkled in the light and smelled of vanilla. How did she do that? Smell of vanilla when she'd been nowhere near a kitchen the last few days?

"There, you're all properly fastened." He placed his hands on her shoulders and spun her to face him.

"Mange takk."

Her damp hair hung in one long twined lock like a golden rope over her shoulder and brought his attention to the creamy skin above the swells of her breasts peeking through lace. He'd purchased this dress not only for the color but the modest neckline. Kelda wouldn't have been comfortable if too much of her neck and chest were revealed. This dress had a high neckline, but where most evening gowns were open from the swells of the breast on up, this one had a covering of pure white lace.

His mouth grew dry taking in the sight of her.

"You're staring." The hesitancy in her voice

broke the trance her beauty cloaked him in.

"That's because I've never seen a more beautiful woman." He took her hand and raised it to his lips. "You are going to turn heads tonight, and I'm honored to be your escort."

Her cheeks tinged a bright red, but the happiness glistening in her eyes warmed his heart.

"Again, thank you for your kind words. I do feel more...soft in these clothes."

Her softness was what his hands itched to touch, but there was no way he'd ruin this night by allowing his randy body to follow through.

He took the clothes from under her arm, and she blushed all over again. "I'll put these clothes in your room and fetch your new boots. Sit in the chair and once your shoes are on, we'll head to dinner."

Kelda loved the feel of the rich carpet under her feet as she padded across to the chair by the table. The warmth of Hank's fingers as he buttoned her dress sent tendrils of excitement skittering across her skin. Then the heat in his eyes as he stared at her...she fanned a hand in front of her face. And he looked wonderful. Freshly shaved and clothed in a fancy suit. No one would know they were from a logging camp.

Hank returned with her boots and knelt at her feet. She gathered the hem of her dress and raised it to her knees. His eyes widened and flared with the same dark heat she'd witnessed moments before.

"You don't have stockings on." The sentence came out more choked than unhappy.

"The feet in them didn't fit well. I wear men's

socks with the work boots." Her large body caused more problems. She'd been surprised when the dressmaker had one that was long enough and wasn't too small for her broad shoulders.

"We'll take them back and get ones that fit you proper." His warm palm held the heel of her foot as he slipped her new boot over her toes.

"Could I take them to the camp and give them to Mor?" Talking about her mother took her mind off the sensations buzzing up her leg from his touch.

"Yes. But you'll still need proper stockings to wear these boots." He tugged on the laces and had that foot properly booted.

He picked up her other foot. His fingers ran over the scar just under her ankle. "What is this?" His gaze drifted from her ankle to her face. His wrinkled brow and narrowed eyes warned her he wasn't going to like her answer.

"When I was learning how to work the chute, I got caught between two logs." She shrugged. Every job she'd worked through the years had given her a scar, but she'd learned from every one of them.

He stared into her eyes. "This is why I won't have you working in the woods. It's dangerous."

She tried to pull her foot from his grip, but he wouldn't release it. "I got that when I was learning. Now I know what I'm doing. Only those who don't pay attention get hurt."

Hank continued to hold her gaze and raised her foot, kissing the scar.

Her heart raced as her body pulsed with excitement. How could she stay angry with him when he kissed her and shimmered wonderful sensations through her body?

"We won't talk of logging the rest of the night. I want this to be a special night for you." He slipped her other boot on and laced it.

Hank rose to his feet and extended a hand toward her. Kelda accepted the offering and stood, her body only inches from his. The spicy scent of his shave soap wafted around her adding to her dizzy sensation.

His hands held her head like a cherished object. Her breathing quickened as his lips descended, inch by inch, until the connection sent shivers of anticipation sparking through her body. His tongue caressed her lips, and she opened.

The initial intimate contact struck her like a bolt of lightning, spinning her senses. She clung to him with a talon like grip on his upper arms. His body pressed closer. The scrape of his clothing across her breasts added another jolt of sensations.

He drew back, but held her head. "Kissing you makes me forget proprieties."

She understood. If he laid her on the bed at this moment, she would welcome his advances with open arms and heart.

Dropping his hands to his sides, he backed away. "I like your hair down like this but you should do something with it before we go to dinner."

Her body flamed with a yearning she didn't understand. She understood there was a need it wanted fulfilled but what that need was...she peered at Hank. Her heart fluttered and the juncture of her legs throbbed. Her body wanted his. Unsure how to fight the desire, she ducked her head and hurried into her room.

She stopped at the bureau and stared in the mirror and gasped. The woman starring back at her didn't look a thing like the Kelda she knew. Who was this striking woman with lips swollen from kisses and eyes shimmering with desire?

Kelda picked up her hair brush and swept the bristles through her hair. The grounding aroma of vanilla filled the air. She sprinkled drops of the extract on her brush once a month to keep her hair smelling good between washings.

The locks shimmered in the light as they dried. She didn't want to braid it, but had never had a need to do any of the fancy upswept styles or even a bun. Gathering her hair on the sides, she twisted and pulled them to the back, using the ribbon from her braid to tie the two together at the back of her head. There, it was up and out of her face, yet down the way Hank liked it.

She felt his presence. He stood at the doorway watching. Kelda set the brush down and walked over to him. "I'm ready."

He skimmed his knuckles down her cheek. "You're beautiful."

His eyes darkened, and she thought he was going to kiss her again, but he stepped aside allowing her to enter his room. He followed and held out her cape. She wrapped the garment around her and stepped out into the hall.

Hank offered his arm, and they walked side by side without talking all the way to the Warhauser.

The magnificence of the hotel stole her words. Inside the door, their coats were taken by a courteous young man. The restaurant was as beautiful and reverent as a church Far had spoken of seeing when he first arrived in America. The high ceiling was stained glass with rich dark wood furniture and accents.

Kelda tugged on Hank's arm as the waiter escorted them into the dining area. Hank bent his head toward her. "This is too expensive."

He placed his free hand over her hand on his arm and his eyes twinkled. "Seeing the admiring looks on all the people seated is worth every penny."

She drew her gaze from his and noticed everyone watched their entrance. The thought so many people were interested in them stumbled her feet. Hank held on tight making her fumble look like she caught a toe in her skirt. Her body shook.

The waiter finally stopped beside a table in the back corner. Hank held her chair and she sat, breathing a sigh of relief that her back was to the room. She could forget all the people in the room.

Hank sat across from her, beaming. "You are sparkling like a star tonight."

Her cheeks warmed. "It's all because of you. The dress and shoes would make any woman feel special."

He frowned. "It's not the dress or the shoes. Your smile captured me from the first moment I saw you. Your warmth and caring is what makes you glow. The new dress only draws more attention to your smile."

He'd noticed her smile first? No wonder when she was moping around he'd caught onto her poor disposition. Since they were making confessions...

"I couldn't stop looking at you that first day.

I'm so used to my brothers round faces, I found your face interesting."

The tips of his ears grew red. "Really? Now that you've met my brothers did you find their faces as interesting?"

Kelda giggled. "You all do have a similar look about you. But I like the way your face crinkles around your eyes when you smile and laugh and the softness of your voice."

Their food arrived and they fell to eating. Kelda glanced over at Hank several times and found him watching her. She'd return to the meal as heat curled in her body.

The waiter was removing their dishes when Kelda noticed Hank's mood shift. He stared across the room. She peered over her shoulder to see what caught his attention. A large group of men and woman were being seated.

"Do you know them?" she asked, her curiosity getting the better of her.

Hank drew his gaze from the family that had just arrived and peered into Kelda's concerned face.

"Yes. That family is our biggest competitor."

"They're loggers?" She turned in her chair giving him a tantalizing view of her profile and drawing his thoughts from the Eccles to her.

"No, they aren't loggers. They hire loggers. Your father said he turned Eccles down but didn't say why." Hank stood and placed his hands on Kelda's chair. "Ready to go?"

She peered at him and his body tightened like a taut rope. Kissing and holding her earlier had made him so randy he'd wanted to bed her.

She still had that hold over him now. He fisted his hands, digging his nails into his palms. He had to control his urges.

Kelda nodded and stood, placing her arm through his. He'd planned to move on by the Eccles family and avoid conversation. He didn't dislike the man, but he did, however, have misgivings about the way the man did business, using his large family and marriages to dovetail businesses and shut out the local businesses.

"Mr. Halsey." The loud voice couldn't be ignored.

Hank stopped, pivoting slowly with Kelda still clinging to his arm. "Yes, Mr. Eccles?"

"I heard you contracted with the Stoddard brothers." Mr. Eccles stood, walking away from his family and toward them.

"Yes, sir. We have a good stand of timber and my wood boss says we can fulfill the contract and more." Kelda's hand gripped Hank's arm.

"If the Stoddard's can't handle all your trees at their McEwen mill you'll need to come see me about using my railroad to haul your trees to our mill." The gleam of proprietorship in the man's eyes shouldn't have rankled. But it did.

Eccles had not allowed anyone to buy into the railroad. Instead he'd used money procured from members of his church and banking partners. Hank and Ethan had looked into getting a piece of the railroad from Baker to Sumpter and had been turned down flat.

"I plan on coming to see you when the railroad is completed."

"Good. I'll be looking for you." Eccles turned

his attention to Kelda. "And who is your lovely companion?" The spark of interest in Eccles eyes along with his slow perusal of her from head to toe flashed heat and jealousy through Hank.

Kelda smiled and extended her hand. "Kelda Nielsen."

Hank wanted to pull her hand back but knew if he needed his timber hauled to Baker City he had to have this man's acceptance.

Eccles grasped her hand. "David Eccles."

Hank placed his body between the two. "We need to be moving on. I'll be by to see you later this summer." He drew Kelda toward the front doors.

They paused to collect their coats. Hank helped Kelda with her cape, making sure all his motions told everyone in the establishment she was off limits. Eccles studied her like he was looking for wife number three.

Out in the cold night air, Hank tucked Kelda close to his side. He didn't care if he was being too familiar. This trip had taught him one thing. He wanted Kelda.

<h1 style="text-align:center">Chapter 15</h1>

Kelda removed her new dress, folding it carefully and packing it in her valise. They'd leave early tomorrow for the logging camp. She liked the silky undergarments so well she decided to sleep in them. As she brushed and braided her hair, she pondered Hank's strange reactions to Mr. Eccles. Hank had been very attentive and very quiet after Mr. Eccles introduced himself, and he'd ushered her into her room with barely a good night.

She'd hoped they would kiss some more. Though the kisses they'd shared so far were enough to keep her happy for a lifetime. The sound of heavy footsteps on Hank's side of the door stopped her hand mid-stroke. The muffled steps grew loud then faded. He paced.

What had him so upset he couldn't sleep? She placed her brush on the bureau and started for the adjoining door. The cool breeze washing over her exposed skin as she walked halted her steps. She couldn't show herself to him dressed in these skimpy undergarments. Kelda grabbed her flannel night dress hanging over the end of the bed and pulled it over the top of the unmentionables.

Drawing in a deep breath, she turned the knob and pulled the door open.

Hank stood in the middle of the room staring at the door. Her gaze took in the wide expanse of bare chest covered with a sprinkling of dark curls, down to his flat stomach and pants hanging low on his hips. Her undoing were his bare feet cushioned in the colorful carpet. Her heart raced and her body heated.

"Do you need something?"

She leisurely ran her gaze back up his body. The heat in his eyes rocked her back on her heels.

"I-I…"

He crossed the room in three strides gathering her in his arms, pressing her against his bare chest. She splayed her hands out, feeling the hard muscles bunch and the hair tickle her palms.

She'd heard of swooning, but this was the first time she understood the word. His mouth covered hers, and she dove into the sensation of floating. The kiss lifted her onto her toes and quivered her body into heated need.

Her hands slid to his back, allowing her body to press against his chest. The heat and hard contours of his body under her palms started a new flood of desire swirling low in her torso. His lips moved over her jawline and down. Kelda tipped her head back allowing his soft kisses access to the hollow of her neck.

"Kelda," he whispered her name so soft and low she almost didn't hear it for the swooshing in her ears.

"Hank." Her throat felt raw and sounded raspy.

He held her tight against his body. The hardness pressing against the juncture of her legs stole into her hazy thoughts. His arms banded around her like a choker chain. He kissed her neck again and his arms slowly released her. "Go to your room and don't come back in here tonight." Hank turned his back to her.

She placed a hand on his shoulder and he flinched. "What's wrong?"

"Go to your room, we'll discuss it in the morning when we're both dressed."

"Did I do something wrong?" Her heart dropped like a falling tree.

He turned but only enough for her to see the pained expression on his face. "You've done nothing wrong. I promised I wouldn't compromise you on this trip, and I'm trying to stay to my word." He waved to the adjoining door. "Go."

"But I like kissing you." She turned him to face her and placed a hand on his cheek.

He kissed her palm and closed his eyes. "I like kissing you. But that's the problem. The kisses lead to more. I won't do that to you. I won't bed you even though that's all I can think of."

Kelda stepped back. Was that what came next after the kisses? Her body heated thinking about lying in bed alongside Hank. She reached out, but he closed his hand over hers before she touched him.

"No. If you touch me I won't be able to stop. Go." He spun her forcefully. When she dug in her heels, he picked her up, carried her into her room, and dumped her on the bed.

"Stay!" he ordered and closed the door to their rooms. The key clicked.

He'd locked her out.

Hank woke surly and tired. He'd spent most of the night lying awake wishing he wasn't so honorable. When Kelda walked through that damn connecting door in her nightdress he'd pushed aside all good sense and sought the feel and taste of her. He wanted her even more now that he'd pushed her to the point where her desire for him was as consuming as his desire for her.

The only honorable way to get what he wanted was to marry her. But marriage was out of the question. He didn't have time in the next two years for a wife. Especially with Eccles watching and hoping he didn't come through on his contract to Stoddard.

Would Kelda wait two years? The heat and passion in her eyes last night said she wanted him but would that passion diminish if they had to wait? He dressed quickly when he heard her moving around. His belongings were packed in his bag and sitting by the hallway door.

A knock on the outside door surprised him. They told Lars they'd meet him downstairs. He opened the door. Kelda smiled brightly at him. Her new cape draped over her shoulders and the deep blue of the day dress he bought her peeked out from under the cape. She clutched her valise in her right hand.

"I'm ready."

"Why didn't you use the adjoining door?" He plopped his hat on and slipped into his coat.

"It was locked." A brief flicker of disappointment dulled her eyes before she caught it and smiled.

"True. Let's get breakfast and then find Lars and head back to camp." He picked up his bag and offered Kelda an arm. They strolled down the stairs and found Lars sitting on a cushioned chair in the lobby.

The new cook jumped up a smile widening his face. "God morgen."

"God morgen," Kelda chorused.

Hank stopped at the desk. "Would you hold our bags, please, and have someone retrieve my wagon from the livery over on Washington?" He slid a silver dollar across the counter to the clerk.

"Yes, sir. Your wagon will be waiting out front when you're ready."

"Thank you." Hank relieved Kelda of her valise, setting both bags at the end of the counter. "Lars, leave your stuff here, too." He motioned to the cook.

Lars nodded and placed his bundle with their bags and followed them into the restaurant.

Hank wanted more time alone with Kelda but having the third party present was a good way to keep him from overstepping and kissing her. He held out a chair for Kelda then sat to her side while Lars took the seat across from Kelda.

If the man wondered at their relationship, he didn't seem interested. He asked questions in Norwegian and Kelda answered tossing an explanation Hank's direction now and then in English.

They finished the meal and collected their belongings. Lars climbed into the back of the wagon without a word. Hank tossed their bags in hurrying to Kelda's side to help her onto the wagon seat. To her credit, she waited patiently for help. Did she like being treated like a lady rather than a logger? The thought settled warm in his chest.

They slogged through the muddy streets and out to the less busy road leading to McEwen and Sumpter.

Hank leaned his head toward Kelda and whispered. "Does Lars understand any English?"

She giggled and whispered. "Some, why?

"I wanted to speak to you about last night, but we don't need him telling your family how familiar we've become."

Her body shifted, leaving more space between them. What had he said? He wanted to reach over and take one of her hands but the gap between them would show his actions to the man in the back of the wagon. "What did I say?"

Kelda's body shifted, her knees banged into his. He glanced over and caught her icy green stare.

"Am I only to gain your attention when we are away from the log camp?" The anger and edge on her voice told him she was about to boil over like an unwatched pot.

"No." He captured her hand in his. "I-I just don't want your family thinking anything about the trip was inappropriate." He played with her gloved fingers. "I won't be forced into marriage."

She yanked her hand back and faced forward. "You think I'd allow my family to force me to marry someone who didn't want me?"

"No. I didn't mean..." Hank sighed deep and long. What was wrong? He couldn't seem to say the right words. "I would be honored to marry you, but not until I've covered my costs of this operation and can provide for a family."

"Honored?" She huffed and turned her body to face the opposite side of the wagon.

Now what? He slumped his shoulders forward and concentrated on driving the horses. He didn't have a clue what he'd said or done wrong but the icy chill coming off Kelda's back didn't bode well for the rest of the trip. He peered at her back. She was the first woman to have him thinking about marriage, but he couldn't add one more person to depend on this venture working. Her family would be paid whether the trees went to the mill or not, but his family would be out money if he failed.

With blurry vision Kelda stared at the trees passing by. She pressed her eyes closed forcing the tears to recede. The cold seemed to seep through her cape and chill her to her bones. Why would Hank kiss her like he did then say he'd be honored to marry her? The way his eyes darkened and smoldered when he looked at her and kissed her was more than honor wasn't it? She knew she'd never marry another. He had captured her body and heart during this trip.

"Hvor langt til leiren?" Lars asked from behind her.

She shifted, putting her back to Hank and peered back at Lars. He'd asked how long of a trip. It looked like he already realized it would take most of the day as he pulled a blanket out of his pack.

"Vi vil ankomme av mørket." Kelda gave him a slight smile. They had many hours to travel yet and would get to the camp about dark.

"Mange Takk." He curled up in the back, drawing the blanket around him and closing his eyes.

She shivered, wishing she had a blanket. The day had turned gray and cold. The winter weather had hung on longer than usual.

"Come here." Hank's soft deep voice warmed her ear as his arm curled around her shoulders, shifting her next to him. "We'll stay warmer if we cuddle."

She wanted to push away, but the warmth she immediately felt softened her resolve, and she snuggled against his side.

"I'm sorry." He kissed her temple. "I don't always say things the way I mean them." He kept his voice low, his chin resting on her head. Kelda didn't want to ruin the moment and remained quiet.

"I promise I won't ignore you when we return to the camp, but we'll need to keep our kisses private."

She tried to pull out of his arm, but he held her tight.

"Don't get upset. Hear me out." He shifted, meshing them even closer. "I don't want your brothers hassling you for consorting with the boss. I might do more than dock their wages if I came to your aide."

She had to agree to that. Her brothers would tease her mercilessly, and she wouldn't want them getting into a brawl with Hank. Far needed them in the woods.

"And I don't want to make your life uncomfortable around the other men. I see how they respect you and would hate to have you lose that respect."

She nodded. Her respect came from how she conducted herself in the woods not in the kitchen or as a woman. If they started seeing her as a women she had no doubt their esteem of her would fall down several notches.

"That's not to say I won't steal a kiss now and then, because there's no way I can see you every day and not crave a taste." He captured her lips in a soft tender kiss that warmed her better than a roaring fire. Hank topped the kiss off with two more short sweet kisses. "I feel a whole lot warmer now. How about you?"

Kelda nodded and smiled, peering into his eyes. She thought his disregard was him being fickle but he was only trying to save her from torment and ridicule.

Movement in the back of the wagon reminded her they weren't alone. "What about Lars, if he mentions our kissing?" she whispered while tucking her head in the crook of Hank's arm.

"I figure you can ask him to keep this quiet. With the way you grab a man's affections, you should be able to persuade him to keep our secret."

She sat up and stared at him. "What do you mean 'grab a man's affections'?"

The smile in his eyes told her he wasn't saying it with any malice.

Hank shook his head. "You don't see it, but when you smile at a man he falls all over himself to help you. "

"Nei." This wasn't so.

"Yes. The clerk at the hotel, the waiters, Lars, even Mr. Eccles." Hank drew her back against his side. "Sweetheart, you capture the attention of every man you come across."

"Nei. It is only my size. They have never seen such a tall strong woman."

He chuckled, rumbling his chest under her ear. "That might be what draws their attention first, but it's your infectious smile that chains their affection." He kissed her temple. "I know. It's what hypnotized me."

"Really?" Kelda smiled, thinking he'd noticed her smile and liked it. But what he said…she'd have to pay more attention. She smiled because she liked people and enjoyed a happy life.

"Yes. Your smile, your eyes, your disposition. Woman, you set your gaff in me and I'm not going to struggle to get away."

She laughed and snuggled closer. Her hand strayed out from under the cape and slipped between the buttons on his jacket. The heat and muscle of his stomach under the flannel shirt he wore warmed her like adding pitch kindling to a fire. Hank sucked in air and his muscles flexed under her hand.

They rode like this until Hank started up the grade to Sumpter. She pulled back and glanced over her shoulder. Lars was sitting up. He smiled and winked. She would have to speak to him before they arrived at the camp.

Entering Sumpter, Zeke walked out of the mercantile and waved at them.

"Come to the house and warm up before you head to the camp," he said, holding the lead horse. "Maeve will have my hide if you continue on and don't dote on the baby."

Hank glanced her way. "Do you mind?"

"I could use a cup of tea to warm up." Kelda peered at Zeke. "We'd love to come see the baby."

Zeke led the horses to his house, and they all unloaded and introduced Lars to Maeve and Zeke.

Lars and Hank went with Zeke to the barn to give the horses a rest from the weather. Kelda followed Maeve into a lovely two-story house.

"Your home is beautiful," she said, running her fingers over a piano that resembled one she'd seen in a traveling acting troupe's wagon.

"Thank you. Before I became with child, Zeke and I hadn't planned to stay in any place for very long, but once we knew a child would be born it seemed best to buy a home and stay in one place." Maeve led her into a cheery kitchen with bright colored curtains of yellow gingham.

"I've never lived in a house. We've been in logging camps my whole life." Once the words were out she wished she hadn't uttered them.

"Did you lack for love or food?" Maeve asked.

"Nei. We had plenty of both."

Maeve patted her hand. "Then you had the most important things. Sit."

Kelda sat and Maeve placed five cups and saucers on the table and a plate of fancy bread.

"The bread looks wonderful." Kelda didn't realize how hungry she was until the aroma of the bread wafted to her.

"I can't take credit. I'm a lousy cook, but

Rachel and Aileen take pity on me and bring me baked goods." Maeve tilted her head to one side. "Your assistant, Lars, I can't believe Hank is going to let you work side by side with that good looking man."

Kelda stared at the woman as her ears burned. "Why would Hank care?"

"Oh, don't you even try." Maeve laughed. "We've all seen the way the two of you look at one another."

"What's so funny?" Zeke asked, entering the kitchen with Hank and Lars behind him.

Kelda sent a pleading look toward Maeve.

Chapter 16

Hank entered the warmth of the house. His gaze landed on the stricken expression on Kelda's face. He crossed the room and placed a hand on her shoulder. "What's wrong?"

"N-nothing." Her gaze flew to Maeve.

"We were just visiting and I brought up a subject that she couldn't deny." Maeve picked up the coffee pot, pouring coffee in three cups and then tea in the cup in front of Kelda and the one in front of her chair.

Hank took the seat beside Kelda. "What can't you deny?"

Kelda shook her head and held the tea cup in front of her lips. Lips he wanted to kiss and take away her discomfort.

"The attraction between the two of you," Maeve said and laughed as Kelda spit tea.

Hank handed Kelda a napkin and patted her back as she coughed. He glared at Maeve. The woman had been a burr under his saddle since he met her. She had a good heart but said things knowing full well they caused discomfort.

Zeke leaned back in his chair, his arms crossed, and smiling like he'd just been dealt a full house.

Lars stared at Kelda. Then started talking to her in Norwegian. They carried on a short conversation that ended with Lars agreeing. "Ja."

"What's that about?" Hank asked, beginning to wonder if hiring a man she could so easily talk with and keep him excluded was a good idea.

"What you wanted me to discuss with him." Her eyes pleaded with him to...what?

"Ah." Hank turned his attention to the couple watching and hanging on their every word. "Where's the baby?" Might as well get their attention focused on something else.

"Brendan is napping." Maeve shoved the plate of bread toward Lars, Kelda, and finally Hank.

"So you decided on a name." Hank had wondered when the newest Halsey would be named.

Zeke picked up Maeve's hand. "We decided to name him after the other man Maeve loved. Her father."

"I didn't get to have him in my life for very long, but I plan to be in Brendan's a lifetime." Tears glistened in his sister-in-law's eyes.

"That is a wonderful tribute. I know Far can't wait for the boys to marry and give him grandchildren," Kelda said, not looking up from her cup of tea. "Of course the boys need to get out of the woods and find a woman for that to happen."

The wistfulness in her voice surprised Hank. Why would she wish her brothers out of the woods?

"They're going to have a tough time find-ing wives around here. Women are scarce." Zeke winked at Maeve. "I was lucky Maeve was prickly or she'd have been snapped up."

They all laughed and settled into small talk about the area.

"We need to get going. The road to the camp is hard enough to travel without doing it in the dark." Hank rose and held Kelda's chair, continuing his gentlemanly treatment that he started in Baker City. He wanted her to remember he saw her as a woman and not a logger. Something that, if he had his way, she would never do again.

"We've kept you too long." Maeve took Kelda's hand. "Come see me or Rachel any time. We enjoy the company."

Kelda's eyes widened in surprise, she glanced at Hank. "I-I'll see what I can do. Thank you."

Hank helped Kelda into her cape. "Thank you for the coffee and conversation," he said, moving Kelda toward the door that Zeke held open. Lars shook Zeke's hand and exited.

Zeke slapped Hank on the shoulder. "Ethan and Gil will be happy to see you. They want their wives back."

Kelda stopped. "Oh, I'm so sorry for this in-convenience. " She turned to Hank. "What can I do to make it up to them?"

"We'll think of something. Come on. Tonight will be the last meal they have to prepare. You and Lars can take over at breakfast tomorrow." Hank placed a proprietary hand against Kelda's back propelling her toward the barn. Lars already had the horses hitched to the wagon.

"Thank you," Hank said as he helped Kelda onto the seat.

Lars smiled and jumped into the back.

Hank climbed up beside Kelda, sliding his body against hers. He started the horses in motion and looked at the house. Maeve and Zeke stood on the porch waving. He nudged Kelda, and they both waved as well as Lars.

"I like your family," Kelda said, snuggling tighter to his side.

"I'm glad. They seem to like you as well." He peered over his shoulder at Lars watching them. "So what did Lars have to say about us?"

Kelda straightened a little. "He thought we were married. I explained we weren't and didn't want our families pushing something we aren't sure of yet." She peered into his eyes. "He said he'd not say anything as long as you treat me right."

Hank should have been angry by the man's words but they only validated his belief every man she smiled at fell under Kelda's spell. He'd be damn lucky to be the one who captured her heart and kept her.

"It's going to be hard to only touch you when others aren't present." He kissed her scarf covered head. Why was she so hard to put out of his mind? He'd never felt this protective about any of the other girls or women he kissed. He'd been randy and would have liked to bed them, but he'd taken those urges to the women that didn't form attachments—the prostitutes in Baker City. With Kelda, he wanted to love her thoroughly.

He jerked straight and stared forward. He

couldn't be in love with her. You've been thinking marriage since meeting her. She shifted next to him, sliding her arm through his and hugging it. His heart thudded. Was it from panic or the thrill?

The horses turned down the road to the camp. Hank cleared his throat. "You better sit up in case anyone happens along."

She sighed, squeezed his arm, and sat straighter, sliding over allowing the cold air to slip between them.

Regret washed over him the moment the cold air circled his body. He could make it so they didn't have to hide their closeness. All he had to do was ask her to marry him and explain it would be a long engagement. He shook his head. No, he wouldn't have her commit to him. There were too many things that could go wrong. He could end up losing everything if the logs weren't delivered to Stoddard on time. He wasn't going to risk Kelda's happiness. If he offered marriage and all hell broke loose he wouldn't have the means to support her or a family. He'd be back living off the family mine and mill. It wouldn't be a bad living, but he'd be a failure and that wouldn't be fair to saddle Kelda with a disgruntled husband.

The evening descended in a gradual gray to dusk by the time they arrived at the camp. A line of men stood outside the cookhouse waiting to wash.

Karl walked over to the wagon a scowl marred his face. "This looks like another logger not a cook."

Kelda shoved his head with the heel of her hand and said something to Lars. The man laughed and replied, making Karl squirm even more.

"I'm missing the joke," Hank said, again wondering about the language connection between the cook and Kelda. He knew her family spoke Norwegian when others weren't present but they spoke only English around him, until now.

"Nei joke. I told Lars what Karl said and he said if he needed to fall a tree to prove he could cook so be it." Her eyes sparkled with merriment and Hank became caught up in their glow.

The wagon wiggled and he continued to peer into her eyes.

"You two going to come eat or sit and stare all night." Karl's gruff voice broke the trance, and Hank motioned to Kelda.

"Go ahead and get down, I'm going to take care of the horses."

Kelda nodded and climbed down from the wagon, aware that more than just Karl watched. She made it halfway when hands grasped her waist and set her feet on the ground. She turned and Lars winked at her.

"Mange takk," she said and glanced at Hank. He gave Lars a brief nod and slapped the horses with the reins. So that's how it would be. Lars, the married man, would look after her while Hank kept his distance. She wasn't sure she liked that arrangement.

The men stood back from the door allowing her and Lars to enter first. Aileen and Darcy were setting platters of biscuits on the long tables.

"You're back!" Darcy practically skipped across the floor. "And what a lovely dress and cape." She hugged Kelda tight and stepped back, tipping her head to look at Lars. "This is the assistant cook?"

Kelda shook her head. "Cook. I'll be the assistant. That way I can have more time for Mor. How is she?" She scanned the room but it was empty.

Aileen came forward and hugged her. "She's been a bit under the weather today. Yer da is in with her now."

"Could you show Lars the supply room and the kitchen? I'll go see how she is." Kelda unbuttoned the cape and headed for her parents' room. "Oh, he speaks very little English," she tossed over her shoulder.

She knocked lightly and entered the room. Mor appeared even smaller and paler than she remembered. Far sat on a chair next to the bed. He looked her direction. His gaze traveled the length of her and his brows raised.

"Where did you find those fancy clothes?"

Kelda's cheeks heated as she knelt by the bed. "Hank bought them for me. How is Mor?"

Far's large hand cupped her cheek. He held her face where he could peer into her eyes. "What favor did you do for the boss that he bought you a dress?" The underlying growl of disapproval turned her burning cheeks to ice.

"Nothing. He said they were an early birthday present. We went to dinner at a fancy restaurant, and Hank wanted me to be dressed appropriately." She sat back on her heels. "Far, how can you ask me such a question? You and Mor have raised me proper."

Tears welled in her father's eyes. "Ja. You are our good girl. I'm sorry. Your mother is getting weaker and remembers little. It is breaking my heart to see her this way."

Kelda drew Far into an embrace. She knew the day would come when she would take care of her parents as they had taken care of her, but she had hoped for more years of good health. "I brought back a cook, not an assistant, so I can spend more time with Mor." She inhaled. "And so I can relieve the boys once a week."

Far held her away from him. "Is this wise? Not only will leaving your mother alone not be good, but it would seem you think nothing of the feelings of a man who has tried very hard to make you happy."

"Mor will be in good hands. Lars, the cook, is Norwegian and can speak with Mor in our native language. I plan on working in the woods."

"You know Hank's feelings about you working in the woods." Far's gaze scanned the length of her. "By the fancy clothes he bought you and the sparkle in his eyes when he watches you, he is smitten. If you continue to push to work in the woods against his wishes you may find he is not so taken with you."

"By working in the woods so my brothers can find wives I am making them happy and with them happy the whole crew is happy."

Far shook his head. "It's too late to shut the stable door after the horse has bolted."

Kelda tilted her head. "What do you mean by that Far?"

"It is one thing to wish your brothers a happy life with families, but you may be shutting the door on your happiness by working so hard to find them theirs."

Her heart stuttered a moment. "You mean Hank? I'm not planning a life with him." She allowed her gaze to wander to Mor looking so poor on the bed. "I wish a marriage like yours and Mor. I'll not settle for less. If Hank doesn't see the woods make me happy, he isn't the man for me." Even as she said the words, she knew no other would make her feel as cherished as Hank Halsey.

Far pat her hand. "Go on telling yourself that. You will have a rude awakening the day he walks away." Far stood. "I'll have one of the women bring in a tray for you and Mor."

Kelda shrugged out of her cape and nodded. If Hank walked away could she survive? Logging was what made her happy. She touched her lips. They tingled remembering the fevered kisses and his touch skimming along her body. Shaking her head, she settled back on the chair by Mor. No man would ever make her feel the way Hank did. She knew that and knew her heart was opening to the thought of being with him, but could she persuade him to allow her to work in the woods?

Chapter 17

Hank didn't see Kelda the rest of the evening. Her brothers and father kept him busy regaling him with the logs downed and his brothers' visits. After the meal, Lars shooshed the women away and began washing the dishes. Aileen and Darcy pulled Hank to a corner of the table and began interrogating him about the trip.

"That's a beautiful outfit Kelda returned in," Darcy said, her eyebrows rising.

"It was an early birthday present. When are your husbands coming to get you?" Hank didn't want to divulge any of his time with Kelda to either his sisters-in-law or their husbands. The three days with Kelda had cottoned him to the idea of marriage. Just not right away. He'd enjoyed their conversations to and from town, watching all the heads turn when they entered a room, and her sense of humor and intellect made the trip memorable and one he would like to take again soon.

"They'll take us home tomorrow when they

arrive to see how things are runnin'," Aileen said, scrunching her brows and staring at him. "You were good to the girl and no' any randy business?"

Heat shot up his neck and flashed like gunpowder on his cheeks. "Yes! I can't believe you're saying these things to me." The outrage he felt that his sisters would question him, nearly shot him to his feet until he glanced at the Nielsen men, all watching him intently. Hank ran a hand over his face. "I was a gentleman. Did she look like she'd been ravaged when she arrived?"

"She's in good spirits." Darcy waved a hand toward Arvid's room.

"Do you think that could have been the fact she was taken away from all her duties and allowed to see and experience things she's not seen before?" He loved showing Kelda new experiences and showing her how a woman should be treated.

Aileen tapped his shoulder, drawing his attention to her. "Aye. 'tis good ye show her life outside this camp. But remember she is who she is and ye cannae change her."

Hank frowned as the two women stood.

"We have a cot set up in the cabin. Send Kelda over when she's ready to call it a night," Darcy said as she and Aileen plucked shawls from the pegs by the door and disappeared.

Hank liked the idea of Kelda in a cabin rather than the supply room. Just as he wiped the smile off his face, the Nielsen men sat down around him. He glanced at Lars who had the dishes washed and put away. The man smiled and saluted as he disappeared into the supply room.

He was left all alone with Kelda's men folk.

"Think we wouldn't see those fancy clothes our sister came home in?" Karl leaned over Tobias to get in Hank's face.

"They were an early birthday present." He didn't need to defend himself, but he'd be damned if Kelda's brothers harassed her because of him.

"You sure you weren't trying to buy our sister's affections?" Dag now leaned into Hank. "If we find out you ruined our sister, you'll marry her."

"I didn't ruin her. I showed her what life could be like outside this camp. We dined at a fancy restaurant and went for a walk, peering into store windows." He nodded his head toward the supply room. "And interviewed cooks."

"About Lars." Karl sat back. "We were hoping for a woman."

"A young woman." Dag's eyes sparkled.

"There were no young women who applied. And once Kelda laid eyes on Lars she was determined to hire him." Had she been attracted to the man at first sight? He hadn't thought about that until just this minute. Hank stared at the supply room. Was he competition? Kelda said the man was married, but he had no proof other than her word. Would she say that to throw him off? Hank thought about their closeness with the man in the back of the wagon. No, he didn't believe the new cook was competition. But why had she wanted to hire this man so quickly?

Karl smiled. "He said he could log. She must have seen him as potential for the woods as well as the kitchen."

Hank caught a brief grimace from Arvid before the old man coughed and stood.

"I'll retire for the night and send your sister out." He peered into Hank's face. "Her belongings have already been moved to the cabin of your brothers' wives. We believed she would be bringing back another woman."

"And now? Will you move her back to the storeroom and have Lars bunk with Paddy?" The idea of Kelda back in the supply room didn't settle well with Hank.

"We'll see what Kelda and Lars wish to do. God natt." Arvid's steps were slower and more labored than Hank remembered as the man moved to the room he shared with his wife.

Tobias sighed. "Mor is not doing well. She took sick while Kelda was gone."

Would Kelda blame her mother's illness on him dragging her away? He ran a hand over his face. She'd known her mother wasn't doing well before they left.

Kelda stepped out of Far and Mor's room, her cape draped over her arm. Mor was so weak and Far...her heart ached as if someone were taking huge bites out of it with an axe.

Her brothers remained seated, but Hank rose as she walked across the room. A smile quivered on her lips. They were back and he still insisted on treating her well.

"You should eat something," he said, taking her by the elbow and seating her at the head of the table nearest the kitchen. He disappeared and returned with a cup of water and a bowl of soup.

"Mange takk." She didn't dare raise her gaze to her brothers who were, no doubt, taking in the way their boss treated her. She took a bite and her stomach growled. With all the wonders of her trip, she'd disregarded hunger pains for giddiness over Hank's attention.

"Your belongings are out at Paddy's cabin. You'll bunk with Aileen and Darcy tonight then the cabin is all yours."

The concern etched in Hank's brow made her want to smooth it with her thumb, but she knew better than to make any moves that would have her brothers speculating about their relationship.

"I'll move into the supply room tomorrow, so I'll be close to help Far with Mor."

He placed a hand over hers on the table, stopping her upward motion of another bite of soup.

"You'll be close by all day. Give yourself a break by living in the cabin." His brown gaze looked deep into her eyes.

What was he trying to convey to her? The warmth of his hand sent heat racing up her arm. His touch kindled the yearnings she'd been tamping down since they arrived at the camp.

The scrape of a bench and heavy footsteps approaching registered as Karl's looming presence threw a shadow on Hank's face.

"I'm finding it hard to believe you didn't ruin my sister the way you're looking at her and holding her hand."

The softness and tenderness in Hank's eyes shifted in a blink to the hard steal of an axe blade.

"I'll not defend our friendship to you, but I take your accusations that you'd believe your sister is anything other than a proper young woman as slander to her." Hank rose to his feet, his eyes dark and angry, his hands fisted at his sides, and his stance...wide, set to swing a blow that she was sure would down a tree in one swipe.

Kelda stood, placing a hand on both their chests. "You know no man thinks of me the way you're insinuating." She purposely kept her gaze on her brother. She didn't want to see the hurt in Hank's eyes. "Hank and I are good friends. It's nice to have someone to talk with who isn't family or a logger." She picked up her cape. "Hank, walk me to the cabin, please."

Hank didn't answer, but by the way Karl backed away she had no doubt he was behind her. His hands captured her cape and placed it around her shoulders. Her bag, from their outing, sat by the door. On their way out, Hank grabbed her bag and extended his arm to her.

She didn't glance back to see her brothers' expressions. All she knew was Hank would always stand up for her against any odds. The idea lightened her mood and sent her stomach fluttering.

"Thank you for standing up for me back there."

"If you haven't figured out you've gotten under my skin by now, you're more hopeless than I first imagined." The playful tone of his words made her laugh.

He drew her to the side of the cabin out of the lantern light shining through the window. Before she could catch her breath, he tugged her close with one hand and lowered his lips to hers. The sensation of their mouths touching and the earnest way his lips sought hers, she melted against him. A thud sounded beside her, but instead of allowing her to pull away, his other arm circled her waist, drawing her closer. She twined her fingers together behind his neck and savored his mouth changing angles and chasing dizzying tendrils of delight from her lips all the way to her toes.

He drew back and her body swayed into his. "You're hard to resist." Hank's whisper rallied another round of delicious vibrations through her.

"I didn't realize a kiss could heat a body so."

"Did you feel it too?" he whispered, warming her ear and neck before a kiss tingled her skin.

"Ja. Very much."

He hugged her tight before setting her away from him. "Good night, Kelda," he said loud enough for the women in the cabin to know they were outside. "I'll escort you to the cabin every night," he said, leaning toward her speaking for her ears only.

The idea of secret kisses every night before she went to sleep excited her nearly as much as participating in the kisses.

The door opened and Darcy's head peeked out. "There you are. We were just wondering if you'd arrive before we blew out the lantern.

Kelda breathed in and out, stilling her racing heart and hoped the women attributed her rosy cheeks for the cold outside and not the heat in her body.

Hank grabbed his satchel sitting inside the office door and went to his room. A few minutes later the outside door opened. The creak of the wood stove door and thunk of wood being added meant Tobias was in for the night.

Soft footsteps stopped outside Hank's door. He glanced up from unloading his satchel. Tobias leaned against the door frame.

"You know Karl and Dag are just jealous that their little sister has found someone and they haven't."

Hank straightened. "What do you mean your sister has found someone? We're friends."

A grin spread the full distance across Tobias' face. "Real good friends from what I've seen."

At least this was one brother that didn't seem to care Kelda spent time with him. Hank ran a hand along the back of his neck and grinned back. "We're not as close as you all seem to think. But I've grown fond of your sister and wouldn't mind having her in my life permanently down the road."

Tobias pushed away from the door frame, his face sobering. "What do you mean down the road?"

"I can't make any promises to her until I know this logging operation will make a profit. That could take a couple years." Hank shook his head. "I can't offer marriage to anyone until I'm sure I can support my brothers' families and one of my own."

Tobias shook his head. "Seems to me you'd be missing out on some good times between now and then if you're thinking with your wallet and not your heart." He turned and ambled into his room.

Hank sat on his bed and stared into the office. Was it wrong to want to be financially secure before settling down? He thought of Kelda's passionate kisses and her sparkling green eyes. Would he be able to hold off claiming her body for that long? Would she wait that long?

Displeasure at thinking someone else might come along and snap her up, sent him stalking into the office to stoke the stove and turn off the lantern. Back in his room, he undressed and slid into bed.

Placing his hands behind his head, he stared at the dark ceiling and ran numbers over and over in his mind until his head ached and he closed his eyes.

Chapter 18

Kelda had fallen asleep grateful the two women sharing the cabin hadn't asked any questions, but as they all dressed and prepared for the day, the two were full of questions.

"Where did Hank take you for dinner in Baker City?" Darcy asked, while lacing her child-sized boots.

"The Warshauer." Kelda's fingers refused to work as expertly on braiding her hair as other mornings. The frustration at her own clumsiness around the two women who went through their morning routine with no mistakes and stood before her glowing and womanly only added to her discomfort.

Aileen stepped forward. "Let me give it a go. Yer all thumbs this mornin'." She undid the braid Kelda had started and ran the brush through her hair. "Ye've beautiful silky hair. Do ye ever just let it hang down yer back?"

"I need it out of my way. A braid is the best."

Kelda stood as still as a pine as the woman's deft fingers moved down her hair. "I really need to go to the cookhouse and help Lars."

"He's a strong man and can manage the mornin' meal by hisself." Aileen handed her a mirror.

Kelda held it up and stared at the elaborate braiding Aileen had put in her hair. She'd woven a satin ribbon inside the braids on either side of her head. Aileen flipped her braid over her shoulder to show the ribbon continued down the main braid as well.

"'Tis good to add frippery to yer hair now and then to feel like a woman." Aileen glanced at Kelda's dungaree clad legs. "Especially since ye dress like a man."

Darcy took the mirror from her hands. "You're a beauty and don't let anyone tell you any different."

"Look at me. I'm taller than both of you and Aileen is tall for a woman. My feet and hands are large. I'm only good for hard work." Kelda shoved her feet into her logger boots. She'd placed the beautiful boots Hank bought in her valise to keep them for special occasions. They wouldn't get worn out from everyday use.

Darcy planted her small body in front of Kelda and stomped her foot. "Look at me!"

Kelda reluctantly dropped the shoelaces and straightened.

"We've seen the way you and Hank look at one another. He is falling for you and you for him. Help him along. Dress like a woman who knows what she wants." Darcy put a hand on her shoulder. "Make him want you so bad, he's cross-eyed. He's going to hold out and do the right thing by you, but if you push him past his control, I can guarantee neither one of you will regret it."

"Aye. When a Halsey loves, he loves with his whole bein'." Aileen winked, "And that is the very best for those of us on the lovin' end."

Heat started at Kelda's toes and flashed like a pitch stump through her body to fuse her cheeks. She slapped her hands over her face. "You're making me uncomfortable."

The two laughed, moving to either side of her, slipping an arm around her waist.

"We're here for you if you need to talk," Darcy said. "You'll find the wives of the Halsey brothers have bonded like sisters, and it's been unanimous that we all think you are perfect for Hank."

Aileen squeezed her middle. "Ye have our blessings to do whatever it takes to pull him into marriage."

Tears burned at the back of Kelda's eyes. Her entire life she'd wished for a sister and now if things went well she could have four. Their suggestions and comments swirled in her mind. How did she make him cross-eyed?

The meal bell sounded. She wiped at the single tear tickling her cheek. "We better head over and see if Lars needs help." Kelda quickly finished tying her boots.

The two women stepped toward the door.

"Remember you can talk to Rachel, Maeve, Aileen, or I about anything if you need to." Darcy snagged her shawl from the peg, wrapping it around her small frame twice.

Kelda nodded, grabbing the man's wool jacket she'd worn every day of her adult life until Hank bought her the cape. Pulling the heavy wool up her arms and taking the weight of the garment onto her shoulders, she shifted from the unsure woman of moments before to someone with confidence and swagger. This was why she found it hard to shed her belief she couldn't be loved. When she was in the woods or among the loggers she knew how to behave and what was expected of her. Being a woman was new and unknown territory.

She grasped the door, pulling it open and slogged out into the muddy camp. The weather had warmed, melting snow and leaving the ground a slippery mess. Falling logs was more dangerous during this transition in the weather. More hazards to watch for with slick footing.

Aileen and Darcy followed her to the cookhouse where the beasts of the woods filed into the building. Kelda waited her turn and entered. The aromas made her mouth water. Lars knew how to cook by the looks of rapture on the faces of the men already forking hotcakes into their mouths.

She hung her coat on a peg and headed to help Lars serve. He handed her a platter loaded with fried eggs. Casting a glance at the table to see where the platter needed to go, she caught Hank watching her. She smiled and he nodded. Her heart pattered in her chest. He wasn't hiding their relationship.

The first platter went to the middle of the table. The second platter of eggs Lars handed her went on the end near Hank. She made a point of leaning into Hank as she set the platter down. A trill of excitement skittered up her back as his hand grazed her side. Her cheeks heated and her body wanted to remain near his touch, but she straightened and returned to Lars who had another platter of hotcakes ready.

She made it a point while placing the platters and bowls at Hank's end of the table to lean into him. If anyone noticed, no one said a thing. When the crew had left to start their day, Kelda sat down and discovered why no one noticed her leaning into Hank. Lars's hotcakes melted in her mouth and had just the right amount of sweetness they could be eaten plain. The whole crew had been in hotcake heaven.

Kelda carried her plates to the drain board and started washing the dishes while Lars worked on cakes for dinner. Aileen and Darcy had returned to the cabin to pack their things while they awaited the arrival of their husbands.

"You asked me not to say anything about you and the boss, but your actions will give you away," Lars said in Norwegian.

Kelda flinched. "How do you know what our actions were? You had your back to us."

He grinned sheepishly. "I wanted to see if you were as bold here as in the wagon." He shook his head. "What is wrong with everyone knowing?"

Kelda sighed and leaned against the drain board. "It's hard to explain. I don't want to lose the respect of the loggers." His eyebrow rose, and he started to open his mouth. "Nei, I don't mean by looking like a loose woman though that wouldn't be good either. I work out in the woods with the men when Far allows. Tree topping is my favorite thing." She crossed her arms and smiled. "And I'm good at it."

Hank's words came rushing into her thoughts. "Hank has forbid me to work in the woods as long as we are working for him. But Far has agreed to let me sneak out once in a while and work for the boys so they can go look for a wife and I can keep my skills honed." She didn't like the disapproving scowl on Lars's face. "That's why I hired you. I wanted someone I could feel good about leaving to work on meals alone. And with you speaking Norwegian you can also comfort Mor if I'm not around."

"If the boss doesn't want you in the woods, it's not a good idea to go against his wishes. He may not overlook your trickery even if he is in love with you."

Kelda stared at Lars. "What do you mean he's in love with me?" Her heart raced with the notion. She knew her feelings for Hank had blossomed past that of friendship. His touch and presence warmed her body and filled her soul.

Lars shook his head. "Only a fool would not see the way you two look at one another." His eyes grew misty. "Your bodies gravitate toward one another, just as I cannot keep away from Asa, my wife, when we are in the same room."

"How long has it been since you've seen your wife?" If Lars felt for his wife what she felt for Hank how did they survive apart?

"Two years. I should have enough money to bring her and our son here by the end of this year." He smiled. "If I continue to work for your family, she will not miss her sisters with other Norwegians around."

"Sisters? What are their ages? Would they be interested in writing letters to my brothers? Perhaps..." If her brothers hit it off with the women they could come over and her brothers would have wives.

Lars nodded his head and smiled. "I see where your thoughts are going. That would make my Asa very happy. I will write to her and see. If her sisters are not interested, her cousins or mine may be."

Kelda's heart hummed. If she could distract her brothers with writing letters to prospective wives, she could have more encounters with Hank.

Hank had planned to learn how to work the chute, but with Ethan and Gil coming to get their wives he decided to stay in camp to see if they had anything they wanted to report to him about the days during his absence. He'd also planned to linger after breakfast to see if he could steal a moment with Kelda. The way she'd leaned into him when placing platters on the tables, she'd heated his need and he wanted to taste her lips.

Tobias had other ideas, asking Hank to come to the office to discuss the books. Now Hank sat in his office, staring at the door, and wishing he could find a good excuse to walk over to the cookhouse. But they had their own coffeepot brewing on the potbelly stove and until the noon meal there wasn't a reason to go over there.

The jangle of harnesses caught his attention. That would be his brothers. Hank stood and crossed into the office. The outside door opened.

Ethan and Gil entered, followed by Colin. The grins on the men's faces told Hank they were glad to learn their wives would be snuggled in their arms tonight.

"You're back. Did you find a cook?" Ethan stepped up to the stove and plucked the coffeepot from the surface. Gil held out two cups and he filled them.

"Judging by the breakfast he cooked, the men should be happy," Hank said, holding out his own metal cup.

"He cooked? I thought you were getting an assistant to Kelda." Gil took a sip of his coffee.

"She decided she wanted a cook while she remains the assistant so she can have time to take care of her mother." He couldn't shake the feeling Kelda had an ulterior motive behind her actions but he couldn't figure it out.

Ethan nodded. "That's a good idea." He nudged Hank with his elbow. "And it will make it easier when you marry her to have a cook already in place."

"Wait a minute. I haven't said anything about marrying. Kelda or anyone." He glared at Ethan. "Don't go putting any notions in your wives' heads or your heads. I can't think about marriage until this project shows a profit."

Gil lifted his cup in a salute. "If you can keep her out of your bed until then you're stronger than I thought."

Hank didn't like the talk or the fact Colin was listening so intently. "Drop it. Did anything happen I need to know about? Karl filled me in over dinner last night, but from your point of view is there anything that could be done differently?"

Ethan shook his head. "From what we saw the last few days these men know what they're doing and changing anything would slow their process."

"Good. That's been my observation too. But I wanted to hear your thoughts." He stared out the window. "I'm heading up to work the chute this afternoon. I plan to learn every job to get a log ready to sell."

"It's dangerous if you don't know what you're doing." The caution in Gil's voice didn't bother Hank.

"I know. But these men are the best at what they do." Hank stared pointedly at Ethan and then Gil. "That's why I hired them. To learn from the best."

The door opened. Aileen and Darcy blew in, smiling at their husbands, their eyes sparkling.

"We can go home. Kelda brought back a very capable cook." Darcy pressed against Gil and his arm circled her waist possessively.

"Aye, and Kelda looks rested from bein' away from this camp for a few days." Aileen stood beside Ethan who pulled her closer with an arm draped over her shoulders. He placed a kiss on her head. Hank wished he were out in the woods instead of witnessing what he couldn't have for a few more years.

"So what did you and Kelda do while in Baker City that relaxed her?" Gil wiggled an eyebrow.

The insinuation ground Hank's teeth together. The hand clutching the coffee cup ached as his fingers squeezed the metal. "We had dinner and walked the streets peering in store windows when we weren't interviewing potential cooks."

"And bought her a beautiful dress, cape, and boots," added Darcy, snuggling deeper into her husband's arm.

"They were early birthday gifts. I didn't want her feeling out of place when I took her to the Warshauer for dinner."

"See anyone there we know?" Ethan asked sarcastically.

"Yes, I did. David Eccles and his family." Hank had planned to put the man's interest in Kelda out of his mind.

"Did you speak with him?" Ethan's nonchalant stance straightened.

"I planned to walk on by him, but he stopped me to make sure I knew he knew I'd contracted with Stoddard." Hank paused thinking about the encounter without allowing his emotions for Kelda to slip in. "He almost made a threat that if I didn't make good on that contract he'd take it over and I'd be ruined."

Gil stepped forward. "He can't threaten us."

Ethan's gaze bore into Hank. "There's more you aren't saying."

Hank shook his head. "Nothing that concerns the rest of you."

"If he said something against you, it does concern the rest of us." Ethan would always be the big brother looking out for the rest of them.

"It wasn't so much what he said, but the way he watched Kelda. Like he was looking for a third wife." The jealousy that ate at him at the Warshauer resurfaced, jabbing its talons painfully around his heart.

Darcy laughed. "You don't have to worry about that."

Hank stared at her. "What do you mean?"

"There is no way Kelda would stand for being married to a man as his third wife."

He had to agree with her. The passion he'd drawn out of her so far wouldn't take second or third seat to anyone else. Hank grinned. "That's true."

"Let's get going. There are some children at Rachel's that are waiting to see their mothers," Ethan said, handing his cup to Hank.

"I've missed my babies." Darcy tipped her face up to her husband. "Our bags are still in the cabin."

Gil kissed his wife's upturned face and disappeared out the door. Ethan loaded the women onto the wagon seat.

"Let me know when I can come work for you, Uncle Hank," Colin said as he climbed in the back of the wagon. Gil returned with the bags and mounted the horse tied to the wagon.

"I'll keep you in mind if a job comes up." There was no way he'd allow Colin to work out in the woods. He might let him come tally the logs, though, when they had more stockpiled.

"One of us will come by once a week to see if you need anything. Or you can send word if you need us for some reason." Ethan turned the horses, heading the wagon down the road.

"Will do. Give everyone my love." Hank waved until they were out of sight. When he turned to go back in the office he caught sight of Kelda watching him from the supply tent.

He scanned the camp and didn't see anyone.

With decisive strides, he crossed to the supply tent that Kelda ducked into. He entered and found her waiting for him.

Kelda slipped into Hank's arms and tipped her face up for a kiss. He didn't disappoint. The open-mouthed kiss jolted her body and heated her skin. She wanted this every day for the rest of her life.

He pulled out of the kiss, resting his chin on her head. "You make me forget my duties."

She giggled. "You set my body on fire with your kisses and your touch."

His hands unfastened the buttons of her coat and slid across her belly making the throbbing low in her body stronger. Hank's mouth captured hers once more. His tongue tasted, his teeth nipped and teased.

Kelda unfastened his coat and pressed her body to his as her hands skimmed up his back. She wanted her clothes off and their bodies to touch. She needed to feel his skin to hers. Her hands grasped his shirt, tugging the tails from his pants only to encounter the softness of flannel. He still wore his winter drawers.

A frustrated sigh slipped from her lips as Hank captured her hands.

"This...we can't do this. It will only make us crazy."

"I like crazy." She stepped toward him, touching his lips with hers.

A tight grip on her shoulders held her back. "We can't do this. We'll regret it later."

She shook her head. "I'll never regret the feelings you've brought out in me."

Hank clutched her to his chest then set her

away and buttoned her coat. "Go back to work. I'll wait for you tonight and walk you to your cabin."

Her lips curved into a smile. "Will you stay and have a cup of tea with me?"

He shoved his shirt back into his pants and buttoned his coat. "That will depend on how proper you are."

"I can be very proper."

Hank exited the tent, and Kelda collected the items Lars sent her to retrieve. Her mind conjured up her and Hank sitting on her bed, wrapped in a quilt talking and touching...She could be proper. But she had a feeling tonight she would be improper.

Chapter 19

Hank was beat. And he'd only worked a little over half a day. He knew working in the woods was laborious but every muscle in his body screamed for relief. Gaffing the logs and shoving them down the chute had taken arm, leg, and back strength. He couldn't fathom how Kelda had done the job. He'd gained a newfound respect for her abilities but it didn't change the fact he still believed she shouldn't be working in the woods. According to Dag she started gaffing at the age of sixteen. That would account for the scar he'd found on her ankle. He'd wanted to ask Dag about the accident but that would reveal he'd seen Kelda's bare ankle.

He glanced her direction as she picked up the dishes from the evening meal. The glint in her eyes curved his lips in response. She had plans for tonight. He could see it in her bouncy gait and saucy quips to the other men. Just lifting the cup of coffee to his mouth required more strength than his arms had at the moment. He set the cup down and focused on the discussion between Arvid and Karl.

"Far, it's so slick the horses are having problems getting traction to pull the logs to the chute." Karl ran a hand through his dark hair and peered at his father.

"Ja. I saw two men go down today just swinging their axes. We'll take two days out of the woods and see if that dries things up enough to work."

Hank jumped in. "Is that wise? To stop cutting for two days will hurt our production."

Arvid held up a hand. "Would you rather have less men working because they are injured working in the slick mud? That would hurt production as well."

"You're right. I'm sorry." There was no way Eccles would take over his contract. But it made sense to not get workers hurt. "What will they do while waiting for the ground to dry?"

Karl's eyes lit as he watched his father.

"Half will go to town with Karl tomorrow and the other half will go to town with Dag the following day. The ones here will sharpen their tools and relax." Arvid stood. "It would be good if you boys came in and visited with Mor. She's had a better day today."

Karl, Dag, and Tobias all stood and followed their father into the backroom. Hank hadn't seen Mrs. Nielsen since his return from Baker City. He wondered if they should have Rachel come out and see her.

Kelda swept by him to gather the platters and bowls on the table. Standing was a chore, but Hank helped her gather the dishes.

"How's your mother doing? I haven't seen her since our return. Do you think we should have Rachel come visit her?"

"Nei. Mor is getting stronger not having to work all day, but her mind is still foggy at times and she believes she's in Norway." Wrinkles on Kelda's forehead and the dulling of her eyes proved the worry she held for her mother.

"Maybe with her body getting stronger so will her mind." He placed the dishes on the drain board next to Lars, who was already washing the plates.

Lars spoke to Kelda and she smiled. "Mange takk." She took off her apron and linked her arm in Hank's. "Lars said I may go, he can take care of the dishes."

Hank wasn't sure if he was pleased. He'd hoped for a little more recuperating time before tangling with Kelda.

"You don't look pleased." Her triumphant smile uncurved and her bottom lip extended just a bit.

He'd never witnessed her pout and it sparked his body like a stick of dynamite going off, warming all his aching muscles and giving him new vitality. Hank grabbed her hand and hauled her into the supply room. The minute the blanket settled across the door, he pulled Kelda into his arms and seduced her pouty lip. The suppleness, sweetness, and her soft moan added to the need flaring in his body and pounding in his head. It took all his control to pull out of the kiss.

Resting his forehead against hers, he drew in fortifying breaths and eased his arms from around her, taking hold of her hands. "What am I going to do with you?"

"Take me back to my cabin and do more of that."

The simple, quiet response aroused and surprised him. Hank laughed and released one hand to lead her back out into the eating area. Kelda never ceased to surprise him.

Lars turned their way and her brothers walked out of the backroom. Kelda pulled a little as if trying to release her hand from his, but he'd made a decision. While he couldn't marry her yet, he wasn't about to let anyone else worm their way into her affections. He was going to make it known she was his. Be damned if her brothers didn't like it.

He peered into her eyes and gave a slight shake of his head. She nodded and smiled.

"What's with the hand holding?" Karl asked, stepping forward.

"It's what two people who are courting do," Hank said.

Kelda drew in her breath, but the sparkle didn't diminish in her eyes.

Karl stalked up to him. "Courting?" His gaze drilled into Kelda. "When did this happen? What did you do in the city?"

"We had the long ride to Baker City to talk. The more time we spent together, we realized what we felt for one another needed to be explored more. So we're courting." Hank released Kelda's hand and held out her coat. She slipped into the garment and he put his coat on.

"Make sure the men you take to town tomorrow don't get into trouble. But be sure and eat at least one meal at Myrle's place. She's got the best cooking and she'd appreciate the business."

Hank opened the door and ushered Kelda out into the crisp night air. The nights were still freezing, but the warm days didn't keep the mud solid long enough to help their logging. Kelda linked her arm in his, and they walked through the camp to the cabin she now occupied alone.

The thought of what they could do all alone simmered his blood. At the door, Kelda stepped in and grasped his hand, tugging him in behind her. She slipped the board into the brackets on either side of the door and smiled.

"This is the first time I've lived in a place all by myself." She slipped off her coat and hung it on a peg.

Hank removed his coat and hung it beside hers. He liked the image of their clothes hanging side by side.

She moved to the potbelly stove and added wood. "Do you want me to make coffee?"

He nodded and sat in the only chair in the room. Two small half log benches lined the small table. Two cots sat on one side of the cabin and a third was shoved into a corner. "We'll get that third cot out of here tomorrow," he said, to make conversation.

"Why not take two out? It would give me more room." She sat on his lap.

The warmth of her round bottom settling on his lap and her arm slung around his neck, pressing her breast against him, drained his brain and engorged another part of his body.

He couldn't speak staring into her glittering

eyes and watching them darken with the same desire scorching his body.

Kelda sat on Hank's lap to be playful. But as soon as she saw the heat of his eyes, felt the bulge against her thigh, and the tingle of her nipple where it pressed against him; her body yearned to be touched by him. Ached with need.

Sitting on his lap made her taller, but with Hank she didn't mind. He made her feel like a cherished woman not a gangly giant. She lowered her head and placed her lips on his. A chaste, testing kiss. Her mind said go slow, but her body raged with need and begged to move fast.

One of Hank's hands gripped her hip, while the other worked at the buttons on her shirt. She glanced down at his hand working the fasteners loose. Her heart raced as each inch of her shirt splayed open. His dark hand against the white of her chemise enthralled her. While her hands were also darker than most women from working outside, her fingers were long and slender and his while not short and stubby were wider, thicker... masculine looking.

He stared into her eyes as his fingers pulled on the tie at the top of her chemise. She shivered with anticipation, and his hand slipped between the fabric and her skin. His warm hand cradling her breast filled her with the sensation of being treasured.

Kelda slipped her hand through the buttons on his shirt and undershirt, touching his warm skin, feeling the tickle of curly hair, and solid muscles that bunched and made ridges. Her mother's words, "Don't let him compromise you" didn't place any guilt on her heart. She wanted his touch, his body. If he bedded her, maybe having created the bond between them he would be more accepting of her working in the woods. For her to give him her body would show she trusted him, and she did. With every vibrating muscle in her body and every emotion in her heart she trusted him.

Hank pushed her chemise down exposing her breast. She sighed as he ran his tongue around the nipple and kissed the end. He took the nipple in his mouth and suckled. The sensation caused her breasts to ache and tingle and the junction of her legs throb. She squirmed in his lap trying to find a way to relieve the pulsing.

His lips released her and he groaned. "Sit still, you're making this hard for me to bring you pleasure."

"I ache." Kelda placed a hand between her legs. She could have sworn she felt the pulsing in her hand.

"There's only one way to take care of that and I'm not going to bed you." He grasped her hips to lift her off.

"Don't leave me like this. You have to do something, I..." She raised pleading eyes to his and fisted her hands in his hair, dragging his mouth to hers. Thrusting her tongue in his mouth she went with instinct and the desire thrumming through her.

The ache between her legs built, and she realized Hank's hand was inside her pants. His palm cupped her, enhancing the pulse and adding the rhythm to the swooshing in her head. A finger slid between her folds, moving back and forth. She rocked against the hand and finger enhancing the sensations. Kelda pulled out of the kiss, closed her eyes, and focused on Hank's touch.

His finger slipped inside of her. One minute her body welcomed and exalted the entry, the next she vibrated and shimmered with sensations that sparkled in her head. She sighed and dropped her head to Hank's shoulder. She'd never experienced anything so wonderful or body draining.

Wet kisses climbed from her breast, up her neck, and stopped in one drugging kiss on her lips. By the time she could open her eyelids, her pants were in place, and her shirt was buttoned up.

"That was incredible. Is that what people who are courting do?" If so, she was going to like courting.

Pounding on the door jolted both of them to their feet.

"Kelda, open this door." Karl's voice bellowed.

"What the hell." Hank crossed the room, pulled up the board, and flung the door open. "What's the matter with you?" he growled, yanking Karl into the cabin by the coat front and slamming the door shut.

Kelda hurried to stand between the two. "What do you want, Karl?"

"The boss has been in here long enough to say good night." Karl's gaze bore into Hank.

Kelda kept her eyes on Karl and his fisted hands. "We were talking. I have coffee on would you like some?" She didn't really want her brother to stay, but she didn't want him to get wind of what she'd just done with the man pressing against her back and heating her body.

"I told you we're courting. We're getting to know one another. It takes more than a ten minute discussion to discover those things." Hank put his hands on her shoulders and squeezed.

Her face heated knowing they hadn't discussed much of anything in the time they'd been in the cabin. But she knew one thing; she liked courting and wanted it to continue.

"I'm taking this courting thing up with Far tomorrow. I still say you need to be chaperoned."

"If we were both ten years younger, I'd agree with you. But we're grown adults who know the consequences of our actions." Hank's tone sent her stomach vibrating. Did this mean he'd take things even farther if they had the chance? "I'm sure your father will agree we're past the age for the need of a chaperone."

Kelda knew Karl's interference came from jealousy she'd found companionship. "Did Lars tell you he's going to ask his wife if her sisters or cousins would like to correspond with you and Dag? If you like them we can help bring them to America."

Her brother's glower lightened and his mood improved. "He didn't say anything."

"Maybe you and Dag should write letters talking about yourselves and what you do. Lars can send them to his wife to let others read and find someone who would like to write back." Kelda stepped out of Hank's hold and opened the cabin door.

Karl sent one more scathing glance at Hank. "I will, but this doesn't mean I won't bring up the need for you two to have a chaperone with Far."

"Do what you feel you must do." Kelda swept

her brother out the door and closed it, placing the board across once more.

Hank's arms circled her waist and pulled her back against him. "That was close. If he'd have shown up any sooner we'd have had a lot of explaining to do."

Kelda spun in his arms. She slid her hands up his back and pressed her body against his. "I'll talk to Far tomorrow and ask him to put a chain on Karl so he leaves us alone." She kissed Hank's scratchy cheek. "I want to spend more time alone with you."

"If I spend too much alone time with you, I'll have to keep a bucket of cold water handy."

"That's a funny thing to say. Why?"

Hank shook his head. "For all the time you've spent around men you sure don't know the first thing about us."

Kelda pushed on his chest. The mocking in his voice irritated her.

His arms banded around her, not allowing her to get loose.

"Let me go."

He pressed his lower body against hers and the moment the hardness touched where his hand had cupped her, the throbbing started.

"What?" She pushed back and rubbed. The sensations were nearly as exhilarating as his hand.

Hank groaned and stepped away. "That is what I'm talking about. A man has needs just like you do."

She stepped closer and put her hand on the hardness. The solidness felt like an axe handle in her hand.

"That's a man's vulnerable spot. Touching me like that I'm ready to rip your clothes off and bed you." His teeth gritted and he stepped back. The pain on his face and heat in his eyes stopped her motions of following him.

The dawning came slowly. She knew a bit about making babies from animals and the conversations between the loggers she walked up on in the woods. The axe handle in his pants was his male member. Her palm itched knowing she'd touched such an intimate part of a man. Her gaze flicked to the area, and she studied the rise in his pants. Hank clearing his throat brought her gaze to his face. He wanted her. She studied his glazed eyes and feral smile.

Heat sparked behind her belly button, spreading and building in intensity.

"If we bedded would you still need a bucket of cold water?" she asked low and husky.

<h1 style="text-align:center">Chapter 20</h1>

Hank couldn't believe Kelda was serving herself up just to ease his discomfort. "I'll not bed you just to satisfy my needs."

She took a step toward him. He put up his hands to keep her away.

"If I bed you, they'll be no going back. Once we've joined that way, you'll have to marry me." He wasn't sure who he was trying to convince—the woman backing him into a corner or himself.

"Why do I have to marry you if you bed me?"

Hank stopped and stared into her round green eyes. Did she really not know about being compromised and how a man covets having a maiden for his wife? And what about her morals? If she was willing to bed him so easily how did he know she hadn't been with other men? Could she be not as innocent as he thought?

He glared at her. "Have you bed other men before?"

"How dare you!" She swung a fist at his face.

Hank caught her wrist in his hand and held her arms behind her back as he peered into her face. "You're being awfully bold for a woman who's innocent." He spun them around, backing her into the wall. Holding her arms together at the wrists he raised them above her head even though his muscles screamed from the added activity. His body pressed her to the wall. He kissed her neck and behind her ear. Her arms stopped straining against his hold, and he released her, running his hands down her sides and settling on the curve of her hips.

He slipped his hands under her shirt and chemise, running his palms up her sides and leaning back to cup her breasts. Her arms rested on his shoulders. Small puffs of air against his cheek proved his hands had her panting. His thumbs rubbed the nubs of her nipples, and she moaned in his ear. The sound charged his senses.

But he wasn't going to bed her until he knew she loved him and planned to spend her life with him. And right now he wasn't sure he was ready to say the words to her. He wanted her with a desire that surpassed anything he'd ever experienced, and he believed he loved her. But he wasn't sure it was the strong lasting love she sought, and he didn't want to give her anything less.

"Kelda, I'm going to say good night now and let you think about what we talked about. I'll only take you to bed if down the road you'll marry me. I don't compromise women and move on."

He gave her nipples one more playful tug. Her fingers wove in his hair, and she pulled his head down to meet her lips. Her aggressive kiss and body pressing to his, he knew she was on fire, but he wanted to leave her that way. Make her wonder about her reactions to him and perhaps have her finding the answers he sought.

Hank unfisted her hands from his hair, kissed her knuckles, and led her to a cot. He gave her a little nudge, and she sat.

"I'll see you tomorrow." He crossed the room quickly, grabbed his coat, and went outside. The cold night air swirled around him, cooling the fever she'd brought to his body. There was a lot to think about and putting distance between them was the best way he could think. He was certain she'd never been with another man, but he'd make discrete inquiries of Tobias tomorrow. If she hadn't, then he'd uncovered the most passionate woman he'd ever had the good fortune to call his.

He stomped into the office and scowled when his gaze fell on Kelda's three brothers sitting around the potbelly stove. He really didn't want to converse with them right now.

Dag kicked the counter stool toward him. "Have a seat."

Hank hung up his coat and took his time situating the stool where he could watch all three brothers at the same time. Once seated, he studied them.

"What are your intentions with our sister?" Karl finally asked when the other two started fidgeting.

"We're working that out." He'd always been the one to keep order among his brothers. So it pleased him to rile the Nielsen brothers.

"What do you mean working it out? Either

you plan to marry her or you quit dallying with her." Karl, again. Hank guessed because he was the oldest, felt the need to exert his authority.

"How do you know she isn't dallying with me?" Hank ran a hand over his face. He couldn't figure the woman out. She was either a good pretender or she was a hot bloodied innocent. "She's been like a mare in heat and makes me think that maybe she's bedded a man or two ..." Three snarls registered he'd said the words out loud.

"Why you—"

All three brothers shot to their feet and made a grab for Hank. The outrage and hurt on their faces couldn't be faked. He'd definitely riled them raw.

"Okay, I'll take that as an answer. Which pleases me. Very much." She was a hot passionate woman, and she felt safe enough with him to allow herself to give freely.

"What does that mean?" Tobias backed off first and sat back down, his brow furrowed in thought.

Dag glanced at Tobias and then back at Hank. "Yeah, what do you mean?"

Karl released the hold he had on Hank's shirt and sat hard in the chair. "It means our sister loves him if she's willing to bed him before marriage." He glared at Hank. "But if you hurt her, I swear I'll bloody your face and make you wish you'd never heard of the Nielsen's."

Hank raised his hands in surrender. "Just because she's willing to be compromised doesn't mean I will. I respect your sister and your family too much for that. But she's damn tempting."

Dag shook his head. "I don't see it."

"What?" Hank sat down letting his body finally relax. He'd known stepping in the door there'd be an alteration, but he'd handled it and they could be amiable now.

"Kelda works like a man—"

"Used to. I'll not have her in the woods." He was firm on that and would remain so.

"Does she know this?" Tobias asked his eyes reflecting skepticism.

"Yes."

All three shook their heads.

"You think she'll stop working in the woods for you?" Dag asked, his tone mocking.

"You don't think so?" Worry skittered up Hank's spine and lodged in the base of his skull.

"Ever since she's been big enough to swing an axe all she talks about is working in the woods." Dag studied him a moment. "I don't think even your pretty face and persuasive words are going to stop her hankering to be out there."

Flashes of the day he followed her into the woods to find her father ran through his head. She'd been one with the woods and the work going on. When she'd taken off her coat and swung the axe, he'd been mesmerized by the fluidity of her body and the precision of her swings. Arvid said she was one of his best toppers. His gut clenched. He refused to allow her to climb a tree dangling a saw from her belt and then saw the top of the tree off. It was lunacy to think she would be allowed to work like that.

"Then I guess she'll have to make a decision." Hank stood and walked into his room. He shut the door and sat on his bed. Hell. He couldn't spend every day wondering if she was safe or not. Would she give up the woods for him? For their happiness?

Kelda rose early having been awake most of the night due to Hank's words and handiwork on her body. He'd left her wanting and unsatisfied. She didn't understand her body's craving his touch or the fact he wouldn't bed her. From what she'd overheard from the men they'd bed anything in a skirt. Yet, Hank said he wanted her and wouldn't bed her for fear of compromising her. The only way he would compromise her would be if he changed his mind and didn't marry her.

She thought back over their conversation for the hundredth time. They talked about bedding and marriage but never love. She knew the act could be done and love never be spoken. That's what the soiled doves did. But could people who were married enjoy their time in bed and enjoy one another's company and not be in love? She thought of how Far and Mor looked at one another and when younger she'd found them hidden in corners kissing and touching much like she and Hank did now.

What she and Hank had for one another was love. The thought of being his wife warmed her chest and tipped her lips into a smile. She crossed the camp and stepped into the warm wonderful scent of breakfast. Lars already had the table set and was frying ham. The smoky aroma filled the room.

"You are a wonderful cook," she said, walking up beside him. While they had become friends, and he was married and knew something about love and men and women's relationships, she decided with today being a down day and some of the men going to Sumpter, she'd ride along and visit with the Halsey wives. Maybe they could help her decipher Hank's thoughts.

"Mange takk. I like cooking." Lars studied her face. "You did not sleep well."

She waved off his comment as Far stepped out of the back room.

"God morgen. Kelda, your mother would like to see you this morning," he said, picking up a cup and filling it with coffee.

"Mange takk." She kissed Far on the cheek and hurried into the backroom. Mor sat propped against pillows in bed, brushing her hair.

"God morgen, Mor." Kelda said, sitting on the side of the bed and kissing Mor's cheek.

"God morgen, my daughter. Far tells me you have brought a very good cook to help us."

Kelda was relieved to see Mor was having a good day. "Yes. Lars makes tasty meals and the men are happy. He also handles the whole kitchen well by himself." She slipped the brush from her mother's hand and brushed her graying locks. "Mor how are you feeling today?"

"I'm tired but otherwise my mind isn't muddled if that's what you're wondering. I don't like it. I lose hours and days of time, I can't remember." Mor's voice rose with anxiety.

Kelda pat her hand. "That's okay. We'll take good care of you always. Don't worry."

"How are you and your man doing?"

"What?" Kelda peered at Mor. For having been fuzzy and not remembering things she asked an odd question.

"You and Hank. Are you getting along better?"

"I thought you didn't like him?"

"I like him and he's good for you."

"But you were lecturing me on not getting compromised and being a good girl." Kelda studied her mother. Her soft cheeks turned a deeper hue of pink.

"That was my selfishness to make sure you stayed in the kitchen to help me. I knew that I couldn't handle it alone anymore. Now that there is someone taking care of things, you can get that man to fall in love with you if he isn't already." The sparkle in Mor's eyes made Kelda giggle.

"Mor, you sly matchmaker." Kelda hugged her mother. "I do have some questions, but I'm not sure I want to ask you. Hank's sisters-in-law have offered to visit with me. I'm going to go to Sumpter today and see what I can learn about Hank."

"That's a good idea. The more we gang up on him, the faster he'll come around." Mor winked and leaned back on her pillows. "I'd like to rest before you bring my breakfast."

Kelda kissed her forehead. "I'll be back when the men have eaten."

The men were seated at the tables when she returned to the other room. Hank wasn't in his place, but her brothers grinned like they'd put a mouse in her boot.

"What's up?" she asked Lars when he passed her a platter of biscuits.

He shrugged and turned back to fill another platter. She set the first platter up by her brothers and Far. They kept grinning, and she hadn't clue what had happened but it made her nervous.

By the end of the meal her nerves were jangling like she dangled from a sixty foot tree with no rope.

"What are you all grinning like fools about?" she asked when everyone had left but her family.

"We had a little chat with Hank last night after he finally left your cabin." Dag nodded his head and her stomach clenched.

"What did you talk about?" She already had a feeling she wasn't going to like where this was headed.

"You, him, working in the woods," Karl said, stirring a spoon in his coffee cup.

"What about working in the woods?" She plopped down on the bench beside Tobias and stared at Karl. Her heart raced.

"He said there was no way you'd be working in the woods from now on."

Kelda spun to stare at Far. "You agreed as long as he didn't know I could work."

He held up his hands. "It will be between the two of you. If you love him you will put his wants first."

"But if he loves me shouldn't he put my wants first?" She stabbed the table with her finger. Why did the woman always have to compromise? She'd tried to get him to bed her last night hoping once they were bound by their hearts and flesh he had to understand how deeply she loved the woods. His adamant demand she not work in the woods was selfish on his part. He was in more danger working in the woods than she was, yet it didn't stop him. This one-sided fear on his part complicated their relationship.

"The woman does what the man wants." Karl crossed his arms and leaned back.

"Not this woman." She stood and placed her hands on the table. "I will continue to work in the woods. If Hank doesn't like it, he can—"

"As long as he is paying us, we do what he asks," Far cut in.

"That isn't fair! He hired us. Us—me, Karl, Dag, Tobias and you to run this logging operation. He can't hire us then tie our hands with how we do things."

Far waved his hand. "Go to town with Karl and the men. When you come back you will have cooled off. I'll visit with Hank today."

Karl stood. "Come on, Kelda. You two need time apart. You both looked feverish last night."

She sent a scathing look at Karl, and he burst out laughing.

"Why are you in such a good mood today?" she asked, following him out the door, slipping her arms into her coat.

"I'm sending off letters Dag and I wrote last night to Lars wife. He added an introduction letter." Karl walked over to the wagonload of loggers going to town.

Kelda climbed onto the seat alongside of him, and they headed down the road. She scanned the camp looking for Hank but didn't see anything that told her where he might be. She refused to ask Karl who sat beside her whistling.

Where could he be this morning and why had he told her brothers about his stupid idea she shouldn't work in the woods? As much as she loved him, she despised him for his shortsightedness when it came to her doing the work she loved.

Chapter 21

Hank left the camp early. After his discussion with the Nielsen brothers last night, he'd decided he needed time to think and talk with an unbiased person. That's how he came to be sitting in Myrle's restaurant one minute after she unlocked her door.

"My, what dragged you to town so early in the day? I heard from Ethan the camp has a new cook. And a right good one, so it can't be the need for good cooking." Myrle patted her gray hair as she poured coffee into his cup. Her fading blue eyes scanned his face.

"I need someone not related to me or Kelda to talk with." Hank took a sip of coffee.

"Let me fix you a plate and then tell the ladies to take over for a spell." Myrle's eyes sparkled when she spun toward the kitchen.

Hank fidgeted with his coffee cup. Now that he was here, he wasn't sure what he wanted to talk about. His feelings for Kelda grew with each meeting, both physically and emotionally. Looking at his life in five and ten years he saw them happy. But when he thought about her brothers' words and the way she'd lit up when voicing how she loved working in the woods, he didn't think his heart could take watching her work in the woods or watching her lose that light when he didn't allow her in the woods. He'd tossed all night trying to determine what would be worse and each time neither scenario came out happy.

Myrle pushed through the kitchen door carrying a large plate piled high with eggs, bacon, and hotcakes and a cup of coffee in the other hand. She placed the plate in front of Hank and took the seat across the table.

"This Kelda you mentioned, she the one Colin gets stars in his eyes when he talks about her?" Myrle watched him over the rim of her cup.

Hank smiled. "Yes, she has that effect on males, though she doesn't see it."

Myrle nodded and smiled. "I can see. Your eyes soften and your tone deepens when you think about her." She patted his hand. "That's a sure sign you're in love."

Hank put down his fork. "Myrle, I am in love but I'm not sure it's good for either of us."

"Does she love you?"

"She hasn't said so, but from her actions, I believe she does."

Myrle stared into his eyes. "Why isn't it good for the two of you to be in love?"

"Her other love is working in the woods as a logger. You should see the way her eyes light up just talking about hanging high in the trees lopping off the tops." He shivered remembering the man they'd watched the one time. "I can't have her doing that. I'd be spending all my time worrying and watching her instead of taking care of my own matters."

Myrle set her cup down firmly. "If you love one another you'll find a way to make it work. You can't take her passion for life away from her, she'll not be the same person you fell in love with."

She pushed the chair back to stand. "I say marry her, love her, and you'll work things out."

"I can't marry her until I get the first load of logs to Stoddard next fall."

Myrle shoved her small fists onto her hips and glared at him over the rim of her spectacles. "That's the most asinine backwards thing I've ever heard come out of your mouth."

Hank thought of Myrle as an aunt but her tone and words lit his anger. "I take exception to that."

"You and your brothers can afford to have a project fail now and then and still provide for your families. Saying the Stoddard contract has to be fulfilled before you can marry is your way of running from commitment." She crossed her arms. "You may need to see if what you feel for Kelda is really love or just the need to have what your brothers have."

Hank sank back against the chair and stared at the woman. Was his infatuation with Kelda only because he was envious of his brothers' lives?

The door opened, and Myrle scurried across the room to seat the newcomers.

Staring at the food growing cold on his plate, Hank reflected on the times spent with Kelda and his feelings. He picked at the food, running the trip to Baker City over in his mind. It was a fact when he was near Kelda his body became inflamed with desire, but the trip to and from Baker City with her tucked against him and talking, warmed his heart and brought a lump to his throat. He delighted in the passion she had for life and for him. The only fault he could find with the infectious woman was her need to be in danger.

Scowling, he stood and walked out of Myrle's. Maybe he needed to see how Zeke dealt with Maeve being in harm's way as a Pinkerton operative.

Karl stopped the wagon at the mercantile. Kelda hopped down.

"Where are you going?" he asked as the men scattered up and down the street.

"To see Rachel and Maeve Halsey." Specifically, Rachel as she felt less intimidated by her even if she was a doctor.

"We'll be leaving for the camp around two."

Kelda waved and continued up the street to Clay and Rachel's two-story house that sat back off the main street in a cluster of trees.

Her strides weren't long-legged and full of purpose. She honestly didn't know what she planned to say or why she had the need to discuss her feelings for Hank with someone, but she was confused and figured a woman was the best person to unburden to.

Climbing the steps, she drew in a long breath and let it out slowly. Her heart raced with panic. This was silly. Shouldn't she discuss her feelings about Hank with him and not someone else?

Her boots thumped on the porch and she spun to retreat.

"Kelda! What a wonderful surprise. Come on in."

Swallowing, Kelda slowly pivoted. Rachel stood at the open door in a bonnet and shawl, little Frankie in her arms.

"We were just going to walk over and visit with Maeve and Brandon, but that can wait." Rachel backed up, opening the door wider.

"I can return later if you have plans." Kelda remained rooted to the far side of the porch.

"Nonsense. I can see them any time. You only come to town once in a while." Rachel stepped out and linked arms with Kelda, drawing her into the aromas of coffee, cinnamon, and yeast.

"Hang your coat on the hall tree and come back to the kitchen. I made sweet rolls this morning."

Rachel strolled down the hallway to the kitchen in the back of the house. Her dress swayed with her steps. Kelda wondered if she'd looked that womanly walking down the street in the dress Hank bought her.

She peered down at the man's shirt billowing over the waistband of the dungarees on her lower half. Nothing she wore revealed she had any feminine qualities. It was no wonder she was going on twenty-seven and hadn't been kissed by a man until the last month. Which brought her back to why she was here—Hank.

The homey aromas she'd always attributed to the cookhouse wafted from the kitchen, luring her down the hall and into the cheery room warmed by the cookstove.

Rachel stood at the stove pouring two cups of coffee. A fresh baked pan of sweet rolls sat in the middle of the table. Frankie was seated in a child's highchair banging a spoon on the wooden tray holding her in place.

"Sit down. I didn't expect to see you so soon after your return from Baker City." Rachel sat opposite of Kelda.

"Far told the men to take two days off because the ground is too muddy and slippery. Half the crew came to town today and the other half will come tomorrow." She wrapped her hands around the cup of coffee and stared into the dark brown liquid. Now that she was here she wasn't sure what she wanted to say or ask. Her mind whirled with indecision.

"Did Hank come, too?"

"Not with us. I'm not sure where he is." She scowled. His disappearance at breakfast still puzzled her.

"Are you feeling better after your trip to Baker City?"

Kelda glanced at Rachel and searched her face. Had she spoken to Darcy and Aileen? What had the other women told her? "J-ja. Why do you ask?"

"You don't look any more rested than when I last saw you." Rachel reached across the table. "Is your mother worse?"

"She was actually better today than she has been. With the new cook, she can stay in bed and rest. The rest is helping with her memory loss." That was one less concern for her right now.

"Good. But if you think it would be a good idea, I can come out and take a look at her."

"If she takes a turn for the worse, I'll send word." Kelda took a sip of coffee. This was more awkward than she'd thought it would be.

"So if your mother isn't keeping you from sleeping it must be Hank."

Frankie tossed the spoon to the floor. The noise jolted Kelda as much as Rachel's direct comment.

"Did you two get along on your trip?" Rachel bent over and retrieved the spoon.

Memories of walking arm in arm with Hank and sharing special moments at the restaurant warmed Kelda's chest. Their intimate moments in the room, heated her cheeks. "We... got along well."

Rachel smiled and her eyes twinkled. "I can tell by the blush on your cheeks."

Kelda slapped her hands over her cheeks.

"Has he proposed to you yet?" Rachel held the spoon out to her cooing daughter.

"Nei. He said we can't marry until the logging operation proves successful." She scowled. Why did they have to wait? He had the money to pay their crew before he began making a profit. Surely the venture wouldn't put his family in that much financial trouble.

Rachel studied her. "Would you say yes if he asked you right now?"

Her question snapped Kelda out of her reverie. "I-I don't know."

"Do you love him?"

His arms and kisses made her feel special and filled an empty void in her soul she'd not known was empty. "Ja."

"Then why don't you know if you'd marry him?" Rachel took a sip of coffee; her dark brown eyes watched Kelda over the rim.

"There's one thing that we don't agree on." The memory of his accursed belief she could get hurt working in the woods fueled her temper.

Rachel set the cup down. "What is that?"

"He refuses to let me work in the woods. I've been working alongside my family since I was sixteen. I have some scars," which was one of the reasons he was so adamant, "he saw one when we were in Baker City, and now he refuses to even listen to my side." She reached across the table and clasped Rachel's hands. "The only place I feel adequate and good about who I am is when I'm in the woods. Topping trees or swinging the axe. The work gives me fulfillment. But all he sees is danger."

"Do you worry about him when he's in the woods?"

"Ja, but only because he's a greenhorn and hasn't learned all the skills necessary to be a beast of the woods. Once he learns everything, I'll know he's prepared. Like I'm prepared."

Rachel wiggled her hands out of Kelda's grip and picked up her coffee cup. "Has he seen you in the woods? Know how good you are?"

"Only once. I took him out to where Far was working. Far handed me the axe and let me work while he talked to Hank." She frowned remembering how he shoved her out of the way when the tree creaked. But her body warmed when she fleetingly remembered the look of adulation on his face when she swung the axe.

"Perhaps he needs to see you working to real-ize you are careful and wouldn't take risks." Rachel put the cup down and peered across the table. "One thing I've learned about the Halsey brothers, they are fair and impartial to women who have jobs usually held by men."

Kelda nodded. "Hank always speaks well of all his brothers' wives, and he told me of their unusual occupations though I do believe Darcy and Aileen are no longer—"

Rachel cut her off. "They aren't in those jobs because they chose to change not because their husband's made them." She nodded her head to-ward the door. "Maeve is worrying herself to death trying to decide if she wants to remain a Pinkerton now that they have a child or settle down here." Rachel leaned closer. "Between you and me, if Zeke asked her to quit she wouldn't because she'd feel like she had given up on her dreams, but if she makes the decision herself, then she'll be happy with it."

Kelda knew exactly how Maeve felt. Per-haps the two had more in common than she first thought.

Stomping on the back porch grabbed their attention. Kelda and Rachel glanced at the door. Clay followed by Zeke and Hank entered the cozy kitchen. Rachel popped up, placing a kiss on Clay's cheek.

"I didn't make it over to Maeve's because Kelda arrived for a chat." Rachel moved to gather more cups from the cupboard.

Hank's gaze landed on Kelda. He couldn't miss

the dark skin under her eyes or her timid return gaze.

"That's why we came over. To see if a patient arrived and kept you." Clay held out his hand and found a chair. He shed his coat and placed it on the chair back and sat.

Hank took the empty chair beside Kelda. "I didn't know you were coming to town today."

"Far suggested it." Kelda held his gaze, but she lacked the usual sparkle.

"I see." He didn't really but could think of nothing else to say in the presence of his family.

"Why are you in town?" Her question shouldn't have rattled him as much as it did.

"I had some people to see." He stole a glance around the table. His family stared at the exchange between he and Kelda like it was a high-stakes poker game.

"Actually, I'm ready to head back to camp. How about we ride together?" He wanted her alone to sit down and have a good long discussion. One they couldn't have with so many people butting in.

Kelda nodded and stood.

Hank turned to Zeke. "I'd like to borrow one of your saddle horses."

"Take Coal, he's sound in this mud."

"Thanks. I'll have the group coming to town tomorrow return him." He turned to Kelda and helped her with her coat. "Ready?"

She faced Rachel. "Thank you for the coffee and conversation."

"You're most welcome. Stop in anytime." Rachel stepped forward and gave Kelda a hug.

Kelda's cheeks redden, and she backed up, running into Hank. He placed his hands on her shoulders and squeezed, trying to infuse her with his support.

Hank took hold of Kelda's hand and led her to the door. He stopped. "If any of the loggers get out of hand while they're in town let me know."

"You can count on it," Zeke replied and waved them off.

Hank left the house, holding Kelda's hand. He didn't want to release her but knew it would be impossible to saddle Coal one-handed.

At the barn, he let loose of Kelda reluctantly and opened the door, releasing the hot, humid animal, dung, and hay aromas. Four horses were stabled in the barn. He found the black gelding and began saddling.

"You're being awfully quiet," he said, trying to start up a conversation. Kelda's silence worried him.

"Why weren't you at breakfast?" Her voice came from over near the door.

He tightened the cinch and dropped the stirrup down. "I wanted to visit with Myrle this morning." Hank walked to the wall where the headstalls hung and picked out Coal's.

"Who's Myrle?"

"The woman who helped us after our parents were killed. She owns the eating place just as you come into town." Hank led the horse over to Kelda. "My horse is tied in front of her place." He held out his arm waiting for her to take hold.

She peered at his arm then down her body.

"What's wrong?" Hank tipped her chin up

with his free hand.

"I'm not dressed like a lady so you don't have to pretend I am." The uncertainty swirling in her eyes dulled their usual spark.

"Kelda, sweetie, it doesn't matter how you dress, I'm always going to treat you like a lady. And you should always feel like one." He placed a quick simple kiss on her lips and wished he knew of a way to help her get passed her inferior feelings about being a lady.

He held his elbow out again, and she looped her wrist through. "That's better. Let's get my horse and head somewhere where we can talk and not get interrupted."

They walked the length of Main Street without saying a word. He tipped his hat to the few women out running errands and said hello to the men he knew. At Myrle's Hank helped Kelda mount and handed her the reins before turning to untie his horse.

The door of the building opened, and Karl trudged down the steps a napkin still stuffed in the neck of his shirt.

"Where are you taking my sister?"

"We're riding back to the camp." Hank mounted his horse and peered down at Karl.

"She came with me and can ride back with the rest of us in the wagon." Karl's arms swung toward the wagon and horses tied at the mercantile.

"We're both ready to leave now." Hank turned his horse and motioned for Kelda to follow.

"Kelda, you be sure and let Far know this was your idea," Karl shouted as they continued out of town.

Kelda raised her hand and waved at her brother, causing Hank to smile.

He kept the horses at a walk and fell back to ride beside Kelda. "We're not going back to camp right away." He took a path that veered to the left off the main road.

"I had a feeling we weren't when you said we'd go somewhere no one could interrupt." She studied him. "Where are we going?"

"To the cabin where I grew up." He watched the information settle in her mind.

A smile curved her lips and her eyes half closed. "I'd enjoy seeing where you grew up." A frown marred her face. "I can't take you to where I grew up. We'd have to travel for months to cover every place I've known as home."

"How long is the longest you've lived any where?" Knowing she'd never had a chance to call a place a home tugged at his resolve to give her a permanent home.

"We spent three years in the same area but pulled up camp a couple of times to be nearer the cutting." She stared straight ahead. "As far back as I can remember the cookhouse has been my home."

Hank placed a hand on her arm. "Would you like to stay in one place?"

Her green gaze peered into his face. "There were times as a child I prayed every night that this would be the last time we moved. That was back when I wished for playmates besides my brothers. As I grew older the wood beasts became my friends, some have been with us for years, others not as long, but we all become a big community kind of like Sumpter. And I don't mind it so much anymore."

"Do you think you'd be happy in a community like Sumpter?" His heart raced waiting for her answer.

She smiled. "It would be fun to see."

Her words lifted the dread that had been sitting on his chest like a stamp press. "Come on." He urged his horse into a trot. He wanted to get off the horses and sit down and talk.

Chapter 22

Kelda dropped down into Hank's raised arms. She wouldn't have allowed herself to drop into another man's arms believing they wouldn't be able to hold her, but she had faith in him. And he didn't disappoint either with catching her or the long, dizzying kiss he gave her before propping her against the barn wall as he took care of the horses.

When her legs regained their strength, she walked to the doorway and studied the cabin fifty feet away. They'd slowly climbed the side of a mountain and rode into a small meadow. A cabin sat at the far side of the meadow and the opening of a mine sat back in the mountainside.

This was where Hank and his brothers grew up. The cabin wasn't big. In fact, it appeared too small for the five large men. But then they had been boys when all five and their parents had lived here.

Arms circled her waist, drawing her against Hank's hard body. "What do you think?"

"It seems too small for all of you."

He kissed her neck and chuckled. "It was getting too small about the time Zeke and Ethan got married. Then Clay. And I found myself living alone. After all those years of bumping into someone every time I turned around, it took some getting used to."

She spun in his arms. "And now you're sharing the office with Tobias."

"It's not the same. We have our separate rooms." He nodded toward the cabin. "That's one room."

"Show me." She slipped from his embrace and holding his hand, led him to the door of the cabin.

"I can't guarantee critters haven't taken up residence since I moved to the logging camp." He tugged on the rope and pushed the door inward.

Kelda stepped in and the first thing that caught her attention were the four beds; two, head to foot, along each wall. They were all longer and wider than a cot and could easily hold two bodies lying snuggled together. The thought galloped heat through her.

A small cookstove sat at the far wall and a table with six chairs sat in the middle of the room.

"I can't believe your whole family lived in this at one time." She glanced up and saw the flash of emotions in his eyes. Happiness, sorrow. Her heart ached for him. Kelda placed a hand on his cheek. "I didn't mean to bring back bad memories."

He closed the door and held out his hands for her coat. "You didn't. There were more happy times here than sad."

She shucked out of her coat and waited for

him to hang it on the peg by the door and remove his to hang beside hers.

Hank grasped her hand and led her to one of the beds. "Sit we'll talk and if it gets cold I'll start a fire. I just don't want to leave a fire in the box when we leave."

Kelda sat. The bed had a real mattress. She'd slept in cots all her life except for their trip to Baker City and the lovely bed at the hotel. She ran her hands over the plumpness.

"What are you thinking?" Hank's deep husky tone sent shivers of anticipation racing up her spine.

"This is only the second time in my life I've been on a mattress. At the hotel and now here."

Hank played with her fingers. "I'll bring you a bed. There's no reason you can't have a proper mattress. There is plenty of room in the cabin for one." He raised her hand to his lips and one by one kissed her fingers. "This size or larger." The flash of desire in his eyes left no doubt before they left this cabin they would spend time together in this bed.

Her breath hitched. "W-what will we tell everyone?"

His gaze caught hers and held as he moved closer, brushing his lips across hers. "That you deserve a decent bed." His lips whispered against hers as he spoke.

The sensation tickled and lit the fire he'd stoked in her the night before. She licked her lips to douse the tingling. He hadn't pulled back and her tongue slid across his lips as well. The intimate contact jolted her charged body even more.

Hank pressed his mouth to hers and drugged

her with another dizzying kiss. When he finally pulled back, they were both panting and her body felt like it floated on a cloud.

"Kelda, I brought you here to talk." His eyes flared with heat and desire. He wanted her as much as she wanted him. The knowledge one kiss could do that to him, made her bold.

"No one knows where we are. Love me now and talk later." Kelda plucked the buttons on Hank's shirt out through the buttonholes, revealing the cotton undershirt stretched across his wide chest.

"Woman." He ground between his teeth but didn't make any moves to stop her from pulling the tail of his shirt out of his pants and slowly exposing the brown curls on his chest.

When Hank's shirts lay on the bed behind him, Kelda spread her hands across his chest and dropped kisses from shoulder to shoulder and down his center, until he caught her head in his hands and pulled her to his lips for a tongue tangling, scorching kiss.

Flames engulfed her body and she wanted her clothes off. Before her fingers could get more than two buttons undone, Hank grasped the bottom of her shirt and pulled it off over her head. The cuffs were still buttoned and her hands caught in the sleeves.

A mischievous grin crinkled the lines around Hank's eyes when he discovered she was "tied up". He leaned down, using his mouth to pull on the bow of her chemise. Then with merriment dancing in his dark eyes, he rolled the chemise down her arms and body holding her arms to her sides and her wrists still inside the sleeves of her flannel shirt.

If she wanted to work herself into a fit she could get loose, but when his mouth drew in one nipple and his hand captured the other one, she didn't want to move. Between the suckling and the tweaking, her breasts grew heavy and tingled in a most wonderful way. The only thing she didn't like was her inability to use her hands. That and the fact his attention to her breasts had started the throbbing between her legs and she found it hard to sit still.

"Please, help me get loose," she panted when she thought her body was going to vibrate right off the bed.

Hank released her breasts, and she immediately wished she'd not said a word. Then his hands skimmed down her sides, and his fingers dipped under her waistband, moving to the front. He unfastened her dungarees, gently pushed her onto her back and removed her boots, and socks, disappearing from her sight. He returned to her view and slid his hands between her skin and her drawers, slowly drawing her dungarees and drawers down her legs until he was once again out of sight, and she lay on the bed bare as the day she was born for his eyes to see.

Heat blazed a path up her neck and into her cheeks. She'd never been naked in front of anyone. Wasn't even sure if her body held all the qualities a man wished in a woman. She knew her breasts were of ample size and her hips curved outward, but what would he think of her muscled thighs and calves?

She gulped in one big breath of air and waited for...what? It seemed like hours passed before a soft whistle of appreciation floated in the air. Her breathing stalled when his hands skimmed up the inside of her legs, brushing the hair at her juncture, jolting her and moving up her stomach.

The fire and admiration in his eyes when she finally glimpsed his face lessened her fears.

"Kelda, sweetie, you are one magnificent lady." He repositioned her onto the bed to lay the length of it and removed her shirt and chemise.

She spread her hands across his bare chest and dipped her fingers under his waistband. "When do I get to see all of you?"

"Whenever you wish." Hank reclined on the narrow bed nearly pushing her on the floor.

Kelda stood and leaned over the bed, unfastening his pants, and sliding them along with his drawers down to his stocking clad feet. He must have removed his boots when she was left naked and wondering on the bed. She tossed his pants and socks to the side and stared down at his muscled masculine body. When her gaze peered at his male part it jumped.

She reached down taking the hot, firm appendage in her hands. The size, shape, and silkiness was very pleasant.

Hank grasped her arms and pulled her body down on top of him. The full body, skin to skin, touching elicited even more wonderful tremors in her. She loved the whole naked experience. She wiggled and rubbed. Pressing her breasts tighter against his chest and rubbing her female parts on his male parts.

Hank growled and rolled, placing her under him, covering her from head to toe with maleness. Her hands skimmed up and down his back and cupped his backside.

His weight pressed in all the places that excited her. Before she could think beyond the feel of his body, his lips descended, pressing against hers in the same manner as his body pressed her intimate places. His manhood to her womanhood, his chest to her breasts, his lips to hers. The intimacy they shared warmed her heart and ignited desires stronger than the night before. She wanted all of this man. Not just to have her body pleasured but to be fully loved.

His lips opened, and she dove in with her tongue and her heart. She wound her fingers in his hair, holding his mouth to hers, taking and giving. Her body wriggled under him, her breasts tightening from the contact of his body to hers, her hips thrusting against his.

She wanted him completely. "Please." She begged not really knowing what she wanted, but knowing he could fulfill her.

His legs slipped between hers and slowly parted her knees. The new position pressed her throbbing parts even more intimately with his. Sensations tingled to her fingers and toes moments before his entry. She stiffened uncertain what to expect.

Hank dropped wet kisses down her neck and drew a nipple into his mouth suckling and causing her to buck and thrust her hips toward him once more. His attention to her body heated her more and he thrust deep. Pain opened her eyes and her body stilled.

"Hold me." Hank's husky voice pulled her back into the moment as his lips descended on hers once more.

The kiss was tender, soft, and so intoxicating she once again took control, but soon found her body bucking against his as he thrust in and out sparking waves of body numbing explosions that finally burst into one volley of energy draining sensations. Moments later, Hank thrust deep and his essence spilled into her. He thrust once more, and she squirmed against him, wanting to remain bound with him. He now held her heart and soul, and she couldn't think of any other man she'd ever met who she trusted with both.

Hank looked down into Kelda's half-opened eyes and saw his future. Even before they'd made love, he'd known he didn't want to spend the rest of his life without her in it. Peering into her love flushed face he believed she felt the same.

He started to pull out, but her hands clasped his backside, holding him firmly inside her body.

"Not yet. I like feeling as if we're one." She licked her lips plumped from their kisses, and he couldn't stop himself.

He captured her tasty mouth once more hoping to convey the emotions buzzing in his chest at the moment. He didn't deepen the kiss but kept it light, sensual, and caring.

Raising his head, he peered into her face. She sighed and her blonde lashes fluttered up, revealing her sparkling green eyes.

"You can kiss me any time you like."

"I'm glad you said that because I plan on taking full advantage of your offer." He kissed the tip of her nose. "We should finish our talk and head back to the camp."

Her hands skimmed down his back and around to tickle his sides at his hips. The sensation twitched his body part still encased in her. Her eyes widened and her mouth formed a perfect 'O'.

"You like that?" she asked, skimming her fingers along his sides and moving down to where their bodies joined.

He twitched again. Her touch excited him, and he couldn't control his erection.

"Oh, I like the way that feels." She ground her hips tighter against his, and his body sparked to life.

"I knew you'd be a handful in bed." He grasped her hands holding them above her head and began suckling her breasts. He loved the way her nipples hardened and her responding mews and moans as he brought her body to life again.

"Nei!" she cried when he pulled out of her.

"Shhh... You're going to like this, I promise."

With more restraint than he'd thought possible, he teased her, pushing in slowly and pulling out slowly then thrusting hard and fast and slowing again until Kelda was panting and begging him to finish. With one hard thrust, he seated himself deep, and her body convulsed as he spilled into her and fell exhausted onto the woman who fully captured his heart.

Catching his breath, Hank rolled to her side and pulled her backside to his front, one arm at her waist, the other below her breasts. Their bodies fit together and their personalities fit. Theirs would be an ideal marriage.

Chapter 23

Kelda woke with a start. Her body was cold on the front and warm on the back. She ran a hand over the coldness and discovered skin. Her eyelids popped up, and she peered at the masculine arms holding her. A smile spread across her face. Her body still tingled from making love to Hank.

She kissed the arm across her chest and twined her fingers with his. Her body felt different. Alive. Womanly. Hank had said her body was beautiful. He'd proven his thoughts by how thoroughly he loved her.

Wiggling her backside, his desire grew. She giggled and spun in his arms.

His hair stuck out all over. No doubt, from her fingers entwined in it during their escapade. She traced a finger across his lips and up to his eyebrows then down to his lips. His tantalizing mouth heated her body with kisses and how he suckled her breasts. Just thinking of it had her squirming to get closer.

She flung a leg over his hip to move her lower body closer and pressed her breasts against his chest as her lips sealed with his.

"I like this kind of dream," he said against her lips.

"If I'm dreaming don't wake me," she said, deepening the kiss. Her reward didn't come as she'd hoped.

Hank pulled out of the kiss and tucked her head against his chest. "We need to talk before you make me forget about talking. Again."

Kelda snuggled in, playing with the dark hairs on his chest. "What do we need to talk about?" Her heart raced. She wanted to stall this talk for fear the subject would upset both of them. She wanted to stay happy and loved in his arms.

"First, I don't want to wait to get married." A soft kiss buzzed her ear.

She squirmed to see his face. "What do you mean by not waiting?" Warmth surged through her body and tickled her heart.

"I love you and don't want to keep hiding it." His hand skimmed down her body and cupped her backside, pressing her even tighter to his body. "I don't want to spend time each day wondering when I can touch and taste you. I want to know you will be in my bed each night." He kissed her cheek. "I want to marry you as soon as we can make the arrangements."

Kelda's heart slammed against her ribs. "Really? Let's go back to town and find a preacher!" She hugged his neck and kissed his cheek. To be married and spend time being loved and sharing the running of the log camp...She released his neck and pushed on his chest with her hands to get a clear view of his face.

"Will you allow me to work in the woods?" Trepidation stomped on her heart as his eyes lost the shine of love.

"No. I can't be worrying about you." His firm unyielding tone sunk her hopes.

"Then I can't marry you." She pushed out of his arms, her heart splitting like a tree hit by lightning, and stood. She groped for her clothes.

He sat quickly and grabbed her around the waist. "Kelda, sweetie, you have to understand. I can't lose you after finding the only woman who can make me a better man."

"Ja, I understand. You can forbid me to do what makes me happy while I can worry about you in the woods." She pried his arms loose and moved farther from him. The ache in her chest grew. She refused to cry.

"You don't have to worry about me." He lurched to his feet and moved toward her.

Kelda sidestepped out of his touch. She couldn't keep her anger if he touched her, and she needed it to keep from falling apart.

"Why don't I have to worry about you? Because you're a man? You're nothing but a greenhorn. You'll come to harm in the woods before I would, and yet, I'm not to worry about you."

She pulled on her undergarments and shuffled to a corner when he reached for her again. "Don't! Don't touch me. If you truly loved me you would allow me to do what I love, not expect me to become something I'm not."

Hank ran a hand over his face and watched

Kelda cover her tantalizing body with men's clothing. He'd unwrapped a treasure and wanted more than ever to spend his life proving she was cherished. But damn! He didn't think he could survive if she worked in the woods, putting herself in danger every day. His talk with Zeke had only confirmed he didn't want to live every day in fear of losing his wife. Zeke said it just made every day they had together more precious knowing that danger could take one of them the next day.

He couldn't live like that. He'd never been a danger seeker and wasn't about to start now. Because she'd grown up with the danger she didn't understand how it iced his blood thinking of her dangling from a tree or having a log fall on her.

She grabbed her coat.

"Don't." He stood, snatching his drawers and pants from the floor. "Don't leave." He quickly dressed as she leaned her forehead against the door frame not looking at him. The defeated slump of her shoulders and resolve to not look at him gripped his heart like a vise and added to his guilt.

Dressed, he walked over to the stove and lit the kindling he always left ready for a quick start.

"Sit. We'll have some coffee and discuss this." He kept his distance but took her coat from her hands and motioned toward the table.

"Will talking change your mind?" she asked quietly.

Hank turned from hanging her coat up. "I don't know, but not talking will solve nothing."

She shrugged. The light and love that had shined so bright in her eyes earlier had flickered out. She reminded him of the month he'd kept his distance and she took on her mother's workload. Only he knew now that it had been more than just him and her mother. The truth gnawed at him like a beaver after a tree. He had the power to put the shine in her eyes and the smile on her face. And it had nothing to do with her love for him. That's what pained him the most.

Heat from the stove slowly filled the room. He added more wood and pulled the pot of boiling water to the side, adding coffee. A sniff behind him now and then was the only sound that told him Kelda remained seated at the table. Watching her would only make her uneasy, but he wasn't ready to start the discussion until they were seated across the table from one another and he could read her face. He had to know if she really loved working in the woods over him, and if so, could he live being second to the dangerous life she craved.

The coffee finished brewing. He filled two cups and placed one in front of Kelda as he took the seat across from her. The sadness he witnessed tore at his heart. Only a short time before they'd both been so happy. He had to find out why the woods meant so much to her. More than him or anything else it seemed.

"I remember when we first met; you told me you loved working in the woods. I saw the excitement light your eyes when you watched someone else topping a tree." He swallowed the lump of fear that lodged in his throat just as it had that day watching the man and seeing the delight in her eyes. "While I might try topping trees, I know I could never hang from the top of a tree like that and not be fearful."

"Do you think I don't understand it's danger- ous? I have fear every time I climb a tree. If I didn't I would be stupid." Her eyes blazed with something short of anger. "Any beast of the woods who tells you they aren't scared of their job is either lying or dimwitted and someone I wouldn't want to work with." She forcefully tapped the end of her finger at the table. "Working in the woods requires vigilance and guts."

"I don't disagree with you." Her conviction to the job showed her passion. Passion. That was what drew his attention to her in the first place.

"Yet you know working in the woods is what I am good at, what makes me happy, and you tell me I can't have happiness."

Hank reached across the table and placed a hand over hers. "I make you happy. You can't deny all the good times we've had." He nodded to the rumpled bed. "Not just here but traveling to Baker City, walking the streets, and talking at the camp."

She turned her hand, so they touched palm to palm. "Ja, you have made me happy since the first day when you looked at me with more than curios- ity. But what happens when you become so busy with work you spend less time with me. What will I have?"

"Babies?" His heart raced thinking of the children he and Kelda would make and love and cherish.

She shook her head. "I do not want only to be a mother. I want to be a wife and a full partner in the logging. I can't be respected if I don't do the jobs."

"Do I have respect?" He hadn't successfully

learned any of the logging stages, but he felt the men respected him.

"Ja. You are the boss." She looked at him as if he'd sprouted two heads.

"You'll be the boss, too, as my wife." He would win this conversation. His logic outweighed hers.

"As your wife I will be expected to warm your bed and make you babies. How does that gain me respect with the beasts of the woods?" She pulled her hand out from under his. "If I marry you, I want to be a partner and help run the logging business. I know the process from the setting up of camp to loading the logs on a railroad car."

If it kept her out of the woods, he had no problem with her being a business partner. "I can agree to you being a partner in business and in marriage as long as you don't pick up an axe or dangle from trees."

Hank watched Kelda's brow furrow as she thought his words through. Could she find enough excitement in making deals for the lumber as she did downing a tree? What was going on in her head?

After his talk with Myrle, he realized he loved Kelda and wanted her in his life. And not just because he wanted what his brothers' had. His discussion with Zeke didn't take away all his fears but he'd planned to ask Kelda to marry him even before their passionate romp. But he believed he couldn't be a success at logging if he worried constantly about his wife working as a beast of the woods.

Kelda finally peered into his eyes. "Can I have some time to think about this?"

Her words hit him like a strike from a sledge hammer. If she had to think about it would that mean she'd turn down his marriage proposal? But if he didn't allow her to think on it she could turn him down right now. Taking the chance that someone might convince her to marry him, he nodded.

"Take all the time you need as long as you give me an answer before your family moves on to a new job," he said jokingly, but the dull flash in her eyes speared fear into his heart.

Her stomach growled, and he peered out the window. Darkness had fallen while they sat talking.

"We better spend the night here. The trail between here and the camp is treacherous with the mud during the day and freezing at night." It was better to have her family mad at him than for the both of them to end up at the bottom of a canyon injured. It could be days before they'd be found and possibly not alive. Nope, facing her family was the lesser of the evils.

Her eyes widened. "But Far and Mor will wonder where we are."

"It's better to be safe and have them worry for a night than have us both hurt at the bottom of a ravine." Hank stood and moved to the cupboard by the stove. He had a half a dozen tins of beans and fruit stored in case anyone from the family needed to hold up overnight in the cabin. He knew Darcy's brother, Jeremy, preferred to stay here when he came to Sumpter with Gil and his family.

"Both of us gone overnight...you know what everyone will think." She frowned and her eyes narrowed. "Are you holding me here on purpose so

I have to marry you once my family finds out we spent the night together alone?"

"No!" Hank stalked to the table and hauled Kelda to her feet. "I'd planned to have you back to the camp by dark and ask your father for your hand in marriage until you went stubborn and re-fused my marriage offer." Peering into her face and wanting to make things right he loosened his hold and dipped his head.

The soft caress of her lips against his filled him with an overwhelming desire to make everything right. He deepened the kiss, seeking entrance to her sweetness. Her lips remained firmly sealed, until he changed the angle and she sighed, opening to him and relaxing in his arms. If only they could settle their difference of her working in the woods with a kiss. He savored the taste and feel of her knowing once the kiss ended she would be back to the stubborn woman he adored even if it infuriated him.

He eased her away, slipping slowly out of the kiss, until she stood an arm's length from him. When her eyelashes fluttered up, he smiled. "You can't ignore how good sharing a kiss is."

Her face flushed a deep red and her eyes flashed.

Hank released her and went back to preparing beans and opening a can of peaches. "Keep an eye on the beans. I'm going to get a load of wood so we don't get cold tonight." If he could talk her into sharing his bed they'd stay good and warm, but he had a feeling she wouldn't go that far while she was still contemplating his marriage terms.

He slipped into his coat and stomped out of

the cabin. Nope, it was more likely to be a frosty night with her stubbornly clinging to her need to act like a logger.

Chapter 24

Kelda shivered and pulled the blanket up tighter around her shoulders. As soon as the beans and peaches were eaten she'd crawled into a bed on the opposite side of the cabin from the one they'd made love on and pretended sleep. Sometime after Hank had banked the stove and blew out the lantern she'd drifted to sleep wishing she could give up topping trees and become the wife Hank wanted. She knew there would never be another man who made her feel the heat and passion he did. Or believe in her and the woman he made her feel. But to give up the one thing she'd loved her whole life to have something else she loved...it didn't seem fair. Mor always said to love only one thing or one person was not being open to everything in life. Why couldn't she love both Hank and logging and participate wholeheartedly in both?

She rolled and the blanket rose allowing even more cold air to nip at her body. Should she get up and add more wood to the fire? In the dark, she wasn't sure where the wood box was situated. In her distraction over staying out of Hank's arms so she could stay mad, she hadn't paid enough attention to the layout of the cabin.

Stomping and voices registered at the same time the door burst open. She sat upright.

"I have a gun. Who are you?" Hank's voice boomed from across the room.

"Zeke and Karl."

Scuffing noises ensued and the lantern slowly glowed in the middle of the room. Zeke and Karl stood by the table scanning the room. Their gaze landed on Hank first then on her.

Zeke smacked Karl on the shoulder with the back of his hand. "See I told you there was nothing to worry about. Hank's in his bed and Kelda's in Clay's bed." He stared at her closer. "And she's dressed. No hanky-panky."

Kelda's ears burned. If she had given into her desire to feel Hank's arms around her, they would have been caught...She didn't want to think what her father would have said or Karl would have done had he found them in bed together.

"What the hell are you two doing here?" Hank moved to the stove and tossed more wood in before his gaze connected with hers for a brief moment.

"When you and Kelda didn't show up at the camp, Far sent me back to Sumpter looking for you. Zeke said you might have come up here to be alone." Karl crossed his arms. "Why didn't you get Kelda back to camp before dark?"

Hank shot her another quick glance. "We were

caught up in a discussion and lost track of time. It was dark, and I wasn't going to take the chance of an accident trying to go from here to the camp in the dark."

Kelda stood and stared at him. "But they seem to have made it here just fine." Her tone was accusing, but she didn't care. She was beginning to believe it had been his plan all along, to keep her here and have her family believe she and Hank had to get married.

"The trail from town to here is better traveled than from here to the camp," Zeke said, jumping in to defend his brother.

"Then he should have gone back to town and then to the camp," Karl said, moving to stand beside Kelda.

Hank sat down at the table. "Yeah, I probably should have, but I was hoping to finish the discussion this morning."

His gaze landed on her and didn't waver. The weight of it held her tongue. She wasn't ready to concede marriage. But she also wasn't ready to walk away. She was even more confused than before they made love.

"It's almost light out so you might as well feed us and we'll head out. I'm sure Kelda's parents would appreciate seeing her as soon as possible." Zeke took off his coat and pulled out a chair. "Take a seat Karl."

Kelda wasn't sure what to do. It was Hank's house but being the woman did they expect her to feed them?

Hank stood, grabbed a bucket and handed it to

Zeke. "Why don't you get some water while Karl takes care of your horses."

Zeke stared at Hank a moment then stood. "Good Idea. Come on, Karl." Zeke put his coat back on.

"Why can't you do both?" Karl asked, eyeing Hank.

"Because it will go faster if we both do it." Zeke grabbed Karl's sleeve and pulled him out of the cabin.

The scene was comical the way the two big men acted like small boys. Kelda suppressed a giggle behind her hand until the door closed. She couldn't hold back the laugh or the silliness of the situation.

She turned to Hank who watched her intently. "I can't believe they came all the way out here to try and catch us..." She blushed.

"In the same bed?" Hank walked over to her. "Kelda, my offer of marriage still stands. If you don't want me to mention it to anyone else I won't, but, I plan to have you as my wife. Sleeping across the room from you last night was a torture I don't want to go through again." He grasped her arm. "Don't fight with me. Just think about my offer, please," he whispered before kissing her.

Kelda fought with herself, reveling in the kiss but refusing to participate completely for fear of losing sight of what he wanted to strip from her.

A horse nickered, and Hank retreated to the stove, banging the coffee pot and opening another can of beans.

Kelda busied herself making the beds and putting her boots on. When their brothers returned, coffee and four plates of beans and hardtack sat on the table. Hank took the seat next to hers. Karl and Zeke sat across from them. No one said a thing as they ate. She felt eyes on her and glanced up to find Karl studying her. What was he trying to see? Did he know she no longer was innocent? The thought warmed her. There should be guilt over what she and Hank did, but the act had proven to her she loved him. She'd never have given her body so readily and wished to give him joy if she had not loved him.

And that was the crux of her dilemma. She wanted to make him happy always. But to make him happy she would be unhappy.

Kelda finished her food and left the table, heating water in a kettle on the stove to wash the dishes.

"I'll head back to town and leave you three to travel to the camp," Zeke said, standing. She turned to say good-bye when she noticed a non-verbal communication between Hank and Zeke. Something she'd witnessed between her brothers.

"I'll walk out with you and saddle the horses for Kelda and me." Hank hurried to the door where his coat hung and left with Zeke.

Karl brought the rest of the plates to her. "Are you all right? You and Hank keep staring at one another but I'm feeling some tension."

"We're fine. There's just a lot of things to work out between us." She sighed and wished things weren't so complicated.

Hank knew Zeke would follow him into the barn.

"So what is this all about?" Zeke caught Coal and started saddling the horse.

"I wish I knew." Hank saddled his gelding and leaned against him.

"You bedded her didn't you?" Zeke said without reprimand.

Hank smiled, remembering the passion and how whole he felt when they were together. He glanced toward the door to make sure Karl hadn't snuck up on them. "Yeah. I also asked her to marry me."

Zeke smacked him on the back. "Congratulations!"

"Don't go telling anyone. We've hit a snag."

"She loves you. She told Rachel. What's the snag?" Zeke slipped the headstall on Coal.

"I told her she can't work in the woods." Zeke sent him a recriminating glare. "I know. You and I discussed the better to have loved and lost than never to have loved, but I feel I can't do my job if I'm always worrying about her. And she is passionate about her need to be in the woods."

Zeke handed him the reins to Coal. "One word, brother. Compromise." He walked out of the barn, mounted his horse, and rode toward town.

Hank stared down the road. It was basically the same thing Myrle had said. How did he find a compromise to their problem?

Kelda and Karl exited the cabin. Hank led the horses to them. "Did you put the fire out?"

"Ja, and all the dishes are put away." Kelda

mounted her horse.

He handed her the reins, making sure their fingers touched. She met his gaze and curved her tasty lips into a slight smile.

His heart thudded faster. It was a start. He'd take small smiles over anger and rejection.

Jitters started in Kelda's stomach. What was she going to tell her parents? They'd stopped at the top of the ravine they traveled down and she'd spotted the smoke from the camp. Up until then she'd not worried about walking into the camp, but now her mind jumped from one scenario to the next. Would the loggers believe she and Hank spent the night together? What about Far and Mor? Would they make her marry Hank even though she wasn't ready?

Karl rode ahead. When the trail widened, Hank held his horse back waiting for her to come alongside.

He reached over, touching her cheek. "I'll take full blame for not getting you home last night. And if you don't want me to mention you're contemplating my marriage proposal, I won't say a word." His gaze remained locked on hers. "But I plan to walk you to your cabin after dinner every night and tell you how I feel about you."

A little bit of the anger she clutched around her heart to keep from saying yes and giving into her desire to be in his arms all the time, melted from his touch and sincerity.

"I don't want to change who I am to be your

wife." She leaned into his touch. "You make me feel special, but that's not enough."

Karl disappeared around a bend in the trail. Hank stopped the horses and cupped her head in his hand, drawing her lips to his. The tender kiss formed tears in her closed eyes.

"We'll figure out what will be enough for you and keep me from going crazy," he whispered on her lips and released her.

Kelda opened her eyes and found Hank's horse walking ahead. Her horse jolted into action and walked fast to keep pace. Maybe with his perseverance and love they would find a way to make this work. But he had to come up with a solution before she agreed to marriage.

Ten minutes later they walked into camp. Tobias jogged out of the office straight to her horse.

"Mor and Far have been worrying about you," he said, holding the headstall of the horse as she dismounted. "Dag's been keeping them company in the cookhouse."

Kelda nodded and started toward the building. "Wait."

She spun as Hank handed his reins to Tobias and jogged over to her.

"I'm not letting you go in there alone. This is my fault." He started to reach for her hand, but she shook her head.

"Let's not start rumors we don't want spreading," she whispered.

"You really think after all they've seen of us here at camp that not holding my hand will stop rumors?"

"It makes me feel better."

Hank shook his head like he didn't understand and motioned for her to start walking. His large warm hand pressed against her lower back and her cheeks flamed. His possessive touch was more incriminating than walking hand in hand to the building.

She pulled in a large gulp of air, and Hank opened the door.

Mor sat in a rocking chair near the cookstove. Far was seated at the table along with Dag and Lars. All stared at the two of them as they took off their coats and walked the length of the building.

Mor pushed out of the chair and walked toward them, her face slack with relief. Kelda hurried to her mother and hugged her tight.

"I'm sorry you were worried." She folded around Mor's small body, hoping her remorse was sensed.

"I'm sorry about not getting Kelda back last night."

Hank's strong voice straightened her body. She turned to the table and the three men eyeing one another.

"We went to my family's cabin to have some privacy to talk."

Karl and Tobias entered and took seats. Hank made a point to peer at each of her brothers.

"Around here we never seem to get a moment to ourselves." Hank reached out to her.

She shook her head two quick shakes. Showing solidarity was one thing but to put her hand in his, she was sure her emotions would show and there would be no way they could tell her family they hadn't made love.

Hank walked to where she stood with Mor tucked under her arm. He drew her against his side and again stared at the men in her family.

"We were discussing our future..."

Kelda moaned and glared at Hank. This was exactly what she didn't want him to say.

"Does that future mean you plan to marry my daughter since you spent the night alone with her?" Far asked with a twinkle in his eye.

Kelda peered at her father. He was far from upset. He appeared gleeful. She studied Hank. Had he schemed this little overnight excursion to force her to marry him?

"I asked your daughter to marry me and she is considering it." Hank squeezed her shoulders.

Kelda ducked out from under Hank's arm and settled Mor back in the rocking chair. The task gave her a moment to get her anger and frustration under control. Had the two men she loved contrived this awkward moment just to get her wed?

She curved her lips in a smile and worked at putting a glimmer of happiness in her eyes. "Far, Hank treated me like a queen while we were alone and he did propose." She made sure she didn't touch Hank so her mind would stay fixed on what she wanted to say. "However, until he agrees to marry the woman I was the day he met me, there will be no wedding."

All the men collectively gasped as she strode across the room, grabbed her coat, and headed out the door. Anger and frustration boiled in her chest as she stomped across the camp to her cabin. She flung the door open, stepped in, and slammed the door shut.

The nerve of the men in her life thinking they knew what was best for her. How would they like it if she started telling them how to live? She flung her coat on the bed and paced. Paddy had started her stove, her pacing and the warmth caused her to perspire. Now she wanted a bath, but she'd have to go to the cookhouse and use the small tub in Mor's room since Lars now lived in the supply room.

Even though she now had her own cabin, this was a time when she wished she lived somewhere other than a log camp so she could take a bath and relax in scented water. Memories of the hotel in Baker City flooded into her mind. If she married Hank there would be more trips like that, and they would share the same bed.

She shook the treacherous thoughts away. That kind of thinking would have her giving in to his proposal.

Chapter 25

Hank woke the following morning grouchier than he could remember ever being. Kelda hadn't come out of her cabin for meals yesterday and refused to answer the door when he'd knocked on it after dinner. He'd wanted to see if she was sick or just avoiding him. It appeared by her silence, she was avoiding him.

He didn't know how much food she'd stockpiled in the cabin, but he hoped she came to the cookhouse for breakfast so he could get a chance to talk to her after the meal. It was obvious something the day before had soured her feelings. He'd had it out with the Nielsen's. Asking them to not say anything to Kelda and allow him to patch things up. The problem was he wasn't sure what had riled her. And why she thought hiding in her cabin would accomplish anything other than drive him crazy.

"You coming?" Tobias called from the outer office.

"Yeah." Hank shoved the papers he'd been reading the last hour into a pile and headed to the office door to retrieve his coat. Tobias opened the door, and Hank caught a glimpse of Kelda hurrying to the cookhouse. He ran out the door.

Hank caught Kelda's coat sleeve moments before she entered the cookhouse.

She spun around and glared at him. "What are you doing?"

"Trying to talk with you since you shut me out yesterday." He stalled his itching fingers from brushing down her cheek. The desire to touch her and kiss away the dark circles under her eyes strangled his throat, making it hard to breathe.

"I didn't feel like company." Her gaze slid to her feet.

"How about now? Would you please talk to me and tell me what I did that has you ignoring me?" He grasped her hand and led her back to the office. She didn't follow him step for step, but he didn't have to tug to get her there.

Once inside, he took her coat and motioned for her to sit in the chair by the stove. She sat, her chin tucked against her chest.

Hank pulled up another chair, placing it in front of her. He sat and tipped her chin up. "What is going on in that pretty head of yours?"

Her gaze searched his face. "Did you and Far set it up so I'd be left alone with you at the cabin? So I'd be forced to marry you?"

Appalled she thought he would scheme, Hank slammed his back against the chair. The high-pitched crack of the back snapping jolted his momentary disbelieve.

"No." He stared into her wide solemn eyes. "Why would you even think such a thing?"

"Far looked too pleased yesterday. Like things had worked out as he'd planned."

Hank grasped her hands between his. "Kelda, sweetie, I promise you, I did not have plans to keep you overnight at my cabin. If you'd have jumped in my arms and kissed me when I proposed, we'd have been back down here celebrating with your family. Instead, we ended up having a discussion that went nowhere and getting stuck on the mountain after dark."

Her eyes snapped with irritation. "So now you're blaming the whole night alone as my fault."

"No." Hell. She was turning everything he said around. His gut tightened at the thought she used the arguing as a means to keep him at a distance. He ran a hand over his unshaven face and listened to the rasp of his whiskers against his calloused palm.

"I'm to blame for the night at the cabin. I should have hauled you down as soon as you refused my proposal. But I wanted to make you change your mind." He leaned forward. She inhaled and pressed her back against the chair. He grabbed the chair seat on either side of her thighs and pulled the chair between his legs.

"I still do." He pressed his lips to hers and waited. She'd either give in or shove him away. His heart raced when she pressed back and opened her lips to allow him to taste her thoroughly.

Deepening the kiss, he drew her onto his

lap and embraced her to his thumping heart. He wanted to start every morning with her kiss and presence in his life. From her response to his kiss, she had the same yearnings.

He ran his hands up and down her back to keep them from straying to parts of her body he'd learned intimately while at his cabin. Now wasn't the time to heat things up. He wanted to prove he was good for her and she could trust him.

With regret, he pulled out of the kiss but kept her seated on his lap. "Not talking won't solve our problem."

"I know."

The eyes he'd memorized and saw whenever he closed his eyelids stared back at him with such sorrow his stomach ached.

"But when you touch me I forget to be mad and I want to stay angry so I can remain firm." She scooted to face him. "I've had few accidents in the eleven years I've been a beast of the woods. I'm good at what I do because I'm cautious and don't have to prove anything like a man does." She grasped his head in her hands and peered into his eyes. The desperation and determination in her green pools sent his heart thudding harder. "Let me prove to you there is no need for you to worry about me every day I'm in the woods. Work with me. Let me teach you how to be a beast of the woods. You'll be beside me and see I don't do anything to put myself in danger."

Hank didn't like the idea, but this may be the compromise they needed. If he could prove she shouldn't work in the woods by working with her then she'd be more likely to stop.

"When your father gives the word to go back to the woods you'll teach me the way of the woods."

She flung her body against his.

Hank placed his hands under her armpits and held her away from him. "But, if you're in danger in any way during my lessons, you have to concede I may be right about you working in the woods."

Her eyes narrowed a moment before she nodded and held out her hand.

He grasped her hand and tugged her against him. "This deal is sealed with a kiss. Our hearts are on the line." Hank met her lips and didn't come up for air until his lungs ached.

Kelda sucked in air and battled to make her fuzzy mind work. Her whole body tingled from the kiss and the fact she'd be back in the woods soon. She peered into Hank's heated gaze. With him beside her. She'd have to take extra precautions with a greenhorn at her side, especially this one who held her heart in his hands. If something happened to him while working with her, she'd never be able to set foot in the woods again.

Her stomach growled.

"That's our cue to get some breakfast." Hank released her.

"We aren't going to talk about marriage until we see how this partnership in the woods works out," she said, slipping into her coat.

His eyes dulled a moment before he nodded. "I'll not say a word." He pulled on his coat.

She ran a finger down his whiskered cheek. "But I'll expect you to continue courting me. Could take more than your brawn in the woods to woo me into being your wife."

A flash of heat in his eyes and a wicked smile on his tantalizing lips drew air out of her lungs like a blacksmith's bellows.

"It will be my pleasure to court you." Hank stepped out of the office and offered his arm.

"I'll take your arm here in camp but once we get out in the woods you have to treat me like any other beast of the woods. If you don't, we could both get hurt."

He stopped and stared at her. "Is my working with you going to put you in danger?"

She wasn't going to lie to him. "It could if you don't keep your mind on the job and forget I'm a woman."

His brow furrowed and his lips pinched. "So my compromise could put you in danger. I can't win with this."

Kelda grasped his cheeks and tipped his head down to make eye contact. "You'll only put me in danger if you treat me like I'm fragile. I'm not. I know my job and can teach you, but only if you can leave your heart in camp and think like a business man in the woods."

His eyes softened. "Can you leave your heart in camp?"

Her heart hiccupped and raced. "If it means keeping you from harm, ja."

"Then I can, too." He slipped from her grasp and continued to the cookhouse.

Her mind spun in a thousand directions at once. Could she leave her heart in camp? Would he be able to treat her different in the woods? What a mess. But if it worked, they could work side by side until they were too old to swing an axe.

They entered the cookhouse and all heads turned their direction. Kelda's face grew warm from the smiles and nods. Hank took her coat and moved her across the length of the room to two open spots next to Tobias.

"I should help Lars." She moved to pass Hank.

"Kelda, sit and eat. You missed several meals yesterday." Far's command stalled her feet.

She studied his stern face. The merriment of yesterday had disappeared. The man she loved and never crossed sat at the head of the table today. His disapproval darkened his face like a shadow.

Her knees wobbled as she stepped over the bench and sat. Hank followed, squeezing her shoulder as he slipped his legs over the halved log.

Butch, one of the older loggers, sat to her left. He handed her the plate of biscuits. She took one and passed it to Hank, keeping her eyes on her plate. Her father had never reprimanded her in front of the others before. Had her turning down Hank put her in disfavor with him?

"Are the men going out to the woods today?" Hank asked, peering down the length of the table. Kelda followed his gaze, trying to read the expressions on the beasts' faces. Many had finished and seemed to be hanging around as if also waiting for word from Far.

"Karl and I are going to check it out this morning. If it has dried up enough we'll get to work this afternoon." Far shoved his finished plate to the center of the table and picked up his cup. "When you finish eating, Kelda, your mother wishes to see you."

Guilt landed like a wedge in her stomach. Avoiding Hank yesterday she'd not been by to see Mor. "I'll go now." She started to rise.

Hank's warm hand rested on her thigh. "After you eat." He pointed to her plate. He must have added the eggs and ham to it because she hadn't.

She glanced at Far fearing he wouldn't like both Hank's hand on her thigh or his command. Far nodded and took a sip of coffee.

Kelda settled back in her seat and ate, not really tasting anything or hearing the conversation between Hank and her family. The buzz of conversation only heightened her feeling she was losing control and not sure how or why.

A stack of plates arrived at her spot. She piled them on hers and passed them to Hank. His hand touched hers and she peered into his eyes. He was asking with his eyes. What did he want?

She leaned toward him and whispered, "What?"

"Do you want me to wait until you come back to tell your father of our working relationship?"

A quick scan of the table proved most of the men had left. Paddy and a couple others were conversing at the other end. "Now," she said and caught Paddy's attention. He smiled and nodded, finishing his conversation and moving up to sit across from her.

She wanted to hold Hank's hand for support, knowing her brothers would not like the idea. They were the ones who trained the greenhorns, only when one of them was busy did it fall to her. But she and Hank had to show they could work together without allowing their emotions to get in the way.

Hank cleared his throat. "Mr. Nielsen and everyone," Hank nodded to each of her brothers and Paddy, "Kelda and I have come to an agreement and I hope you'll consent." He glanced at her, and then back at Far. "We'd like to work together in the woods. With Kelda teaching me the jobs of a woodsman."

Karl reared back his eyes narrowed and angry. "I don't—"

"That's a great idea," Far and Paddy cut in at the same time.

Karl shot to his feet, pushing the bench holding Dag and Paddy away from the table. "It's a bad idea. They'll be mooning over each other or doing who knows what in the woods and not carrying their load."

Kelda shot to her feet. "That is mean even for you. I need to prove to Hank I can handle myself in the woods, and he needs to learn the trade and how to stay alive. We have the best incentive to be safe. The other's life."

Far waved them both to be seated. Hank's hand rested on her thigh when she sat.

"I agree. You two need this time together in the woods to understand one another." He pointed to Hank. "All you see is the fragile woman you want her to be." Then Far's eyes hardened, and he stared at her. "You think working in the woods defines you. You are more than a beast. You are a woman, a daughter, a sister, and a compassionate friend. Until you see that you'll not make a good wife."

Sorrow as damp and veiled as fog filled her. Far had never spoken so harshly about her. Hank squeezed her leg. She knew it was to reassure, but it only compounded her sorrow. Would she learn to be a good wife?

"Go see your mother," Hank said, releasing her leg and nodding toward the back room.

Kelda nodded and stood. She couldn't walk fast enough to leave the room. Even when she'd had to square up against new arrivals and prove her worth, she'd never felt as inadequate as her father's words just made her feel. She slipped in the room and studied Mor.

Her color was better and she sat in a chair, dressed. Her graying hair hung about her shoulders in a tangled mess.

"There you are, Kelda. Could you be a good daughter and brush my hair?" She held up her hands. "Not using my hands every day they are getting stiff." She smiled. "But it has been a wonderful relief to not get up at four to start preparing breakfast."

Kelda took the brush from her mother's lap and pulled it through the thinning hair. "You look better this morning, Mor." She noticed a bowl and cup on the table beside the bed. "Lars is feeding you well."

"You did good bringing him here. He has tales from home, and he makes a good bowl of porridge." Mor twisted her neck and peered up at Kelda. "Tell me about your night with Hank."

Air rushed out of Kelda's lungs, and she plopped onto her mother's bed. "It was a long night. We'd quarreled, and I couldn't get past my anger."

"And now?" Mor patted her hand. "Have you discovered the true reason for your anger?"

She stared at Mor. "How did you know I wasn't just being peevish?"

Mor held up a finger and smiled. "When one is angry with someone they love it can usually be fixed by talking it out." Her eyes twinkled. "After all, if you love someone it is only the one obstacle that must be moved to make things right."

Kelda hugged her mother. "You're so right. Hank and I are working on the obstacle." She released Mor and sat back. "But I've upset Far with all my childish behavior."

Mor shook her head. "Nei. You're finally behaving like a woman and he doesn't know how to handle you." She touched the tip of Kelda's nose. "Keep him on his toes. It's good for the man."

Kelda spent most of the morning telling Mor about the pact she'd made with Hank to show him how to log and that he was courting her. In the back of her mind, she saw the two of them spending many interesting evenings enjoying the courting side of their relationship.

Chapter 26

Hank spent the morning on paperwork in the office, knowing he'd be out in the woods every day after today until he could convince Kelda it wasn't the place for her. He'd have to cut his courting time short in the evenings to do the paperwork he'd be neglecting.

He hoped Karl and Arvid made them wait until tomorrow to go back to work. He needed the half a day to get Tobias trained to do a few of the tasks he'd no longer have time for.

Kelda wandered into his office before noon. "Far's back. He said we'd wait until tomorrow to start back up."

The disappointment lacing her words brought his full attention to her.

"That's good. It gives me more time to get things settled here so my mind can be fully focused on what you teach me."

She stood by the desk looking down at the numbers he was manipulating to make sure he wasn't over spending until the logs were actually sold.

"Tobias is good with numbers. You should let him do that."

"He does all the other numbers. These are for my eyes only. I have to stay within my budget." He shoved the papers to the side and leaned his forearms on the desk. "What else did you come in here to say?"

"I want to learn what you have already done in the woods so I know where to start with you tomorrow." She sat on the corner of the desk since the only chair in the room was under him.

Hank ran his finger along her thigh. Her eyes widened, and he couldn't suppress a sly smile. His touch brought her to life in so many ways.

Kelda cleared her throat. "What have you learned in the woods so far?"

He pulled his hand back. If he wanted to keep a clear head while working with her, he'd have to make sure they didn't touch. "I've set chain and gaffed logs down the chute."

"Have you done any axe or saw work?" The furrowing of her brow wasn't a good sign.

"Only chopping wood for the stove out there." He tried to make light of the fact he couldn't wield an axe as well as she.

"I guess we won't be heading to the woods tomorrow then. We'll hang out down here around the camp and work on teaching you proper swinging and how to gauge where to fall a tree." She stood. "I'll go scout out some trees for you to practice on."

"Why do I have to practice here at camp? Wouldn't it be more time efficient to teach me on trees that we need?" He didn't like the idea of yet another wasted effort when they should be piling up logs.

"To have you practice where everyone else will be could cause harm to someone other than you." Kelda stepped around the desk. "I want to only have to watch your hide and not everyone else's." She bent and kissed his cheek.

Her show of tenderness without his initiating the exchange started his heart racing. After the kiss, she straightened but didn't move away. He snaked an arm around her middle and spun in his chair to draw her between his legs.

"You're growing bolder with your affections." He peered up into her face.

"With you agreeing to my working in the woods I feel we may have something lasting." Her eyes sparkled.

"We may just at that." He stood, sliding up the front of her and pressing his lips to hers. This was a scenario they could do every day once she married him. Her arms tightened around his middle, and he deepened the kiss. The bed came into his view as if he'd searched the room just for that piece of furniture.

Kelda pulled out of the kiss, her chest heaving and a smile curving her delightful lips. "I think I need to find somewhere else to be before..." Her sentence dwindled as she peered into his eyes.

His desire must have shown in his eyes. Her cheeks turned a deep red, and her body pressed tighter to his at the hips.

A light rap on the open door jolted them apart. Hank ran a hand over his face and turned to the door. Tobias stood in the doorway looking like he'd just found a hunk of gold the size of a rabbit.

"What do you need?" Hank asked, shifting his gaze to Kelda who kept her back to her brother. He was the one who should be hiding his front side. Instead, he crossed his arms and waited for Tobias to stop smiling and find his tongue.

"Pa's rounding up everyone for a meeting. Thought you...two might want to attend."

Hank waved him away and placed a hand on Kelda's shoulder. "Next time you enter my office it might be a good idea to close the door behind you," he said softly in case Tobias was hanging around outside the door hoping to catch them in a compromising position, again.

She stared up at him. Merriment danced in her green eyes and a hand covered her mouth. Kelda removed the hand and giggles burst forth followed by laughter.

He thought she was embarrassed, but it appeared she found their getting caught funny.

"Did you see the look on Tobias's face before he started smirking? And you...you looked like you were caught stealing cookies." Kelda's comments started Hank laughing.

Once he gained control, he grasped her shoulders and leveled his gaze on hers. "We have to make sure we only kiss and embrace in camp. If we were to kiss and forget where we are in the woods it could be disastrous." He stared into her sobering eyes. "Promise me you'll keep your distance and just instruct me."

She swallowed and nodded. "I promise. I know work comes first and everything else is kept to the camp. The beasts know you play jokes in camp not out where someone could get hurt. It's respect for forces beyond your control."

Hank placed a hand on her back. "Then let's go see what your father has to say."

The next morning after breakfast, Hank followed Kelda out with the rest of the men. Everyone else started up the path to the area they were logging at the top of the chute. Kelda led him to a small stand of pines over a hundred yards from the camp.

"Do you know the different type of trees?" she asked, setting her axe and a crosscut saw on the ground beside a tree.

"Yes."

"Then pick out the tallest, straightest pine tree in this group and tell me which direction it needs to fall to not damage other trees or the one your falling." Kelda leaned against the tree where her tools reclined at the base.

The vision of her smiling like a cat with cream and relaxing against the tree had his mind starting to move in the wrong direction. He mentally slapped himself and walked around, looking up each one of the pine trees in the group. When he determined which pine fit her description, he walked around the tree seeing what obstacles would hinder it when falling to the ground.

"This one and it needs to fall that way." He pointed in the direction of the clearest path to the ground.

She smiled and nodded. "Now what do you need to do?"

"Cut a wedge in the tree on the side I want it to fall and then saw this side." Hank dropped his axe from where it rested on his shoulder and took a swing at the tree. It didn't sound like the sharp crack he'd heard when others swung at the trees.

Kelda sprang away from her resting spot and thunked the tree with the blunt head of a small hatchet she took from her belt.

"Hear that. This tree is rotten in the center." She continued tapping the tree until she was nearly standing on her tip toes. "It doesn't sound solid until up here." She stepped back and peered up the tree. "There's plenty of good wood up above. We'll go back and get some springboards, and you'll get your first lesson on those."

Hank didn't miss the gleam in her eyes as she placed her hatchet on the ground and started back toward the camp. He propped his axe against the tree and followed, wondering how he'd get through this first test of watching her work over ten feet off the ground.

Kelda's feet were as weightless as fall leaves striding back to camp. Not only was she back swinging an axe, she'd be on a springboard soon and be experiencing the rush she loved.

Hank's steps behind her were slow and heavier. Her excitement didn't rub off on him. It almost seemed to be the opposite. The more excited she became about working, the quieter and sullen he became.

At the supply tent, she thrust two boards six feet long and hewn to three inches thick and ten inches wide in Hank's hands and picked up two for her. She'd found the exact healthy spruce tree, cut it down, cut the six foot long slabs from the center of the tree, and then planed them to the three-inch thickness. Everyone in the camp knew these were her boards. Some beasts used whatever board they could find, but she'd found by hand making her springboards they lasted, and she had less worry of one breaking forty feet in the air.

She stopped at the base of the tree and studied the wind and the lean on the pine. Using the hatchet she tapped the trunk again surmising the extent of the rot. Could it hold two of them until they reached the solid wood fifteen feet higher? Remembering she was here to teach, Kelda handed the hatchet to Hank.

"Tap the tree every ten inches and listen. You'll hear the difference when you hit solid wood." She stepped back and watched him tap the tree.

At first he leaned his ear close to the trunk, listening. But he soon caught on that not only the sound informed but the bounce of the hatchet head off the trunk was a telltale also.

Hank twisted his neck and peered at her a smile tipping his lips. "I can hear and feel the difference."

She nodded. "The next problem is to determine

if the rotted bottom will hold both of us." Kelda picked up her axe and swung it at the trunk five feet from the ground, making a wedge-sized notch to fit a springboard.

Stepping back, she pointed to the notch. "You want the notch to be slightly larger than the springboard on the outside edges but smaller in the back." She picked up a board, shoved it into the notch, working it back and forth until the board held firmly. With a flick of her wrist, she lodged her axe in the tree as high as she could reach and put her palms on the springboard.

Hank's hands gripped her waist. Kelda swatted at him.

"I've been doing this for years and don't need you hefting me too hard and making me go on over the board." This was exactly the type of problem she foresaw with him working with her. He had to treat her like another logger.

"Sorry." Hank backed up, holding his hands in the air. His tone and guilt in his eyes told her he realized his mistake.

Kelda repositioned herself at the springboard and pushed off the ground, using her arms to propel her knees onto the board. She stood, caught her balance, and grasped the axe. Her feet were braced shoulder width apart as she swung the axe to make the next notch.

"Hand up a board," she called down to Hank after the notch was made.

"You're as agile as a cat," Hank said, handing her the board. The awe in his voice let loose bees buzzing in her belly. Far handed out praise like a card dealer dealing cards, so hearing the words didn't inflate her head. But praise from Hank warmed and excited her. He'd been so against her working as a logger, that today could be the day she proved to him she belonged alongside him and the other men in the woods.

She set the board in the notch and climbed up. The hatchet hung from a leather belt around her waist. Using the hatchet, she tapped the trunk. The springboard was ten feet off the ground. Starting at the board, she tapped up to shoulder level. To get the best wood from this tree, she needed to go up another springboard.

Kelda picked up her axe and made another notch. "Hand me up another springboard then go back to camp and get two more boards and rope. You picked a tree that's going to teach you everything you need to know."

Hank handed the board up. "You sure it's safe to leave you alone?"

She laughed at the worry in his voice and shook her head. "There's not much trouble I can get into sitting on this springboard waiting for you to come back."

He watched her for several heartbeats as if determining she would be safe. Kelda responded with a playful smile and waved him off. He turned and headed back to camp.

Kelda set the third springboard and climbed up. She sunk the ax into the tree and straddled the board peering out through the trees. This was what she enjoyed about the woods. Sitting at heights only birds flew and watching the wildlife scurry across the ground below. The trees grew thinner back toward camp, and she could see patches of the buildings and the chute disappearing up the side of the mountain.

Tomorrow, she'd take Hank up the mountain. They'd work with the other beasts, falling trees. Today, she'd keep it easy and make sure he handled an axe well and kept his wits about him.

Hank returned with the boards and rope.

"Make the notch for the first board opposite the first notch I made." Kelda watched him pick up the axe and swing. "Whoa! It's not so much strength, even though you do need it, but accuracy and a sharp blade that gets the chips flying. Take your cuts only an inch apart so it chips away at the tree. It goes faster and uses less energy than taking big bites and having to swing multiple times at the same spot."

Hank took an experimental swing.

"Ja, like that. Use your arms and keep it accurate." Her heart swelled when a grin slipped across his face. The determination in his eyes showed he wanted to learn.

He swung the axe and smaller chips flew out of the notch.

The fact he listened to her instructions and followed them without question vanished her fears of them butting heads while working together.

"Try the board. Remember you want it tight but you also need to be able to wedge it in."

He planted the first springboard and looked up at her grinning like a boy with a slingshot.

"Good." The pride expanding her heart made

her chest ache. He learned quickly and had the patience it required to do a good job. "Lean the next board against the tree on the other side of the springboard. You have to be able to get a hold of it once you're on the wedged board."

He placed the board as she instructed. "Now, tie the rope around the last springboard and then the saw and toss the loose end up to me."

Once the items were tied to the rope, Hank tossed the end up to her.

"Climb up on the first board and make the notch for the second one."

She sat on her board, her feet dangling down, watching Hank work from the springboard. Her stomach clenched a couple times when the board started bouncing the opposite of his strokes and he nearly toppled off.

"Work with the bounce. Use it to help propel your swing."

"You've gained a lot more of my esteem. You made putting in a springboard and working from one look easy." He peered into her eyes as he wiped at the sweat beading his brow. The sincerity would have toppled her off the board if she hadn't been sitting down.

Finally, the second notch was ready, and he wedged the board in and climbed up higher. The tree was large enough that she could no longer see him, only hear him as he worked.

"I'm ready for the other board," he called from the far side.

"Coming from the north," she said, untying the board and holding it out toward the north end of the tree. This would be the hard part. Could he reach the board without falling? Or her stretching to help him?

The board tugged. "Let go."

She released her end and watched the end dip then disappear. The screech of wood rubbing against wood signified he was wedging the board in. After a few moments and a grunt, Hank's face appeared around the side of the tree.

"Now what?"

"We work at making the notch to fall the tree. Work in rhythm, chipping away at this side of the trunk." She stood and yanked her axe out of the tree. "I'll start and you follow."

She swung the blade, biting into the wood. Hank followed with a swing, and they started a syncopated rhythm that tossed chips to the ground and matched the beat of her heart.

Fifteen minutes later, the tree had a notch two feet high and a third of the way into the tree. Kelda stopped. "Now we saw."

Hand over hand, she pulled the rope up, until the saw handle was the next thing she grasped. She turned her back to the notch and swung the saw to the rounded side of the tree. "Catch!"

There was a tug. "Now what?" Hank called.

"We start sawing. Just like with the axes, we have to get into a rhythm to make it work." Again, her heart soared as they fell into an easy rhythm. She'd worked with some who never could get a smooth motion going with the saw. They usually ended up working the chute, dragging the trees, or being a whistle punk.

When the tree started leaning, Kelda shouted, "Two more strokes and drop down to sit on the board." She heaved the saw his way and he heaved it back. The saw slacked, she wiggled it out and dropped to the springboard as the tree slowly descended to the ground with a loud thwhump and shook the fifteen foot stump.

She peered across the cut. Hank's lips curved into a huge smile, his eyes glint with excitement, and his flushed face beamed.

"Feels good doesn't it?" Kelda said, lifting one brow and smiling back with as much exuberance.

"Yeah!"

Chapter 27

Hank was still buzzing from the excitement of cutting down five trees. Three he worked with Kelda and the last two she let him do on his own. He'd begun to see why she was adamant about working in the woods. When they weren't sawing or chopping, the quiet and the scents invaded his thoughts more than when he rode through the trees. There was something about harvesting the trees that made them more than just an object to look at or use for fuel or building.

He understood the excitement that followed the men in to dinner every night. Rather than stand in line with the others to clean up before dinner, he washed up in the office. Knowing he'd walk Kelda back to her cabin after dinner, he wanted to wash away the sweat and put on a clean shirt. Courting required he clean up and make a show of caring about his appearance.

Crossing the office, he caught sight of Kelda out the small window. He stood at the window watching her stride toward the cookhouse. Her hair looked freshly combed and her face glowed. His heart picked up pace as she laughed and talked with the others. The respect the men gave her came from her prowess in the woods and not that she was a woman.

After witnessing the strength in her both mentally and physically as she taught him the fundamentals of falling trees, he understood that respect. He couldn't believe how easily she went from springboard to springboard. If she could have seen him when he was getting from the second board to the third she would have fallen off laughing at him. The board had started bouncing, and he'd had trouble getting his balance to swing up to the next board. He was surprised she hadn't called out asking what was taking so long. He smiled. Perhaps she knew and planned to torment him with knowledge tonight when they were alone.

He quickly donned his coat and headed to the cookhouse. Everyone stood at his entrance, taking him by surprise. Arvid waved him to his seat between Tobias and Kelda.

"You are officially a beast." Arvid raised his coffee cup. Everyone cheered and raised their cups before drinking, what Hank discovered to be akevitt when he tipped his cup to his lips.

Lars placed the platters and bowls of food on the table.

"I had a very good teacher," Hank said, gazing down at Kelda's blushing face.

The men all cheered again.

"What else is she teaching you?" a call asked

from down the table.

Silence filled the room like a gust of cold air.

Anger washed through Hank, pushing him to his feet. He scanned the length of the table looking for the man who sullied Kelda's reputation.

"Sit." Arvid's command wrenched his attention from his hunt to Kelda's father. The firm set to his mouth and glint of steel in the old man's eyes told him, the culprit would be dealt with.

Hank sank back down on the bench but not before sending a glower down one side of the table and up the other. He thought he saw Peder flinch. Could he be the one who uttered the comment?

Kelda placed her hand on his thigh. He peered into her face. She shook her head and turned to accept the bowl of potatoes from the man on the other side of her. Hank put food on his plate and ate, but he didn't remember the act of eating. His mind ran down the line of loggers at the table figuring out who had said the comment and if he should give out a punishment. He'd not have anyone yelling out rude comments about Kelda.

The pile of dirty plates arrived in front of him and he passed them to Tobias. The commotion of the men leaving distracted him from his thoughts. Kelda placed her hand on his arm and leaned into him.

"Are you walking me to my cabin?" she whispered in his ear.

He wanted to turn his head and kiss her, but after the comment he didn't want to show her any affection with others around. It was bad enough Tobias caught them the day before kissing in the office.

He nodded and she stood.

"Kelda, Hank, I want a word with you," Arvid said, holding his cup up. Tobias jumped up and snatched the coffeepot off the stove, refilling his father's as well as Kelda's, Hank's, Karl's and Dag's cups.

The refilled cups meant they'd be discussing something. Hank raised the cup to his lips and studied the Nielsen men. The younger men appeared fidgety. What was the old man up to?

"Kelda tells me you did a fine job today, and you're ready to work with the rest of us." Arvid motioned to his daughter with his cup.

Pride once again swelled Hank's chest. His ability to learn things fast had come in handy today. "Thank you, sir. Like I said earlier, I had a good teacher. I can see why you take so much pride in your children. I've learned a lot about this business from every one of them."

Arvid's eyes glistened, and his grin ran from ear to ear. "Ja, they are good children who make me proud." His gaze landed on Kelda and his expression sobered.

"Because of the comment earlier in the meal, I feel you two should not work together." He held up his hands as Kelda sputtered. "I believe you when you say you worked hard. It can be seen by the logs Smithy dragged from that small grove and the dulled blades on your axes." He sighed. "But because goodwill between all my workers makes for less problems, Hank will work with Dag from now on. Kelda, you will work with Peder, he's still not as well trained as he should be. Perhaps he will listen to you."

Hank's gut twisted. He was positive Peder had made the comment. Arvid had to have seen the man utter the words from his vantage at the head of the table.

Kelda's hand sought his and squeezed.

"I don't want to overstep since I'm new to logging, but wouldn't it make more sense to put Peder with Karl since he has an interest in Kelda, too?" Hank didn't want to sound jealous, but he wasn't happy with the match up.

"I'll keep an eye on them and if things don't work, I'll make changes." Arvid downed his coffee and stood. "Kelda, Mor would like to visit with you."

Hank stood when Kelda stood. "I'll wait for you."

She nodded and walked into the back room with her father.

"Kelda was impressed with your work." Dag took a sip of coffee and eyed Hank.

"It was harder than I figured, but I now understand the draw." Hank sat back down and finished off his coffee wondering how long Kelda would be.

"Don't worry about Peder. Kelda will treat him like she does everyone else, and he'll get the message she's not interested in him," Tobias said, picking at the bread still sitting on the table.

Hank turned to Tobias. "He's the one who made the comment isn't he?"

Tobias glanced across the table at Karl and shrugged. "I was taking a drink and didn't see who said it."

What was Arvid up to putting Kelda and Peder together? It didn't make sense. Hank studied the brothers and realized none of them were willing to make any guesses. He walked over to the drain board to hand Lars his cup.

"Did you see who shouted out that comment?" Hank asked, knowing Lars was on their side.

"Nei. I was working." The regret on Lars face told Hank he would have helped him knock some sense into whoever uttered the words.

Hank slapped the man on the back and sat back down. The unease in him wouldn't settle. He stood back up and paced to the door and back. He'd be better off to go to the office and have To-bias tell Kelda that's where he went. Solitude was better company than the three men staring at him.

"Tell Kelda I'll be at the office when she's done." Hank raised his hand to grab his coat.

"Tell her yourself."

Hank spun around as Kelda walked away from the backroom.

"Are you leaving without me?" she asked, hur-rying across the room.

"I-I was going to wait for you at the office." His heart skipped witnessing the disappointment on her face. "But now that you're ready to go, I'll escort you to your cabin."

He held out her coat, Kelda slipped her arms in and flashed him a heart-stopping smile. Hank hustled her out of the cookhouse and across the camp to her cabin without a word. The moment they were behind the closed door, he pulled her into his arms and kissed her. Long and hot, the way he'd been dreaming about all day.

Kelda's body sagged into Hank's arms. Her mind fogged from the heated kiss and roaming hands of Hank. She'd dreamt of their coming together all day, but the reality was far better than any dream. Her coat was suffocating with the heat swirling in her body. The kiss was heavenly, but she needed out of the coat before she burst into flames.

Leaning out of the kiss, she drew in great gulps of air. "Please. Out of my coat. Hot."

Hank backed up. "Sorry. I didn't want to wait any longer to kiss you." His hands unbuttoned her coat and hung it on the peg in one fluid movement. His coat followed, and they sat on her cot their lips locked once again.

Her heart hammered in her chest as his hands slipped under her shirt and chemise, scorching her skin with his calloused palm. The roughness scraped her nipple. The contact extracted a moan and her body arched into his hand. She craved his touch, his kiss, his body.

Kelda worked her fingers down his shirt buttons exposing his chest to her palms. The heat and solidness fascinated and enhanced her need to touch more. She pushed the flannel and the undershirt down his arms, gliding her fingers over the muscles of his arms and marveling at the shape and how they'd worked the axe today.

Hank pulled his hands out of her shirt and leaned his forehead on hers. "We can't go any farther. Not here in camp. I won't have someone catching us." He kissed her nose and slowly pulled his shirt back up on his arms.

"Put the bar across the door and no one will see." Why did he always have to be so staid and worry about her reputation? If they married there was nothing sullied.

"You weren't all that quiet at the cabin." His feral smile and heated gaze vibrated her body and started the throb between her legs.

"I can be quiet. Love me and I'll prove it." She raised an eyebrow, daring him.

"Woman." He grasped her shoulders and kissed her senseless, again.

How she loved the forcefulness and starvation of his kisses. It was as if her essence was all that kept him from starving and he could do nothing to keep from kissing her. His need for her was an elixir she would never outgrow.

Her hands rubbed against the hardness in his lap. He groaned in her mouth, nipped her lips, and set her away from him. She watched his eyes slowly open as he stood. The darkness and heat curved her lips into a knowing smile. He wanted her as much as she wanted him.

She reached out to him, but he took a step back.

He ran a hand over his face and stared at her. "I'm making a rule. One that will not be broken." The steel in his eyes revealed this was a rule she'd better follow.

Kelda swallowed and nodded slightly.

"We will not make love in the camp until we're married." She started to say something, and he held up a hand. "I'll not have any more comments like was uttered at the table tonight. If I knew who said it they would be nursing a beating right now."

She'd felt the anger in him when the comment was uttered. She also knew the voice and wasn't happy Far had paired her up with the man. But she'd go to her grave before she'd let Hank know the person. She feared for both men. Peder, that he would be beat to within an inch of his life, and Hank, being able to cope with that kind of anger afterwards. She'd hold her tongue to save them both.

Kelda cleared her throat. "Forget about the comment. If it makes you feel better, I'll try to keep control." She pouted and glanced at him from lowered lashes. "But it will be hard to stay focused when my body and heart wishes to have all of you."

Hank took a step toward her then fisted his hands at his sides as his eyes danced with desire. "That kind of talk and flirtation makes it hard to stand by my rule."

She stood and took a step, placing her body toe to toe with him. "Then maybe it's a rule that should be broken now and then."

"Woman..." Hank yanked her against him and kissed her open-mouthed and hungry, just the way she liked it.

Before she could sneak her hands under his shirt, he stepped back.

"Good night, Kelda." He backed to the door, took down his coat, and opened the door swishing cold air all around her, but it didn't cool the fever he'd lit.

"Good night, Hank. I hope you toss and turn as much as I'm going to." She smiled sweetly, and he closed the door, leaving her wishing they were married and could forget about proprieties.

Chapter 28

The week passed quickly with the days filled with falling trees and the evenings spent pushing each other over the brink of sanity and parting before their bodies were sated. Kelda decided rule or no rule tonight she wasn't letting Hank leave the cabin until he'd put out the fire that smoldered in her day and night. His kisses and groping hands had her up half the night and sleeping fitfully the rest. Even Mor had commented on her agitation.

Today, the group was spread farther apart. She didn't mind, it was easier to concentrate on her work when she didn't get glimpses of Hank swinging an axe or working a saw.

Peder was also becoming more of a nuisance, using excuses to touch her inappropriately and she'd caught him ogling her more than once the past week. It made her wish she was back in the cookhouse. She'd never had this problem before. If a new logger made advances, she set him straight and that was that. But Peder didn't seem to understand. She'd told him every day that she wasn't interested in him. He'd just laugh and moments later touch her.

Mid-day Kelda couldn't take any more of Peder's actions. "I'm going to find Far and talk with him," she said and picked up her knapsack with her mid-day meal, her axe, and her coat. The spring days had grown warm enough she shed her coat mid-morning and worked the rest of the day without it. She didn't tell Peder why she wished to talk with Far, but from the scowl on his face he probably had a clue.

She crossed through the area where Hank and Dag worked. They both stopped sawing a huge tree. Hank walked toward her.

"Is something wrong?" He touched her cheek with the back of his gloved hand.

"I'm going to visit with Far while I eat my lunch." She tried to keep her tone light and not get him guessing the reason. The last couple of nights she'd almost told him about Peder, but to keep Hank from getting into trouble she refrained. She could tell he knew something wasn't right.

"You're sure?" His compassion welled tears in her eyes.

"Ja. But if you'd make love to me it would help."

He pulled her into his arms, hugging her. "Sweetie, we'll tell them we're going to see my family in Sumpter on Sunday and we'll spend the whole day at my cabin."

"Really?" Her heart slammed into her chest, and her hopes sprung to life like bouncing on a springboard.

"Yes. I promise." He released her. "Go talk with your father. Dag's in a grouch today, so I better not dally any longer."

Kelda's steps were bouncier as she made her way to Far's area. He and Butch were working on a large tree. Far spotted her and shouted at Butch to stop.

"What brings you here, Kelda?" Far asked, taking a drink from his water flask.

She glanced at Butch and back at Far. "I need to speak with you in private."

Far turned to Butch. "Take a break. I'll be back as soon as Kelda and I finish our conversation." He led her thirty yards away from Butch. "What's on your mind?"

Kelda sat on a downed log and pulled out a slice of bread. "I can't work with Peder." She stared at Far. "He makes it a point to touch me where he shouldn't. He stares at me. At areas of my body that makes me uneasy. And he's listening less and less to my advice and doing what he wants."

Far sat down beside her. "I thought maybe by working with you he'd understand you didn't have feelings for him."

"That's the problem. I've told him every day that I only think of him as another logger and nothing more, yet he treats me like a-a woman who sells her body. Far, I can't take the stress of working with him."

"I've noticed you haven't been sleeping. I thought maybe Hank was keeping you up." He studied her.

She bowed her head as her cheeks flamed. "Hank does keep me up but in a good way. Between the two I've not been sleeping well."

Far laughed. "I'm glad Hank keeps you awake in a good way. Finish today with Peder and tomorrow I'll pair you with someone else."

Kelda kissed Far's cheek. "Mange takk, Far."

He slipped an arm around her shoulders and hugged her. "I have to keep my good help happy." He winked and stood. "Back to work. We have a daily quota to hit."

She stood and walked back toward the area where she and Peder had downed six trees and worked on the seventh for the day. Passing Hank and Dag's area she noted the big tree they were sawing as she went by lay on the ground, but she didn't see either of the men. Perhaps they'd wandered off to relieve themselves.

An unusual sound floated on the gentle breeze. A human groan. Kelda walked slower, listening and following the sound. She noticed something colorful by the large end of the cut tree.

The plaid of the shirt registered in her mind, and her heart stopped as well as her steps. Hank had on a red and green shirt.

"Nei!" She shouted and raced to the spot. The log pinned Hank's legs to the ground. He was breathing. His eyes popped open when her shaking hand touched his face.

"I don't think they're broke, but I can't feel much below my waist." His eyes closed and then popped back open. "I love you," he whispered and his eyes closed again.

Agony ripped through her. She had to save him. It was her fault he was in the woods.

Fear for him froze her thoughts.

He moaned, shedding her of fear and pushing her to action. She needed help.

"Dag! Dag!" Kelda stood, shouting for her brother. Where was he? How did this happen? They had to get the log off, but to roll it would surely crush his legs and feet.

"Far! Far!" she shouted and ran back toward her father. He and several others came running.

"What?" he asked, grasping her shoulders.

Hot tears poured down her face. "Hank's under a tree. Can't find Dag."

"Show us." Far turned her, and she ran back to the log.

At the tree, she fell to her knees and cradled Hank's head in her lap. Her tears dropped on his cheek, and she brushed them away. She couldn't lose him, not now, not when they'd finally worked out their differences. Fear twisted her heart.

"We'll have to make a spar tree, set guide lines, and use a pulley to lift the tree off him." Far crouched beside her. "Kelda, you have to make the spar tree and set the guidelines and pulley. You're the only one with the skill right here to get the tree ready by the time Butch returns with the cables and pulley."

Kelda's heart raced. Could she climb a tree when her heart and mind were with the man under a log? She peered at Hank. Love and fear twined together. Love won out. She had to do this for Hank. Easing his head to the ground, she rose to her feet.

"Which one?"

Far pointed to the only close tree.

She scanned the length of it. Not too many limbs to take off. Not the best tree to use for a spar, but they didn't have much choice.

Kelda watched Far check a length of rope before he handed it to her. "I'm not happy we don't have the cable reinforced rope for you to use to climb, but we can't wait for one to be brought up here."

"I'll be careful." She glanced down at Hank. "Far, take care of him while I'm up there."

"I will, child, I will."

Feeling for her hatchet on her hip, she picked up her axe, hanging it from the other side of her belt. She stared down at her boots. She'd rather have cleats but those were at the camp.

"Wait, wait!" Sven ran up, a pair of cleats dangled from his hands. "I always carry my cleats with me. You never know when you need to dig in on a slope."

Kelda hugged the man and sat down to strap them onto her boots.

Now she was prepared.

With one more glance at Hank, she strode over to the tree Far picked. Sven helped her loop one end of the rope around the trunk, and she began, one step at a time, walking up the tree. Digging in with her cleats, she leaned forward, swung the loop father up the tree and walked up two more steps. At the first low limbs, she pulled the axe out of her belt and lopped off the limbs with three strokes.

She stopped mid-way and looked down.

It was a mistake.

Seeing the small shape of Hank pressed under the large tree made her queasy and her sight blur. Fear, unlike any she'd ever had, rushed through her cold and icy as a winter storm.

Her hands shook and her legs weakened.

The rope slacked, and she slid down several feet before catching herself.

"Don't look down. Stay focused!" Far shouted up to her.

Kelda swallowed, forced her gaze to the bark scraping her shirt and on up to the limbs she still had to knock off to reach the height needed for good leverage.

Hank couldn't feel his legs. Musty ground, pine, and pitch scents filled his nostrils. Hushed voices caught his attention, and he opened his eyes. Looking straight up, he caught sight of someone climbing a tree, knocking off the limbs as they climbed.

"Who's that?" he asked as loud as his voice would go.

Arvid stood over him, blocking his view. "The only person talented enough to climb the tree and set a pulley for us to lift this log off you."

Panic squeezed his chest. He raised an arm to push the man out of the way. "You shouldn't have sent her up there. It's too dangerous."

"She's the only one who could do the job fast enough. You could end up losing your legs if we don't get that tree off you quickly." Arvid moved.

Hank forgot about his legs. The pounding of his heart whooshed in his head as he followed each movement Kelda made.

"Stand in front of him, she's ready to top." Arvid walked over to the long rope hanging to the ground and tied on a saw.

"Sven, step to the side," Hank said, craning his neck to watch Kelda pull the saw sixty feet into the air. His gaze remained riveted even as his stomach clenched when she leaned back against the rope holding her to the tree and worked the saw back and forth.

"Now," Arvid said as Kelda hooked the saw to the rope length and then pushed on the tree top and dropped the rope circling the tree, plummeting her down the side of the tree. Her cleated boots stopped her fall as the tree top whooshed and tumbled to the earth on the opposite side Hank was pinned.

If it had been anyone but the woman he loved maneuvering at the top of the tree he'd have whooped with the others. But the clamp of fear squeezing his chest barely allowed him to breathe.

Butch, Tobias, Karl, and Dag came loping up on the draft horses.

Butch and Karl hauled the wire and pulleys over to the base of the tree.

Arvid stalked over to Dag. "Where were you? You were supposed to be watching out for the man you're paired up with."

"Peder came over and said Karl wanted to talk to me. Said since Kelda was talking with you, he'd help Hank while I talked to Karl." Dag's voice held contrition.

Hank hadn't thought about how he was under the tree, but it all came rushing back at Dag's comment. He and Peder were sawing on the tree. Peder walked around to the dangerous side and fell to his knees, saying he'd sprained an ankle. When Hank went to help him, the man slammed a limb against his head, knocking him out. Hank came to, couldn't feel his legs, and realized a log had him pinned to the ground.

"Where's Peder?" he asked, drawing the men back to him. "He did this. He lured me to the down side of the tree then hit me with a limb. I came to and this tree was on me." Anger replaced his fear for Kelda. Not only had the man nearly killed him, but he'd put Kelda's life in jeopardy too.

Arvid's face darkened with rage. He turned to Tobias. "Go to camp. Tell everyone what's happened then ride to town, get the doctor, tell Hank's family what's happened, and telegraph for a marshal. I want Peder found."

Tobias nodded and swung up onto a horse.

"My brother's will find him," Hank said, knowing with one brother who was a marshal and one a Pinkerton agent Peder didn't have a chance.

He looked skyward watching Kelda haul first the guide lines up with the rope and secure them as men below pulled on the tree, arching it slightly away from his position. Then she dropped the rope again and hauled up the pulley, securing it.

Men dug under the log near his legs and hooked a chain around the tree.

His gaze remained riveted to the tree as Kelda

checked everything and then began the descent. His heart lodged in his throat more than once, watching her fall and catch herself in a leaping motion as she came down the tree. Her arms and legs had to be tired from all the work.

Ten feet from the ground he lost sight of her.

The few minutes between losing sight and her face showing in front of him dragged on for an eternity.

"How are you doing?" she asked, her hand resting on his cheek.

"Better now that you're on the ground. How are you?" he placed his hand over hers.

"I'll be better when this tree is off of you." She leaned down and kissed his lips.

"Move away." Arvid pulled Kelda to her feet. "We're ready to lift this tree. Kelda, you and Munson pull Hank out when we get the log high enough."

"She has to be tired, get someone—"

Arvid glared down at him. "Do you want out from under that log? We use the manpower we have." He winked. "And there's no way she'll back off."

Hank had to agree with that when Kelda's face set with determination loomed over him as she grasped him under one arm and Munson grasped him under the other arm.

Slowly, inch by inch the weight of the log lessened. With each inch it gave, pain seeped into his legs until he wanted to cry out. But his arms jerked and his body slid out.

"Got him!" Kelda shouted, and the ground

shook as the log dropped. Her hands moved down his legs.

Sharp pain sliced through his legs in bursts. He bit his lip to keep from yelling out.

"I can't find any broken bones." She peered into his eyes. "Is the pain awful?"

He couldn't even nod. Hank focused on her face and slipped into dark oblivion.

Chapter 29

Kelda paced back and forth in the office. Rachel had been in with Hank for nearly an hour. Now she knew the fear Hank had tried to explain to her. Having never had a loved one injured in an accident, she hadn't realized the horror and unbridled fear that racked a body. This was what she'd put Hank through every time she mentioned working in the woods. His fear for her had been real, and now she knew the full force of it.

She didn't like the feeling. Hated the not knowing. And loathed herself for putting him in danger. Her insistence to work in the woods had put him in danger. If she hadn't insisted, she wouldn't have been paired with Peder, and he wouldn't have retaliated by hurting Hank.

Aileen stepped through the outside door with a tray. "Tea to settle yer nerves."

Kelda didn't have the heart to say she couldn't keep anything down. Aileen and Maeve had dropped everything and came with Rachel. Gil and

Zeke were out looking for Peder. Her hands fisted and her body shook knowing she caused Peder to harm Hank. She'd known he was no good. Why couldn't Far have seen that before it was too late? Why didn't she stay in the cookhouse where she belonged?

"Sit. Yer no' goin' to be any good to Hank if yer all tuckered out." Aileen pulled her over to the stool at the counter and plopped her on it.

"Why's it taking so long? I don't think he broke anything." Kelda had held his hand as they waited for Rachel. He'd been in excruciating pain but had worked as hard at keeping her cheerful as she'd tried to keep him in good spirits.

"Rachel will be thorough and make sure he's well cared for." Aileen poured the tea and handed her a cup.

Kelda took the cup and sipped. It was sweet and did calm her a bit. "Thank you. I'm just..."

"Worried. We all are, but you more than anyone else. Yer love for him is new, easier to hurt." She patted Kelda's hand. "Ye'll learn that when ye give yer heart and soul to someone, when they hurt, ye hurt twice as much because ye feel helpless." She smiled. "But love is what will pull you both through this. Ye'll see."

Karl, Dag, and Tobias stomped through the door.

"And family." Aileen smiled and passed the boys. "Gentlemen, keep yer sister calm."

Dag walked toward her his head bowed. "Kelda, I'm sorry. I didn't realize—"

She put a hand on Dag's arm. "You didn't

know the meanness in Peder. I'd just realized it and was discussing it with Far. That's why he was left alone."

"But I should have known better. I should have known he wouldn't be telling me Karl needed to see me."

"That's for sure." Karl said, stepping up. "I'm sorry for giving you such a hard time over Hank."

Tears welled in her eyes. "It's okay. We needed a good laugh."

The door behind her creaked. Kelda spun around as Rachel stuck her head out.

"Kelda, I could use your help."

She'd started across the floor before Rachel had even spoken. Now she stepped into the room that held Hank's bed and desk.

Hank's eyes were dull and a crooked, sloppy smile wiggled on his lips.

"I have him sedated to keep him still and take away the pain. " Rachel took her hand. "I don't really need your help but thought you'd like to hear he'll be fine after a couple weeks of rest."

Relief swelled in Kelda's chest and erupted out her mouth in a hysterical laugh.

Rachel folded Kelda into her arms and held her as she sobbed and laughed with relief. When the episode ebbed, she backed away, wiping at her eyes.

"I'm sorry. I just..."

"It's okay, I understand. When you love someone and you find out they'll be all right the emotions you've held bottled up come out. You're entitled to a good fit." Rachel smiled.

"W-what's-s-s goin' on over-r-r ther-r-r. I'd-d-d lik-k-ke to hug Kel-l-lda-a-a." Hank's slurred words made Kelda giggle.

"I gave him laudanum to help with the pain. As far as I can tell, he didn't break any bones. That's probably due to the mud. But he is badly bruised. His legs are purple and are swelling due to the damaged muscles. You'll need to keep them wrapped tightly to keep the swelling down." Rachel walked over to the desk. "This is the laudanum. Only give it to him if he seems to be in unbearable pain. We don't want him to become dependent on it."

She scanned Kelda. "Why don't I sit with him a little longer and now that you know he's going to be fine, you go change and get dinner for both of you?"

Kelda walked over to the side of the bed and bent. She pushed the dark brown lock off Hank's forehead and kissed him. "I'm going to clean up and get us dinner. Rachel will sit with you a little longer until I come back. Then I won't leave you. I promise." Kelda kissed him again and dodged his hand that came up and grasped for her arm. She knew if he pulled her down, she wouldn't get up. The need to be wrapped in his arms and feel his life and love filled her.

"Thank you," she said to Rachel and hurried out of the room before she changed her mind.

The office was empty. She crossed to the outside door and stood in a daze watching her brothers and Ethan pack buckets of water into her cabin. Immobility wouldn't get her cleaned up and back with Hank. Kelda shook her head and walked through the camp, stepping through the cabin door.

The bathing tub sat in the middle of the room. Steam curled in wisps up from the surface of the water.

Darcy stepped away from the potbelly stove. "We heard all about you climbing that tree to save Hank and figured you could use a hot bath to relax and get washed up. You're going to have some long days nursing him. You should start it off clean." She set two towels over a chair and walked to the door. "Don't worry. No one will disturb you." Darcy stepped out, and Kelda dropped the wood bar across.

Within minutes, she stripped and sat in the tub. It wasn't as luxurious as the tub at the hotel, but she relished every warm drop. She stepped out and donned one of her Sunday dresses. When Hank came out from under the haze of laudanum, she planned to tell him he'd no longer see her in dungarees. She would be his wife and not take any more chances out in the woods. But he would also have to keep his business to the camp. She didn't want to relive today ever again.

Kelda stepped out of the cabin and headed to the cookhouse. Inside, she found Ethan, Clay, Aileen, Maeve, Darcy and all their children as well as Mor, Far, and her brothers and Lars serving them all coffee and small cakes.

Everyone looked up with anticipation.

Ethan cleared his throat. "How is he?"

She peered around at all the expectant faces.

"Didn't one of you go in and ask?"

"That's not our place," Clay said and everyone nodded.

"Not your place? He's your brother."

"He's the man you're going to marry, so that makes it your place," Darcy said, handing her a cup of coffee. "You decide who is informed."

Kelda shook her head. "It's everyone who loves him who should know the outcome. Rachel said he'll be fine. He is badly bruised, but she doesn't believe any broken bones. She said he needs to stay down and resting for two weeks to keep the swelling down and allow the muscles to heal." She smiled, remembering his goofy smile. "She gave him laudanum so he's kind of goofy."

"He's always goofy," Collin said and the group burst out laughing.

Kelda looked at Lars. "Rachel told me to get dinner for Hank and myself then she can go home. Do you have anything I can take over to the office?"

"Ja." Lars turned to the stove and began rattling and clanging dishes.

Maeve walked over to Kelda and put an arm around her. "Your father says you're a hero for climbing a tree and setting the rigging that pulled the tree off Hank."

Kelda's cheeks heated. "I'm not a hero. It was something I knew how to do and it needed to be done." Her mind went to the sight of Hank on the ground and the tree on his legs. "It was climb the tree or lose Hank."

Her body shook reliving the moment she

stared down.

"I didn't mean to upset you." Maeve led her to the bench and sat her down next to Far.

He put his arm around her shoulders and drew her against him. "Skatten min, you did a man's work today. I'm proud of you." He kissed her temple.

"Far, I could have lost Hank today." She peered into her father's eyes. Understanding sparkled back at her. "How do you and Mor not go crazy every day with all of your children working in the woods?"

"Because I trained you and trust you to know what to do. Just like today."

She shook her head. "No more. I learned today why Hank hasn't wanted me in the woods."

Kelda took the basket Lars brought over to her, and she walked back to the office.

Rachel sat in Hank's desk chair working on a piece of handiwork.

"You can go now. Thank you for coming so quickly and taking care of Hank." Kelda hugged Rachel.

"He's family and so are you because Hank loves you." Rachel returned the hug and picked up her doctor's bag. "I'll come by day after tomorrow. He'll be wanting to get up by then and I'll give him a talking to."

"Thank you. See you then." Kelda followed Rachel to the outside door and hurried back to Hank's side. She wasn't hungry, so she left the basket of food sitting on the desk and lay down beside Hank. Snuggling up to his side, resting her head on his chest, she listened to his steady heart beat, and placed an arm across his undershirt clad chest. This was where she'd remain for the rest of her life. By his side.

Hank woke from the throbbing in his leg, but it was heat and scent of vanilla that stirred him to awareness. The shape of Kelda's body registered in his senses as he peered down and spied her golden hair flaring across her body and his. He reached out and sifted his fingers through the soft strands.

His heart ached with love for the woman, remembering the way she climbed the tree and fastened the rigging. She had to be exhausted. Hell, he'd be exhausted if he'd had to make that climb. And she'd scaled the tree as agile as a cat. He understood why she didn't see his fear for her. Her confidence today proved she knew how to handle herself in the woods. He was the one who was hurt. The greenhorn who should have known better when Peder said he had to look at the cut to see why the tree wasn't falling.

Hank mentally slapped himself. If he hadn't been worrying over what was eating at Kelda, he would have thought twice before believing the man.

Kelda moaned and her arms tightened around his chest.

"Shh... dream sweet, I won't let anything harm you," he whispered, wishing he could reach her head and kiss her.

The door to his room opened, and Tobias's

head peeked in. Hank didn't move or say anything. Tobias just nodded and closed the door softly.

The lantern on the desk was slowly dying. He didn't have a window, but he'd guess since Tobias just looked in, the man had been heading to bed.

Hank wrapped both arms around Kelda and used happy thoughts of her to chase away the pain in his leg.

Hank woke again. This time the pain had him gasping. Kelda sat, pushing her hair out of her face and peering at him in the dimness.

"What's wrong?" she asked, placing a hand on his forehead.

"The pain. I need something." His legs throbbed and ached. He'd never experienced such piercing pain.

"I'll give you the medicine then check the wraps." Kelda hurried to the desk and returned with a spoon and a small bottle.

He took the foul tasting liquid and squeezed his eyes closed to keep the tears forming from rolling down his cheeks.

"My!" Kelda gasped as a cold breeze blew across his legs.

"What?"

"Rachel didn't tell me you were naked from the waist down." The lift to one of her eyebrows and quite possibly the medicine working brought a smile to his face.

"You like doctoring naked men?"

"Only when they're you." She stared down

at his legs. "I'm not sure how tight to wrap these around your legs. I'll check the one on the far side first. If I'm hurting you too much, let me know."

Her straw colored hair hung down tickling his maleness as she worked with the bandage. He wasn't sure what was more painful, the bandage or the hair.

She pulled back and checked the other leg. "There, that should hold a while longer." Kelda peered over her shoulder then back at him. "Are you hungry? I brought food."

"More thirsty than hungry." The medicine was working. His eyelids were as heavy as a log.

A hand raised his head, and the taste of tin tingled his lips before wetness lingered. He opened his mouth and drank until not another drop hit his tongue.

"Hungry?" Kelda's voice floated above his head.

He wanted to say no, but you eat, only his tongue couldn't form the words so he moved his head side to side slowly.

Her body slipped back beside him on the bed, and he disappeared into the blackness he was learning to enjoy. The void that took away the pain.

Kelda stood back as Rachel unwrapped the bandages. She'd cut the legs off a pair of drawers and placed them on Hank when he was able to use the chamber pot. Kelda didn't want anyone to move the blanket and see she'd been tending a man naked from the waist down.

His legs had turned green and purple, but they weren't as swollen as earlier.

Rachel probed his legs and he grimaced. "There are some knots that will need to be worked out." She nodded for Kelda to come to the side of the bed. "Put your hand here." She pulled Kelda's hand down to Hank's leg.

The initial contact sent shivers up Kelda's arm and heat ringing her heart. She'd been sleeping on the bed beside him every night and checking the wraps but to touch his skin like this was different.

Until, she felt the lump. It was as hard as a knot on a tree. "Does that hurt?" she asked, probing the lump with her fingers.

"Yesss," Hank hissed.

"But you'll have to massage all the lumps in his legs several times a day. If you don't they could cause permanent damage to the muscle and nerves. The blood has to stay flowing in those areas." Rachel shifted her gaze to Hank. "I know Kelda working out the knots will hurt, but if you can get through it without the laudanum you'll be better."

Hank nodded. "I can suffer pain from her hands."

Kelda's heart double-timed as his gaze remained on her face. He'd woke this morning with less dulling pain in their brown pools. And he'd spent the better part of the morning trying to pull her back into bed. She'd known Rachel was coming and didn't want to be caught in a compromising position.

"Keep him in bed for the rest of the week. The

longer he stays off the legs and doesn't use the muscles, the quicker they'll heal." Rachel snapped her doctor's bag closed. "I'll be by on Sunday to check on him."

"Rachel, have you heard anything from Gil and Zeke." Hank had asked Kelda every day if they'd caught Peder yet.

"They sent a telegraph last night saying they found him and were bringing him back." Rachel grimaced. "Not sure I'd want to be Peder."

Kelda studied Hank's face. Satisfaction was the word that came to mind watching his features soften and set.

"He'll be sorry he messed with a Halsey," Hank said, a wisp of a smile tipping his lips.

Rachel nodded. "See you two on Sunday."

Kelda followed her to the outside door and returned to the office. Hank had pulled his body up to a sitting position. He patted the mattress next to him.

"Do I need to lock the door?" Kelda asked, hoping he'd say yes, but knowing too much activity wouldn't be good for him.

"No. We're going to talk." The tone of his voice hooked her attention.

"What do we need to talk about?" She sat on the bed and laced her fingers with his.

"Our future." His eyes held love and devotion.

"I like the sound of that." She kissed his cheek. "I have something I wanted to tell you, but was waiting until you were no longer sleepy from the medicine."

His free hand rested on her belly. "Did we already start a family?" The hope shining in his eyes made her wish that was the news.

"Nei, but I'm sure it will happen soon." She inhaled deeply and played with his fingers. "I'm sorry I pushed to make you let me work in the woods. If I hadn't been so insistent, I wouldn't have been paired with Peder and he wouldn't have taken my rejection so harshly to cause you harm." Having said her peace the guilt shifted to a lesser ache in her mind.

"This had nothing to do with your pushing to do something you love. I've seen the way you light up when sawing and your expertise at climbing trees. You have every reason to want to work in the woods." Hank lifted her hand and kissed it. "Your love of the woods is what makes you so special."

Kelda shook her head. Tears burned behind her eyes as she peered into his adoring eyes. "After experiencing fear that nearly froze me from helping you, I realized why you were so against my working in the woods. I learned the fear and panic associated with seeing someone you love in danger." Hank opened his mouth, but she placed a finger on his lips. "Having discovered this, I don't want to ever see you like that again or feel the helplessness and pain. I've decided I won't work in the woods again, to save you from the torment. I also wish you to only work here in the camp, not out in the woods." She held his cheek and peered into his eyes. "I love you and don't want to worry every day that you'll be hurt or not come home to warm my bed." She kissed his lips chastely. "Or to know you worry about me."

Hank's arm circled her waist and pulled her snug against him. He chuckled. "Watching you shimmy up that tree gave me a new appreciation for your skill. You know how to handle yourself, and I would be honored if you kept working in the woods."

Kelda peered at him with disbelief. "How can you say that? Won't you fear for my safety?" How could watching her climb a tree change his mind?

"It's like your father has said all along. You are talented, and you know how to handle yourself. I got hurt because I was a greenhorn and didn't think before I followed. That comes with time. You've grown up falling trees. It's second nature to you. You know the dangers before they happen." He kissed her forehead, and her heart melted anew for him. "But if you want to stop working in the woods I won't mind either. It will give us more time to be together."

She spun in his arms, pressing her breasts against his chest and moving her lips close to his. "How about we get married and see what happens from there?"

"I like that idea." He pressed his mouth to hers.

Her heart soared as he kissed her until they both needed air.

Chapter 30

Kelda stood in the cabin, which, after the ceremony today would be where she and Hank lived until the logging on the Halsey property was finished. After that they'd decide if they would go in partners with her brothers or stay in Sumpter.

Darcy and Aileen fussed with her hair while Rachel and Maeve made a fairy ring out of the delicate buttercups Shayla and Sadie found. Hank had suggested they get married on Kelda's birthday. She agreed he was the perfect gift.

Her heart buzzed with excitement. Once the wedding was set, he'd made another rule. They wouldn't make love until their wedding night. They'd spent many an hour exciting one another in many ways, but the coming together would happen tonight, in this cabin. And the following day they would go to Baker City for a weeklong celebration.

"There, 'tis ready for the flowers." Aileen stepped back, and Rachel placed the ring of buttercups on her head.

"You're beautiful!" Maeve said, tears glistening in her eyes.

Kelda sniffed back tears. "It's wonderful having so many sisters after all these years of men in my life."

The women pressed around and hugged her.

"We'll be sisters as long as we're alive," Maeve said and the rest agreed.

"Come on, Hank isn't going to wait much longer." Darcy took Kelda by the hand and led her to the door.

Kelda smoothed a hand down the satin dress Hank bought her in Baker City and she wore to dinner at the Warhauser. She clicked together the heels of her women's boots he also bought her. Wearing these items was the perfect reflection of their love and commitment.

Aileen opened the door, and the four women scurried out, taking positions alongside their husbands and families at the front of the crowd of loggers and Halsey friends from Sumpter.

Kelda scanned the crowd and down the opening in the center of the people. Hank stood at the end of the opening, tall and handsome beside a preacher. Her gaze locked on his.

Far stepped from the side of the door and held out his arm. He cleared his throat, and she slipped her hand around his elbow, smiling at him.

"Skatten min, I'm proud of the woman you've become and the man you chose to share your life with."

"Mange takk, Far. I think we'll have as wonderful a life as you and Mor." Her heart skipped as her gaze reconnected with Hank. His strength, love, humor, and commitment would fulfill her every need.

Far led her through the crowd and straight into Hank's hands. The warmth of his hands clasping hers and the love shining in his eyes, told her their life together would be wonderful.

Hank didn't hear the words spoken by the preacher. His gaze held only Kelda, and his heart thundered in his chest knowing she was his from this day forward to love.

Kelda's eyes danced with merriment. She leaned forward and whispered, "Say I do."

"I do."

The crowd laughed.

Kelda said loud and with commitment, "I do." Her eyes glistened with love and good humor the qualities that drew him to her.

"You may now kiss your bride."

She leaned forward. "Did you hear that?"

"Yes, I did." Hank embraced Kelda to his heart and kissed her deep, long, and with the heat he planned to show her on their wedding night.

Whoops from the crowd broke his kiss, and he swung her around twice before planting her by his side and facing their guests.

"Ladies and Gentleman, may I present to you Mr. and Mrs. Hank Halsey." The preacher said, and the crowd erupted in applause.

His heart couldn't get any happier. He pulled Kelda back into his arms. "I love you and plan to spend the rest of my life showing you."

"I love you and plan to show you just how much." She raised onto her toes and kissed him with the unabashed fervor he loved.

Epilogue

Christmas 1893

Kelda bumped into Darcy and Aileen as the three put the finishing touches on the Christmas dinner being served in the house she and Hank bought in Sumpter. Her growing stomach pressed against the work table in the middle of the kitchen. Another month and she'd present Hank with a child. The idea settled warm and fuzzy in her chest.

Rachel pushed into the room carrying a messy Samuel, her newest baby only six months old.

"Kelda, sit down. You've been on your feet all day." Rachel sat Sam in the high chair she and Clay brought over as a gift to Kelda and Hank.

"I'm fine." Kelda enjoyed being with child. She hadn't suffered from any sickness and the special treatment she received from Hank made her feel even more womanly than she ever thought possible.

"She's nesting," Aileen said. "Leave her be."

"Nesting?" Kelda put the last roll in a basket

and peered at Aileen.

"'Tis when a woman gets close to her time. She gets lots of energy and does nestin' activities."

Kelda nodded her head, but she still wasn't sure what the woman meant. She had another month before the baby came.

Shayla walked through the door with Sadie in tow. "Can we help?"

"You two lassies can carry in the food." Aileen placed bowls of potatoes and green beans in the girls' hands.

Soon all the food including two turkeys and two hams were on the long table made from their table and Maeve and Zeke's put together. Kelda still had to pinch herself when she walked through this house. Her home. The large house they'd purchased had been built for entertaining. The men had opened the large double door between the dining room and parlor. The huge combined rooms made the perfect place for the Halsey family to eat Christmas dinner.

Ethan as the head of the Halsey family sat at one end of the long table which reminded Kelda of the long table at the logging camp, and Hank as the head of this household sat at the other end.

She sat beside Hank near the kitchen door.

"Do you miss your family?" Hank asked, his concerned eyes scanning her face.

Kelda smiled and reassured him. "Nei. I have your large family to keep me company. Knowing the boys are happy with their new brides fils my heart."

"You know any time you ask we'll go visit

them at their new camp." Hank grasped her hand and squeezed.

"I know. I'm sure Lars and his wife are taking good care of everyone." Her eyes burned with unshed tears. "I'm happiest Far took Mor to Norway to visit their family."

"We've had many blessings this year." Hank's gaze drifted to Kelda's growing stomach.

"Ja, we have."

Everyone linked hands, and they all bowed their heads to thank the Lord for all their blessings.

As the food was passed around, she couldn't help but smile at the conversations and camaraderie among the whole family.

"So Maeve, what's this I hear about you helping Zeke after the first of the year?" Gil stared across the table at Maeve whose face glowed from the wide grin on her face.

"We have a job to do for the Pinkertons, and we can take Brandon with us. It won't be dangerous and being a family will make us look even more undercover." Her eyes danced from the excitement of the opportunity.

"That sounds exciting." Kelda passed the cabbage to Hank and noticed Darcy wasn't as bubbly as normal. She knew part of it was because Darcy's brother, Jeremy, wouldn't be home for Christmas. He'd met a man earlier in the year who talked him into becoming partners mining gold in Alaska. They'd had one letter from him so far and that was three months ago.

The smaller children were all placed between adults. Little Frankie sat between Kelda and Rachel.

Kelda reached to take hold of a serving dish from Rachel and a pain shot up her back. She couldn't catch her startled cry before it interrupted the conversation.

"What's wrong?" Hank sprang to his feet and knelt by her side.

"Just a twinge." Another pain shot up her back. "Uff da!"

Rachel stood and moved to her other side. "Let's get her upstairs."

Hank placed his arm under Kelda's legs and cradled her next to his body.

"I can walk," Kelda said, swatting half-heartedly at his chest.

"What's happening?" Sadie asked.

"Uncle Hank and Aunt Kelda's Christmas present is about to arrive," Aileen said, also standing.

"Everyone go back to eating. It's her first and will take a while. Aileen, you know what I need." Rachel's voice carried up the stairs as Hank stopped on the landing and looked at Kelda.

"Sweetie, I think we're going to become parents." His eyes glistened with happiness.

Kelda's heart swelled, and she kissed his cheek. "Ja, do you want a boy or a girl?"

He continued carrying her to their room. "Either as long as they have your sparkle."

Hank placed her on the bed and situated the pillows behind her back.

Rachel walked into the room smiling. "Well, we must have been off by a month with your due date."

"Is that a problem?" The worry in Hank's voice

started Kelda worrying.

"No. The baby should be fine. Kelda is strong and in good health. Now, I know why she has been growing larger than I thought she should." Rachel picked up Kelda's night dress. "You'll need to put this on." She glanced at Hank. "Do you want to help her?"

"Can I? You usually kick the husbands out." Hank moved to the bed, hovering over Kelda.

"I'll kick you out when the baby is closer to arriving. You can stay if it will help ease your fears." Rachel walked from the room, closing the door.

Kelda peered up into Hank's concerned face. She pulled him down and kissed him. "Don't worry. Mor birthed the boys and I and look at how tiny she is. I can handle a child we've made."

A pain sliced down her back and she winced.

Hank started unbuttoning her blouse. This was a routine she knew well; his large hands unclothing her body and taking her to inspiring heights. Only this time she'd present him with a child.

Once she was in her nightgown with nothing else on, he plumped the pillows once more and sat on the bed beside her. Another pain streaked up her back and she moaned.

"Let me rub your back." Hank leaned her against his chest and rubbed her back with slow warming caresses.

Rachel returned along with Aileen, a bundle of sheets, and a large pan of steaming water.

"How's she doing?" Rachel asked, placing a hand on Kelda's protruding tummy.

"She's had several pains since you left." Hank

continued rubbing her back and another pain ripped through her back and squeezed her belly.

Rachel glanced at Aileen. Kelda wouldn't have seen the exchange if she hadn't been staring at Rachel waiting for her to say something. She didn't want to panic but the expressions told her something wasn't right.

"What's wrong?" She clutched Hank's hand, pulling reassurance from his solidness.

"Your contractions are coming fast for just starting labor." Rachel turned sympathetic eyes on Hank. "I'm afraid you'll have to leave. I need to take a look and see what's happening."

Hank's hand squeezed Kelda's. "Is something wrong?"

"I won't know until I examine her. Please, Hank. Go downstairs. We'll keep you informed." Rachel drew him off the bed, and Aileen escorted him to the door.

He turned at the door. His eyes remained locked on Kelda. "They'll both be fine won't they?" he asked. The concern in his voice and fear in his eyes had Kelda sitting up to go to him.

Rachel held her down. "Yes, they'll be fine. Go. Please."

Hank left the room, but he didn't return back downstairs. It wouldn't be right to ruin the others meal by showing his concern for Kelda and their baby. He retrieved the rocking chair from the baby's room and sat in the hall outside the bedroom. If he lost Kelda and the baby now...His body tightened in fear. It couldn't happen. Not after they'd built such a wonderful life together. Her family had moved on, but he and Kelda now ran the logging on the mountain with a small group of loggers. They harvested only the largest trees each year keeping a steady flow of income. They'd made enough on the Stoddard contract to set them up comfortably here in Sumpter. In this house. He promised Kelda he wouldn't move them around. They would both die in this house.

He ran a hand over his face. They had many more years together. She was strong. She'd survive having a baby, and they'd live here as a family.

An hour past with him listening intently to the sounds inside the room. Ethan appeared at the top of the stairs.

"What's happening?" he asked, stopping next to the rocker and placing a hand on Hank's shoulder.

"I don't know. Rachel acted like the pains came too fast and kicked me out." He peered up at his older brother. "You're lucky you haven't been through this. It's agony waiting to hear if they're both fine."

Hank dropped his head into his hands and prayed, again.

Ethan raised his hand to knock when a lusty baby's cry came from inside the room. He slapped Hank on the back. "I think you'll get to go in soon."

Relief washed over Hank and love for the baby he'd yet to see warmed his heart. He stared at Ethan. His face felt like it would split in two from the smile he couldn't have stopped if his life depended on it. Another cry not as strong and a higher pitch joined the previous crying.

Hank turned his attention to the door. Two cries? Two babies? How?

The door opened and Aileen stepped out. "Oh! Ah dinnae expect to find you sittin' by the door." Her surprise dissolved, and she folded a hand around Ethan's as she peered down at Hank. "You have a boy and a girl."

"Twins?" Hank's legs melted like butter next to the fire. "A boy and a girl?"

Ethan grabbed him by the arm and hauled him to his feet. "I bet your babies and their mother would like to see you right about now." He pushed Hank to the door. "We'll go tell the rest of the family."

Hank put his hand on the door knob and turned. The door swung open and there on the bed sat Kelda, a baby in each arm. The love shining in her eyes drew him across the floor. He peered into her loving eyes before soaking in the sight of his son and daughter.

"Now I know why they came early," Rachel said, bundling up the used sheets and toweling. "Twins usually come a month early."

Something bumped the back of Hank's legs, and he plopped down on a chair. "Which is which?" he asked.

Kelda raised her right arm. "This is the boy. He's bigger." He had sparse dark hair and a round scrunched up face. She jiggled her left arm. "And this is our daughter." The small baby had a heart shaped face, small puckered lips and hair so light he could barely see it.

Hank placed a hand on her head and kissed

her. Then he leaned over Kelda, kissed their boy and planted a long thank you kiss on his wife. He'd barely sat back down when noise in the hall announced they had visitors.

Everyone crowded into the room to admire the twins.

"How did we have twins?" Hank asked Rachel.

Kelda cleared her throat. "Mor had twins in her family. A brother and sister."

"Have you thought of names?" Shayla asked.

Hank peered into Kelda's eyes and they both grinned. "Sawyer and Lily."

"The new family needs some time alone." Rachel shooed everyone out of the room and turned to the bed. "If they start fussing you should feed them."

Kelda nodded and Rachel left, closing the door behind her.

"Thank you." Hank kissed Kelda. "You've made my life complete in so many ways."

Kelda's eyes glistened with tears. "You have given me more than I ever dreamed of having. Love, a home, children."

"I'd say we're two lucky people to have found the person who makes our lives whole."

"Ja. You make me happy and feel loved."

"I plan to do that for many, many years."

About the Author

All my work whether it's my romance or my mysteries have Western or Native American elements in them along with hints of humor and engaging characters. My husband and I raise alfalfa hay in rural eastern Oregon. Riding horses and battling rattlesnakes, I not only write the western lifestyle, I live it.

I love to hear from fans. You can find or contact me at:
patyjag@gmail.com
or my website – www.patyjager.net

Continue to the next page to find a listing of my historical western books or visit my website:
https://www.patyjager.net

Historical Western Romance
Gambling on an Angel
Improper Pinkerton
For a Sister's Love
Christmas Redemption

Halsey Brother Series
Marshal in Petticoats – Gil's story
Outlaw in Petticoats – Zeke's story
Miner in Petticoats – Ethan's story
Doctor in Petticoats – Clay's story
Logger in Petticoats – Hank's story

Halsey Homecoming Trilogy
Laying Claim – Jeremy's Story
Staking Claim – Colin's Story
Claiming a Heart – Donny's Story
A Husband for Christmas - Shayla's Story

Letters of Fate Trilogy
Davis
Brody
Isaac

Silver Dollar Saloon
Savannah
Lottie Mae
Freedom

Contemporary Western Romance
Perfectly Good Nanny
Bridled Heart

Historical Paranormal Romance
Spirit of the Mountain
Spirit of the Lake
Spirit of the Sky

Thank you for purchasing this Windtree Press publication.
For other books of the heart, please visit our website at www.
windtreepress.com.

For questions or more information contact us at info@
windtreepress.com.

Windtree Press
Hillsboro, OR

www.ingramcontent.com/pod-product-compliance
Lightning Source LLC
Chambersburg PA
CBHW030710190726
48286CB00001B/255